I0699855

Books by C.B. Wilson

<u>The Gem Hunters</u>

The Fire Diamond

<u>Barkview Mysteries</u>

Jack Russelled to Death
Cavaliered to Death
Bichoned to Death
Shepherded to Death
Doodled to Death
Corgied to Death
Aussied to Death
Dachshund to Death
Labradored to Death
Puppied to Death
Retrievered to Death (Coming 2025)

PRAISE FOR BARKVIEW MYSTERIES

See what readers are saying about Barkview Mysteries in these five-star reviews:

"If you are looking for a mystery to tax your clue-connecting skills then Doodled to Death is one novel you should read. Its quirky humor and intelligent banter give it the feel of a Nancy Drew and Miss Marple murder mysteries hybrid with an even more exciting conclusion."
—Reader's Favorite, 5-star review

"I couldn't put the book down! The writing is top-caliber, the characterization three-dimensional, the concept clever, and the plot is compelling. (Not to mention the cute, opinionated dogs...) This cozy mystery will enthrall both dog lovers and history lovers."
—Lori H, Amazon

"CB Wilson is a fun, fresh voice on the cozy mystery scene."
—Sherri I., Amazon

"C. B. Wilson has done it again. Her cozy mysteries are full of charisma, they are entertaining, full of life, and very descriptive! Every one I read captivates me until the very last page. Love these books!!"
—babygirl, Amazon

"Fast-paced, well-written and clever mystery that will tickle the fancy of dog lovers and non-dog lovers alike."
—BH, Amazon

The Fire Diamond

A GEM HUNTERS MYSTERY

CB WILSON

Character List

Almaz—Russian CVD diamond manufacturer

Amber & Kyan—Hope's twins

Angelina—Ivan Medved's wife

Chad the Cad—Hunter's ex-husband

Chili Pepper—Fire Chief

Crystal Cummings—Owner, Canary Café

Dale—Bank president

Dee the Decoy—Hope's dachshund

Edward Blackwood—Diamond acquirer

Goldine Block—Reporter, *Peak Examiner*

Gram (Anne) Hunter—Taylor & Hope's grandmother

Grant Peak—Founder of Sunset Peak

Hank Allegro—Hope's husband

Hope Hunter Allegro (*ma espoir*)—Hunter's twin sister

Ivan Medved—Head of Medvedya cartel

Jasper Washburn—Head security, Peak Mine

Karo—Diamond acquirer

Katarina—Angelina's twin sister

Kathy—Bank president's assistant

Le Renard Argente—Hunter & Hope's father

Marvel—Hope's Appaloosa horse

Nikolai Volkov—CVD diamond creator

Officer Mason Pepper—Chili's son. Sunset Peak PD officer

Opal—Front desk, Amethyst Inn

Pop—Hunter & Hope's grandfather

Rico Lobo (Two Socks)—Mine IT guy

Rocky Rockman—Police chief, friend of Taylor's ex-husband

Ruby—Mayor, owner Amethyst Inn

Sindikat Krasnogo Medvedya—Red Bear Syndicate

Sophie—Intel from Sterling & Sons LTD

Sunny Dias—Office manager

Taylor "Hunter"

Uncle Richie—Rockman's uncle, in diamond business

Vajra—Hunter's horse (Indian God of Diamonds)

Windy Dias—Librarian

Diamond Terms

AGS—American Gem Society. Provides a diamond grading report. Now merged with GIA reports.

Carbon pattern—The specific arrangement of carbon atoms within a diamond's structure gives it unique characteristics.

Cleavage plane—Cleavage is the weakest plane in a gemstone where the gemstone can split. Cleavage is caused by weak atomic bonds.

Culet—A diamond culet is the tiny facet at the bottom of a diamond's pavilion, serving as the tip or point where the gem's facets converge.

Color zoning—When two or more colors are present within the same stone.

Commodity diamonds—Common sized diamonds used as investments.

Conflict diamonds (blood diamonds)—Diamonds mined in a war zone and sold to finance an insurgency.

Cross-hatching strain pattern—When a diamond is placed under filters a strain is revealed in a strong, almost cross-hatch-looking pattern of intersecting parallel shadows.

CVD (Chemical Vapor Deposition) diamonds—Man-made diamonds that are identical to natural diamonds and are considered 100% authentic diamonds.

Diamond plot—A map of a diamond's inclusions drawn by a diamond grader.

Diamond rough—A diamond that has not been cut or processed. They come in a variety of naturally occurring shapes.

Diamond seed—Seeds are crushed diamond powder. The seed is made up of carbon and may also contain other chemicals, such as nitrogen.

Feather inclusion—"Feather" inclusions are small breaks in the diamond crystal lattice.

GIA—The Gemological Institute of America is a world-renowned institute based in Carlsbad, California. It is dedicated to research and education in the field of gemology and the jewelry arts.

Girdle—The part of the diamond that creates the outer-edge outline.

HPHT—HPHT stands for high pressure and high temperature. It is one of the main methods used to form diamonds. A diamond seed is placed in a large press producing high pressures of above

870,000 pounds per square inch at very high temperatures (1300-1600 °C).

Inclusions—Diamond inclusions are small imperfections within a diamond.

Photomicroscope—A microscope having an illuminator and a camera mechanism for producing a photomicrograph. Straining—Strain in diamond can result from lattice defects such as dislocations, impurities, inclusions, precipitates, cracks.

Striations—Similar to grain lines in a natural diamond. It can also appear similar to twinning wisps, a common feature in natural diamonds. Strain in the crystal lattice is another factor common in lab grown diamonds, especially CVD grown, and relatively rare in nature. It can also appear similar to twinning wisps, a common feature in natural diamonds.

Table—A diamond's table is the largest facet seen when the diamond is viewed face up. In other words, it is the flat facet on the diamond's surface that you can see when you look at the diamond from above.

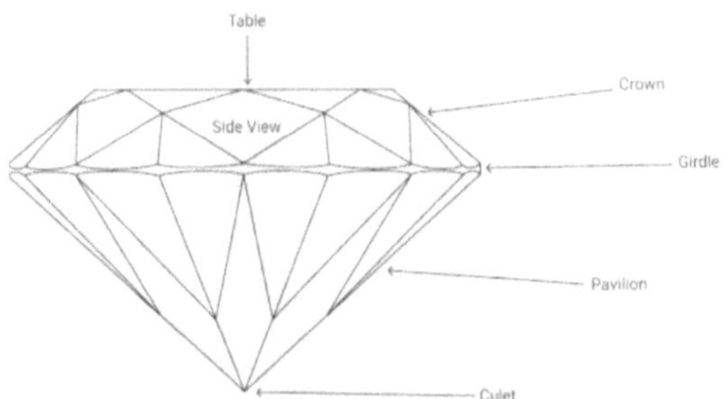

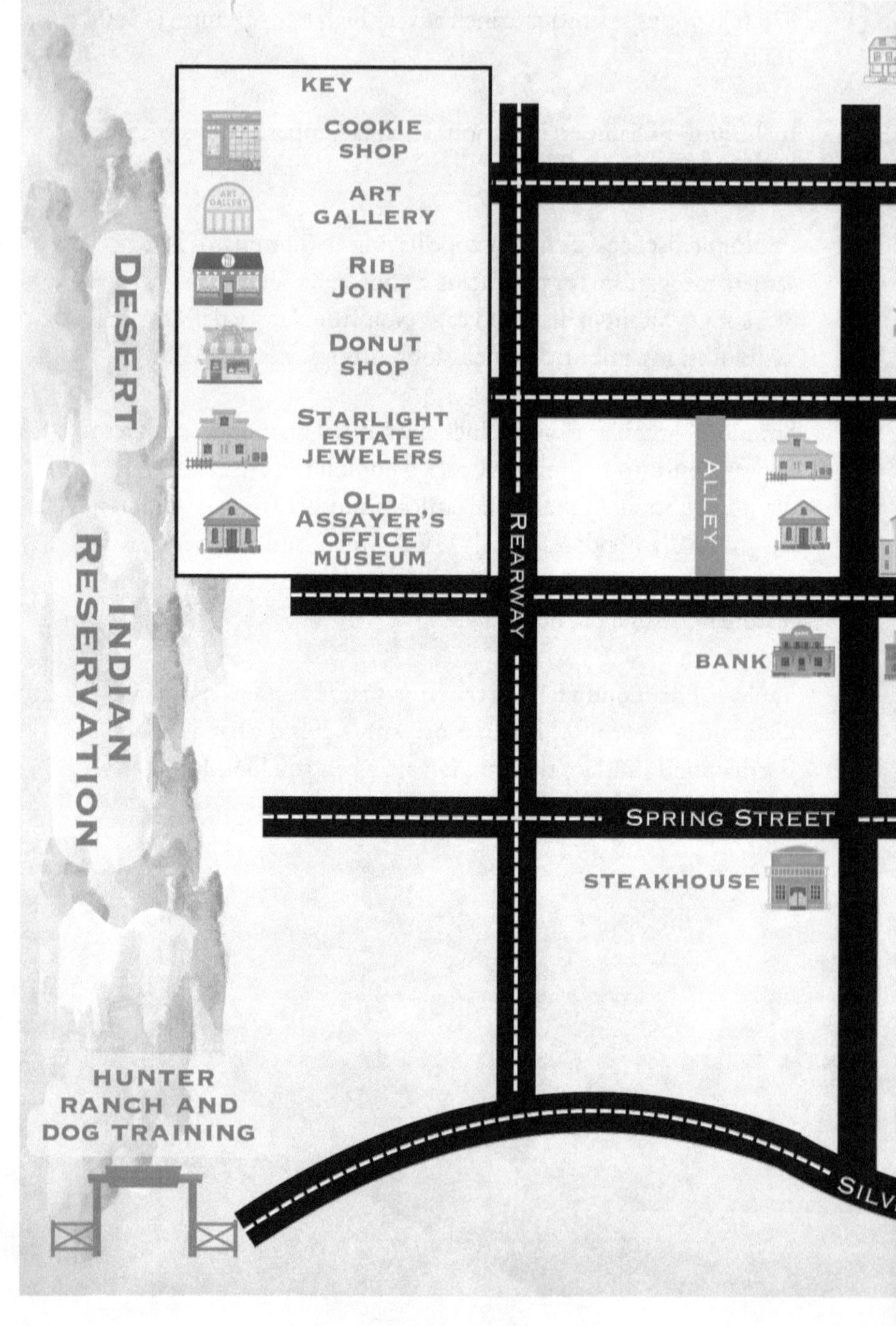

DESERT
INDIAN RESERVATION
HUNTER RANCH AND DOG TRAINING
KEY
COOKIE SHOP
ART GALLERY
RIB JOINT
DONUT SHOP
STARLIGHT ESTATE JEWELERS
OLD ASSAYER'S OFFICE MUSEUM
REARWAY
ALLEY
BANK
SPRING STREET
STEAKHOUSE
SILVE

N
W
E
S
DE HOMES
CRYSTAL
MIA'S ITALIAN
WINE TASTING
FIRE DEPT
LIBRARY
POLICE DEPT
RY TRAIL
D MINER'S BRONZE
E HORSE
Y HALL
OUNTAIN OF DREAMS
ART GALLERY
KEY ROW
PICK YOUR BREW
SOUVENIR SHOP
HANAH'S HOTEL
OLD MINERS TRAIL
QUARRY ROAD
AMETHYST INN AND SPA
TURQUOISE RD
OLD MINE MUSEUM
NEW MINE
E MOUNTAIN RD
DESERT

Chapter One

TRUST NO ONE, ESPECIALLY FAMILY—WISDOM FROM A JEWEL THIEF

Most sixteen-year-olds dream of getting a car for their birthday. I just wanted my life to be normal. You see, my absentee father was a jewel thief. Not your everyday smash-and-grab variety, either, but one that the FBI called a heist master. Yes, my dad made the Gentleman Thief look like a choirboy. I suppose, deep down, I'd known. From bedazzled jean jackets to glitter nail polish, I've always been a blingaholic.

My name is Taylor Hunter, chosen, according to my grandmother, because of the 68-carat Taylor-Burton diamond. Given my genetic predisposition, I pursued the only logical career. No, I'm not a cat burglar. Acrophobia ended that fantasy. My twin sister, Hope (two important minutes younger), and I buy and sell estate jewelry. What sets me apart is my side hustle. I have one of those dream jobs coveted by gemophiles everywhere. I am a diamond detective employed by insurance and law enforcement agencies when baffled by the most daring jewelry thefts.

From recovering royal regalia to foiling an Ocean's 8 Las Vegas heist, I'd solved it all. Recovering one priceless 7.5-carat orange diamond should've been a cakewalk, right? There's a reason doctors don't operate on family. I just hadn't learned that lesson yet.

SUNDAY, 9:35 A.M.

Eyes clenched shut, Glimmer, my weiner dog, tucked under my arm, I stumbled down the alley stairs from my apartment above Starlight Estate Jewelers. Two Nespressos hadn't lifted my mental fog any. My skull throbbed. What was wrong with me? I couldn't possibly have a hangover. I'd nursed a single cocktail at last night's Founders Day celebration.

"Well, look what the cat dragged in." Glimmer, my long-haired dachshund's, head prodded my ribcage at the sound of Hope's sunshine-and-rainbows voice. Acrylic nails scratching an old-fashioned chalkboard couldn't be more annoying. I admit it. Years of trying to beat the morning-perkiness out of my twin had failed.

I raised one eyelid to glare at my mirror image. Like me, she'd worn dark pants and a light blue Starlight Oxford shirt, with her sun-kissed hair, more blonde than brown, tied back in a low pony-tail. Normally, two halves of a whole, few people could tell us apart. Not so much today. Hope's hazel eyes danced with anything but empathy.

"Not a word," I growled. No apologies. My ex-husband called me the Morning Monster for a good reason. Not why we divorced, incidentally.

Another aromatic espresso appeared like magic in my hand. "How much did you drink last night?" Hope asked.

I sank into the coveted back room's butter-soft swivel chair. Visited by a select few gem buyers and sellers, the room had been designed as an elegant haven to view captivating jewels. Today, the jeweler's lighting—the bright, blue-tinged light that added pizzazz to polished, well-cut gemstones—no doubt made me look like Elphaba from Wicked.

I took a long swallow of the coffee. The thick and velvety texture coated my tongue like a comforting blanket. I'd pay the jitter price later, but, for now, life stirred within. "I drank one Arizona Statehood." I emphasized with my left forefinger. "One."

Hope's brows arched in skepticism. "You're a martini drinker. What did you expect mixing Dubonnet Rouge and rye whiskey?"

To be my normal self. "Whatever that bartender put in my drink was a killer."

"Sweet wine, whiskey, gum syrup, bitters, and ginger ale," Hope replied drily. "I warned you not to mix alcohols."

Maybe she had. I couldn't swear to it. She did make a point. Mixing wasn't a grand plan. I hadn't overindulged since my divorce was final. No doubt she remembered that celebration. My sister remembered everything.

"Did you ..."

"I ate a plate of deviled eggs and meatballs." I finished her sentence. We did that a lot to the annoyance of everyone around us.

"That was smart," Hope admitted.

I hardly felt it now.

"I ordered the Statehood, too. I started feeling lightheaded after a few sips and switched to sparkling water," Hope added.

Of course she had. My perfect twin had a way of making me feel like a deadbeat.

"Hank was happy to leave early. So was Gram," Hope added.

My brother-in-law and our eighty-five-year-old grandmother could never be accused of being social with humans. Dogs, on the other hand ...

"I really don't like dropping Gram off at her house. She shouldn't live alone. I still have nightmares thinking about that call from the Mayo Clinic."

I did, too. We'd been at the Tucson Gem Show when she'd been rushed to the emergency room.

"I have plenty of room at my house. She can have her own wing," Hope said.

I agreed, in theory. In practice, though, when dealing with Gram, it tended to be tricky. She loved her great-grandchildren, but chaos surrounded my sister and the dozen dogs undergoing law enforcement training on their ranch. "Two saguaros and a hedge separate your houses," I pointed out.

"Yes, but I can't see ..."

"... in the windows," I suggested.

"Exactly. What if her heart ..." Hope's voice caught.

"She's too ornery to let that happen." I believed that. I had to. The truth was, I appreciated Gram's desire for peace and quiet. While Hope's maternal instincts had developed over the years, I'd chosen to be the cool aunt with great stories. Some true, some embellished, but all based on fact.

Hope crossed her arms. "You didn't drive home last night, did you?" Her manicured finger shake signaled a full-blown mom lecture coming. I empathized with her preteen daughters as I looked for cover.

"I didn't feel the least bit impaired," I retorted. I'd felt great—euphoric, actually, like I could conquer Mt. Everest, even with my bad knee. "I made it home. That's a win."

Hope crossed her arms. "What about my ulcer?"

"You don't have an ulcer."

"I could. I should. Worrying about you ... and Gram."

"You worry enough for me and Gram combined."

Hope's huff wasn't a pass, but I appreciated the reprieve when she changed the subject. No pithy retort from me. I scooped my mini doxie into my lap. The royal princess tossed her head, the sparkle from her pavé diamond collar dancing off the ceiling like a waterfall of brilliant stars. I groaned.

Hope chuckled. "You were right about the new lighting. We'll sell more fine diamonds under the blue tint. I should've listened sooner."

No I-told-you-so today. My sister's slow-to-embrace-change lifestyle balanced my passion for shiny new toys, making us perfect business partners. Good thing, because owning a downtown retail shop meant working together seven days a week.

Hope glanced at her phone. "No estate appointments today. Go back to bed. I'll ask Sunny to come in."

"She hasn't had a day off this week." It wasn't fair to ask our office manager to cover for my bad decision.

"She's twenty-five. She functions just fine with no sleep and strong coffee. She'll appreciate the overtime."

I barely remembered those days.

"Don't worry. We can handle today's tourists. I doubt anything meaningful will happen."

The comic relief to my sister's seriousness and my frequent absences, Sunny's outgoing personality made her a better salesperson than either one of us. I wanted to believe Hope, but the coffee curdled in my stomach a split second before my cellphone tinged with my grandmother's number. Before church on Sunday morning? This couldn't be good news.

I fought the urge to ignore it, but my conscientious sister snatched my phone and turned it to speaker. "What are you doing up this early? The doctor said you were supposed to be taking it easy."

"Uh, I ..." Not Gram's voice. Was that the mayor speaking?

I bolted upright, displacing my donut-curled dog. Glimmer's unladylike snort conveyed annoyance with a commendable panache. We were a pair. Of what exactly, opinions differed.

"What's wrong? Where's Gram?" Hope's panic telegraphed to me.

The clunk indicated that the caller's phone hit a hard surface. The ensuing dead silence didn't help my now-throbbing headache any.

"For heaven's sake, Ruby, give me the phone." Gram's raspy, no-nonsense voice stilled my racing pulse until she added, "Taylor, stop what you're doing and get over to the Mining Museum right now."

I jerked my fingers through my shaggy, shoulder-length mane. Everyone called me Hunter, a nickname that had stuck since childhood when I discovered my knack for finding lost things, especially Gram's reading glasses. These days, Gram only used my real name, Taylor, when I'd committed some unforgivable sin. What had I done wrong this time?

"The Peak Diamond has been stolen," Gram announced as if delivering the weather report.

"Stolen?" Hope and I squeaked in unison. This had to be a nightmare. Our town's legendary diamond necklace should be safely inside the Sunset Peak Bank's Jesse James-proof vault.

"Stop exaggerating, Anne. It's only broken. I didn't mean to drop the diamond. It's my arthritis. I'm telling you, getting old is…" The mayor's whine-worthy comment took a minute to sink in.

"Exactly why you shouldn't touch anything valuable," Gram retorted. "This diamond broke below the girdle."

A bucket of ice-cold water in my face couldn't have cleared the cobwebs faster.

Not fast enough. Hope spoke first. "That's impossible. Diamonds are the hardest stone known to man. The Peak has a single hairline feather so minute it's not even visible to the naked eye. I assure you, as the diamond's grader of record, the Sunset won't break if you drop it."

"Yup. This stone's a fake. Bring your 30x loupe and kit. You'll want to document the crime scene," Gram ordered with drill sergeant precision.

The mayor's outcry nearly drowned out Gram's admission. "It can't be a fake. It looks exactly the same."

"To the naked eye, visually it's identical," Gram admitted. "This stone's workmanship is good. Real good."

I didn't want to believe her, but my grandmother, the founder of our family's jewelry store, Starlight Estate Jewelers, had practically written the diamonds' four C's grading system.

The whole scenario still felt out-of-this-world. "Why isn't the stone in the bank's vault?"

Ruby's high-pitched voice again. "That vault requires a cornea scan. We couldn't get in last night without the bank's president, and Dale was, uh, indisposed."

"Passed out in a heap," Gram added.

"He did his spaghetti-western ancestors proud," Ruby added. "His assistant poured him into her car right after my remarks. He swore he was drinking water."

Hope huffed. "He's been drinking too much again. Kathy drives him home from Whiskey Jack's a least twice a week."

"It's going to be a long day for a lot of people," Ruby replied.

Me included, but an alarm still fired. "Are you telling me that the diamond spent the night at the museum without security?"

"No. No. Since we couldn't get into the bank's vault, we put it in the museum's safe," Ruby insisted.

A joke of a 1960s relic anyone with a stethoscope could crack. Could this be a meticulously planned heist?

"There are security cameras all around the building," Ruby added.

"Designed to deter teenagers from sneaking into the old mine shaft," I added under my breath. Not protect a mega-million-dollar robin egg-sized gem.

"The chief assigned Officer Pepper and the newbie to watch the building last night, too," Ruby replied.

Of course, he had. Police Chief Rockman, Rocky, to a select few of whom I wasn't one, always appeared to do the right thing.

"This investigation is going to get complicated," Gram announced with her usual understatement.

"Has the chief closed off the area?" There had been two hundred people at the gala last night. All within a few feet of the stone. Sunset Peak's five-officer police department would be hard-pressed to handle the witness interviews.

"Not yet," Gram replied.

"What? Why?" Every minute counted when recovering stolen diamonds.

"I graded the stone thirty days ago for the insurance update." Hope's announcement hit me like a sucker punch. My sister had been the last person to officially handle the real diamond.

"I'll have Rocky fetch coffee." Gram's nonchalance didn't fool me. A grizzly didn't stand a chance against my grandmother protecting her young.

But order the chief to run errands? "That's poking the bear," I remarked.

Gram harrumphed her opinion. "Bring Glimmer." The doxie's sensitive ears twitched in acknowledgment, yet she still covered her head with her furry front paws in denial.

"I need to wait for the official request." In this case, the insurance company. Chief Rockman would not allow me on site without it.

"Consider yourself hired," Gram said. "By order of the mayor."

"Yes. By my order," Ruby chimed in. "Your dog can find it."

"Yes, ma'am." I knew better than to question Gram issuing orders. My dachshund wasn't your everyday wiener dog, but a trained ore dog—a dachshund capable of sniffing out diamonds better than modern alluvial rock scanning equipment.

"If this, by some miracle, was a crime of opportunity, Glimmer should solve it straight away," Gram stated.

"But a fake jewel indicates …" My grandmother disconnected the call before I voiced my doubts. Although my investigator's mind churned with too many possibilities, I felt Hope's tension. Like I always did when something mattered. And this mattered.

"I'm going to be the primary suspect. I had means and opportunity." Hope grasped her vulnerability right away.

The voice might be my sister's, but the words were our grandfather, Pop's. A retired Phoenix PD detective turned rockhound, he'd called out every TV police procedural's inconsistencies. "You don't have a motive." Our jewelry business paid the bills, and the gem recovery fees made our lives comfortable.

"I have the contacts to sell a priceless diamond," Hope added.

"So do a lot of people in Sunset Peak. This is a gem lover's destination." To the tune of tens of thousands of annual visitors. Honest to a fault, stealing wasn't in Hope's DNA. Anyone who knew her would swear to that. The problem would be focusing resources away from the obvious suspect. "I can think of ten unsavory suspects …"

"… who'd been ogling the Peak diamond at last night's celebration," Hope finished my sentence in twin fashion.

"Ruby put the stone in harm's way when she coerced the city council to allow the diamond to be displayed at the gala," I pointed out. My investigative success came from treating everyone as a potential suspect until evidence proved otherwise.

"Ruby felt our centennial celebration and the reopening of the historic Sunset Peak Mine demanded an exhibition," Hope said.

I suppose I agreed, too. After a fifty-year hiatus, the mine that founded our town was back in business, mining industrial-grade silver, turquoise, chrysocolla, and azurite.

"It's not right to hide a priceless orange diamond like that in the bank's vault forever. Its beauty should be shared." Those exact words, reflected in the city council meeting's minutes, made my sister a party to the plan.

"It's been shared all right," I muttered. "It's theft, no doubt, commissioned by a private collector."

"Hunting stolen jewels has jaded you," my eternally optimistic sister said.

I suppose it had. Statistics didn't lie. Most jewelry thefts relied on insider knowledge. As the problem-solver between us, I leaned toward practical cynicism while Hope lived up to her name, always seeing the good in people. We balanced each other well.

"Is there any chance this is a crime of opportunity?" Hope asked. "There was a lot of drinking going on last night."

"My gut tells me it's more than that." I felt rather than heard my sister's exhale. She'd felt it, too.

"Stop at the Amethyst Inn and have Opal keep an eye on a couple of our out-of-town guests," I requested. Our resident nosy neighbor, who manned the hotel's front desk, could be a big help.

"Blackwood and Karo?"

It wasn't really a question. Two opportunistic diamond

dealers showing up at our small-town gala couldn't be a coincidence. Both men made my eye twitch. A sure sign of something I didn't want to think about.

"Give me enough time to smooth things over with the chief before you show up at the museum." My jaw clenched involuntarily. Collaborating with my cheating ex's best buddy qualified as pure torture.

Concern crept into Hope's tone. "You'd better put on your big girl pants, Sis. Like it or not, Sunset Peak is his jurisdiction. And I, as the prime suspect, prefer not to get railroaded because of your bad attitude."

"My bad attitude ..." My denial ended there. I really hated it when she was right. Somehow, I needed to work with the womanizing jerk for Hope's sake.

I picked up Glimmer and headed toward my apartment. "Call Sunny in. It's going to be a long day."

Chapter Two

TIME IS NOT YOUR FRIEND—WISDOM FROM A
JEWEL THIEF

SUNDAY, 10:00 A.M.

No cop liked a civilian poking around their cases, and Chief Rockman tended to be more territorial than most. To say I was not at my best today would be an understatement. My skull still pounded like a bongo drum. One question consumed my thoughts: had the thieves who swapped the Peak Diamond for a counterfeit simply been unlucky that the stone had been damaged and subsequently discovered, or was there something more deliberate at play?

Back in my apartment, I navigated around the wrinkled heap of last night's borrowed flapper dress to the bathroom, where I swallowed two more Nuprin. Looking in the mirror confirmed my fears. I looked like something a hungry bobcat had dragged in. I scraped my shoulder-length hair into something resembling a ponytail and changed into dark jeans and the sky-blue button-down that Hope insisted made my eyes pop.

Standing at the short side of five feet, heeled footwear served as my eye-to-eye equalizer.

As I zipped up one fancy artisan ankle boot, Glimmer snatched the other and darted into the bedroom, the chunky heel

"

making a rhythmic thunk against the wood floor with each doxie stride. Though far from a fashion enthusiast, I had one weakness: shoes—the more unique, the better. My collection boasted dozens of pairs in wildly impractical colors and heel heights, an odd choice given the rugged mountain terrain around me.

"Not today!" With one boot on, I lunged after my bandit-dog, caving to the catch-me game. The mini-dachshund easily dodged under my king-sized bed. The boot followed, validating the doxie's magic. Retrieving her thievery always brought a blister packaging battle to mind.

I didn't bother today. Instead, I retreated to the closet and chose another navy, leather-tipped, patchwork fabric pair. Miffed, the weiner dog stretched across the doorway, the runaway boot dangling from her mouth. Before she could take revenge on my boots, I removed her embroidered investigator's sweater from the drawer.

Glimmer's head snapped up. Her tail wagging, she abandoned her prize. Her insistent bark ordered me to quit dallying. We had a job to do.

I grabbed my Diamond Investigators jacket. April in the desert might invite afternoon sunbathing, but nestled between the New River Mountains and the Black Hills, Sunset Peak's morning lows chilled me to the bone.

Like me, Glimmer preferred breakfast closer to noon. I packed her Fresh Pet in a soft cooler and let her do her business on a patch of artificial turf outside the garage door. I deposited her on the passenger seat of my white Bronco and clipped the dog's harness to her special seat belt beside me. She settled into the leather seat, her coloring blending in perfectly.

I backed out of the garage into the alley behind our jewelry store. Although the court had awarded my ex our suburban ranch home located midway to Phoenix, it wasn't a point of contention. Living in the two-bedroom apartment on the northwest corner of our historic town square felt like working from home.

I headed east onto Canary Trail and drove past the White

Horse—Sunset Peak's courthouse and home to our legislative branch, which occupied the Grecian-columned masterpiece. I bowed my head as I passed the Lost Miner's Bronze statue on the east corner before turning right onto Quarry Road.

Two blocks beyond downtown, Craftsman-style homes nestled beneath the yellow canopies of palo verde trees and bright orange ocotillos. To my left, streets wound through vibrant spring wildflowers toward the boulder-spotted hillside.

I tapped the brakes at the Spring Street stop sign and followed the road until it became Old Miner's Trail. A left turn brought the Old Mine Museum into view.

The one-story adobe building, a nod to our territorial past, housed both offices and museum displays. Today, a medieval-style pole tent enclosed the courtyard between the original mine shaft and the museum's building. Evidence of last night's Prohibition-era bash lingered everywhere—metallic streamers tumbled like drunken tumbleweeds across the stone threshold and draped the bronze mining cart like exhausted party guests.

I squeezed into a parking space at the glass-fronted entrance, sandwiched between Gram's pickup and the mayor's luxury SUV. Something was off with Glimmer.

My dachshund had gone rigid the moment we'd passed Spring Street, and her soft, humming growl made no sense.

Breaking her usual routine, she didn't wait for me at her door. The instant I released her seatbelt, she vaulted over the center console, scrambled across my lap, and hit the ground running. Within seconds, she'd raced to the museum's glass double doors and sprawled her long body across the entrance. Her sharp double bark made my blood run cold. We'd been drilling this response for months. My dog's talent for detecting carbon diamonds also made her exceptionally skilled at sensing other dangerous gases.

I didn't stop to think. I leaped over my irritated sausage dog and yanked open the glass door with enough force that it slammed against the wall. "Gas leak! Everybody needs to evacuate now!"

My grandmother, the trail-dusty cowgirl, and the mayor, the Texas beauty queen, gaped at me like I'd lost my mind. Maybe I had. If the situation wasn't so dire, I'd have laughed.

No time to explain. Glimmer was never wrong.

"Where's Dale?" I asked. Gram and the mayor couldn't move the Peak Diamond to the vault without the bank president. It would be just our luck that he was holed up inside somewhere.

"When we found the fake diamond, I called and told him not to rush. That Ruby was running late," Gram explained.

"Is anyone else inside?" I asked.

Gram shook her head. Ruby agreed.

Relieved, I ordered, "Cover your noses and move. Now!"

"But the alarms ..." The mayor pointed to the black boxes mounted on the mine-facing walls, the green lights indicating a safe environment. "I don't smell anything."

Not exactly an accurate indicator. Most noxious gases were odorless.

"We've been here for some time. I feel fine. No shortness of breath. No headache," Gram added.

Yet my dog thought something was wrong. The dachshund's sharp bark silenced further protests, her warning unmistakable.

The mayor turned tail and marched out the door, her heels tapping on the stone floor. Gram's eye roll said it all. Of course, she'd had the peace of mind to protect the diamond. Whatever was unfolding could well be connected to the diamond's mysterious disappearance. The question wasn't if there was danger, but how close it had already come.

As Gram stepped outside, I yanked the fire alarm and brought up the rear, pulling the glass doors shut behind us. Glimmer planted herself in front of the entrance again, every inch the guardian. While Gram supported our hyperventilating mayor, I called mine security. The silence from the substance detectors worried me. Was it just faulty sensors, or something worse in the reopened mine? A gas leak could explain why last night's party had gotten so wildly out of hand.

Although mine safety and security teams historically responded to gas leaks, Sunset Peak's fire and rescue crews were equally well-trained. Lights flashing but sirens silent, the hook-and-ladder truck arrived on the scene a scant five minutes later. Chief Pepper, Chili, to his team—more because of his award-winning, four-alarm chili than his standing-on-end carrot top—had outlasted me last night. Any wonder his eyes looked more red than white. "This better be good," he growled.

I pointed to the doxie protecting the doorway.

Chili's curse bounced off the rock hills. We'd trained together often enough that he knew exactly what was going on. Another deep growl from him sent his team scrambling about the same time as the mining panel van careened into the parking lot, jumping the curb and lurching toward Gram's truck in an exaggerated slow motion. Chili and I held our breath until it finally stopped right on top of a cholla cactus.

Jasper Washburn, the new Peak Mine's security chief, emerged from the passenger side. With his miner's hunch and paunchy middle, his thick shoulders and gruff exterior brought a bulldog to mind—a snow dog, to be exact—since he'd dressed in a creased PPE hazmat suit with only his shiny bald head exposed. His pasty white skin tone reminded me of a man long in the shadows.

Four additional suited figures fell in behind him with military precision, their unfriendly faces unfamiliar—strange in a town where privacy tended to be more myth than reality.

"What's all this about?" Washburn's accent puzzled me. Not quite British or exactly South African, despite what his resume suggested.

Chili studied the tablet Washburn handed him. "Systems show normal," he conceded, returning the device to me.

Sure enough, the green bars beneath the electronic images confirmed his statement. I glanced at Glimmer, who watched us warily from her post, not moving an inch. She sensed something. I'd wager on it. "Who's monitoring the air quality?" I asked.

"Our MIT computer genius." Washburn's gaze darted toward the van. A shadowed figure, obscured behind a computer screen, now occupied the seat Jasper had vacated.

Chili wasn't impressed. He stroked his jaw. "The dog says otherwise."

"That's a load of rubbish. Our state-of-the-art system doesn't make mistakes," Washburn insisted.

In true doxie defiance, Glimmer popped to her feet and barked, daring him to question her further.

"Neither does Glimmer," I shot back. At least, I thought so. The dog had been meticulously tested but never truly tried.

Washburn's narrowed gaze belonged to a man unaccustomed to being questioned. I didn't back down. Safety was paramount.

Unrattled, Chili made his decision. "We'll let the dog do her job."

"Ag, man, the hell you will. That mine's on private land." Washburn's jaw set.

His overprotectiveness triggered my investigator's paranoia. What was he afraid we'd find? Was this somehow related to the missing Peak Diamond? Or simply the new guy posturing?

"Well," Chili stroked his chin with remarkable good-old-boy charm, "the judge may have a thing or two to say about that in due time, but I'm callin' this a public safety issue. There were a lot of revelers last night. No saying if anyone passed out in a corner." He turned to Gram. "See anyone inside, Mrs. Hunter?"

Gram hid a smile, barely. "Can't say I looked in all the crevices, Chief."

"I was afraid of that." He motioned his team to suit up. "Our team will clear the premises. Your team fixes the problem."

Defeat not in his vocabulary, Washburn motioned his team to fill the space behind him. Chili's boys held their ground, too.

The standoff between mine security and local law enforcement had all the makings of an Old West showdown. Where was the police chief? Both emergency response departments had been dispatched at the same time.

Chili's slow smile spelled trouble. "Madam Mayor, the museum sits on public property, correct?"

"It does indeed," Ruby confirmed. "Chili, please ensure no residents are in harm's way." Although married to the owner of the Amethyst Inn, Ruby's take-charge attitude made it clear why the community had chosen her as their leader.

"Yes, ma'am. We'll clear the path to the mine." Chili turned to me. "Taking point, Hunter?"

As Glimmer's handler, I had no choice. I still hesitated. I wasn't afraid. I'd known the risks of working with a detection dog and had trained for this day. Something else nagged at me.

While Gram helped my dog into her four-legged alien suit at the back of my car, I squeezed into my own puffy safety gear. Looking like the Pillsbury Doughboy wasn't exactly how I'd planned to run into the seriously tardy Chief Rockman. Of course, that's exactly what happened. When I turned the corner of my SUV, I crashed right into his rock-hard chest.

A bear of a man, he towered a good foot over me. His strong hands seemed to linger at my waist as he steadied me. The unwelcome warmth that shot through my body shocked and annoyed me. This guy was trouble. Anyone who called my ex "friend" required a healthy distance.

"I should've known you'd be in the thick of this." His deep voice rumbled as his eyes locked with mine for a beat too long.

I sensed his disdain. *That egotistical* ... I bit back my objection as he systematically lifted me aside, his fingers trailing across the small of my back as he moved on toward Chili. I exhaled slowly, trying to ignore the ghost of his touch as my sister filled the space he'd vacated.

"We have a problem." Hope's tight voice pulled me back to reality.

My gut twisted in reaction as her words sank in, the momentary distraction forgotten. Panic bubbled deep within her. I felt it as if it were my own.

"Blackwood's been murdered."

"Murdered!" Not exactly shocking. The man played both sides of the law with equal exuberance. It also explained the chief's delay.

"... and my fingerprints are all over his room."

I'm sure my jaw hit the ground. A priceless stolen gem, a murdered diamond broker, and a noted diamond grader's fingerprints at the crime scene? The series of events weren't too hard to figure out. My sister was in a world of trouble—the kind I wondered if even I could get her out of.

Chapter Three

ALWAYS HAVE AN EXIT STRATEGY—WISDOM
FROM A JEWEL THIEF

SUNDAY, 10:30 A.M.

"It's not what you're thinking. I didn't shoot him."

The calm, matter-of-fact way she said it terrified me. Where was my upbeat, oftentimes emotional twin?

I couldn't begin to process this yet. My honorable, too-good-to-be-true sister having an affair? And with short, stout, reptilian Blackwood of all people? I shuddered. The mental image turned my stomach. I'd even understand if her mousy husband bored her, but to cheat with a man on police watch lists?

Of course, my gaze found the chief almost without trying, like a compass finding north. There he was, deep in discussion with Jasper Washburn. No doubt explaining the rules.

Hope must've read my mind. Her hand flew to her mouth. "Oh! I would never! You know me better than that."

I wanted to believe her, desperately, but our twin telepathy wasn't talking. "How did he die?"

"Shot," Hope replied. "I don't know anything more."

Just as well. Gram handed me my ready-to-go dog. Time to work.

Glimmer stood in her protective moonwalk-ready space suit, looking like a bright yellow beacon. The contrasting black booties gave her an oddly endearing bumblebee appearance. I'd chosen the colors intentionally so I could spot her anywhere. Thank goodness she enjoyed dressing up—in anything except those frilly little dresses she turned her nose up at.

Chili's wave indicated the all-go to breach the building. With a possible gas leak looming, I had no choice. Hope's bombshell situation would have to wait. Glimmer concurred. The dog's elongated snout, extended by a small breathing mask, batted my shoulder. She was ready, too. "We'll ..."

"... figure this out later," Hope finished my thought. She hugged me impulsively. "Be safe. I couldn't possibly live without you."

Nor I her—despite her admissions. I hugged her back. While I potentially walked into an explosive situation, she was the one in peril. Her fingerprints at the murder scene meant Chief Rockman would give no quarter. "Take care of each other." I waited for both Gram and Hope's nods before Glimmer and I walked toward the museum's front door.

Each step ratcheted my anxiety higher. It didn't matter that we'd drilled this exact scenario countless times. This time, death possibly waited on the other side.

Like I had a choice? I took a deep breath and pulled down my face covering, but a wave of claustrophobia crashed over me. The panoramic vision helped, but the metallic-tasting bottled air from the tank strapped to my back made my heart race, causing me to breathe in short, shallow gasps.

Glimmer's sharp, get-it-together head toss ended my spiral. Our eyes met, and something in her unflinching canine stare steadied me. My breathing slowed, even deepened, the moment we approached the glass doors.

Chili crouched to the dog's level. No easy task fully suited in his protective suit. "I've got a filet on ice waiting for you, girl."

Glimmer's wiggling butt signified her willingness. Heck, my motivation upped a degree, too. The man grilled steak better than Ruth's Chris.

He rose and forced my wild eyes to meet his. "This is the real thing, Hunter. You know what to do."

I did. The realization set in. So did the knowledge that the entire town had his nickname wrong. He should be called Chill, a master at calmness under duress.

On Chill's—I mean Chili's—signal, I opened the door. Glimmer shot inside like a bullet. I followed, my heart hammering again as she weaved around the bronze statue and passed the Peak Mine's historical display. At the exit, she waited, poised with purpose, as I reached for the door to the tent-covered courtyard.

The utilitarian concrete area, usually dotted with weathered picnic tables and rotating exhibits, had undergone a stunning transformation. Last night, an opulent 1920s speakeasy, complete with a well-stocked mahogany bar, had stretched the length of the space. Sepia-toned posters of flapper girls and jazz musicians still adorned the fabric walls. Above, art deco chandeliers dripped with crystal pendants from the vaulted ceiling, creating an atmosphere alive with Jazz Age glamour.

This morning, vintage posters loomed in the shadows above the long bar while the light fixtures swayed ominously above. The festive decorations now seemed to mock the danger lurking around us.

Glimmer sat facing the long bar, her nose twitching frantically. On command, she began her search, snuffing upward, darting right, then left. She circled the perimeter twice, eventually returning to the same place she'd started in front of the bar. My confidence cracked. Gas was a treacherous enemy, seeping through rooms and walls with deadly stealth. But Glimmer always found the source in record time. Today, she seemed uncertain. Had she been wrong? Chili trusted her. We couldn't fail him.

Suddenly, Glimmer's body tensed. She darted beneath a pair

of gold-draped tables, straight to the bar. My pulse pounded when the doxie planted her front paws against the wall and barked twice. She'd found something—but what?

I moved in closer. The dog pawed at a knee-high air conditioning vent. Inside the tent, it was a mine sensor's blind spot—an exploitable weakness known to only a select few.

"Can a gas leak affect a tent enclosure?" I asked, eyeing the high roof and the unsealed, weather-resistant fabric that should allow for ventilation.

"Doesn't seem plausible, does it?" Chili muttered as he pried off the vent cover.

Before I could stop her, Glimmer vanished into the opening, her low-to-the-ground weiner body disappearing in the flexible tubing. Terror struck! My brave, focused dog, crawling through what could be a death trap.

Hope's words echoed in my head: A mother's fear. At that moment, I understood the crushing weight of it. No wonder my sister got testy. I forced myself to breathe, but dread still gnawed at me.

"A gas leak at the center of last night's party could explain the drunkenness and disorderly conduct." Chili's observation interrupted my panic attack.

The man read my mind.

"It makes no sense. Methane, carbon monoxide, carbon dioxide, hydrogen sulfide, and nitrogen dioxide kill. Euphoria was not a side effect," I countered, clinging to facts to keep my concern at bay.

He shrugged. At least, that's what I thought the crinkle in his protective suit meant.

When I called Glimmer back, she did not emerge through the vent. Instead, I heard barking. Faint at first, then louder. I traced it quickly to a spot between the tent and the rock wall. Chili cut away the fabric siding.

Inside, we found the doxie in a rock alcove squeezed between two empty canisters of nitrogen oxide. Laughing gas?

The truth hit me front and center—we hadn't been drunk last night. We'd been systematically gassed into euphoria with sweet air found in most dentists' offices.

No doubt about it. The Peak Diamond heist had been orchestrated with terrifying precision.

Chapter Four

NEVER SHOW YOUR HAND—WISDOM FROM A
JEWEL THIEF

SUNDAY, 11:00 A.M.

The moment we located the laughing gas, Chili removed his hand and head gear and radioed in Glimmer's find. I followed his lead and practically ripped off my mask. I sucked in my first unencumbered breath with the exuberance of a smoker just off an overseas flight. I freed my hands to help Chili record the manufacturer's identifying numbers on the gas tank. No need to remember the string of numbers interspersed with letters—he took a photo and forwarded it to me.

"Find the ..." His cough barely covered his curse as the mine team poured into the area. This crisis averted, I scooted out of the way. No need to be around as another loomed.

Of course, I ran into Chief Rockman again. Not literally. This time, he politely held open the courtyard door for Glimmer and me as we passed him. I thanked him with a nod. The mini pulse, more like a tic in his brow, indicated he wasn't in a chatty mood anyway. While he pursued the murder investigation and hunted for whoever had released laughing gas at last night's gala, I had a window to study the counterfeit Peak Diamond before it became official evidence. A temporary reprieve, certainly. For how long, I couldn't say.

Resounding applause and congratulations awaited Glimmer and me as we exited the museum. The recognition made perfect sense—the doxie had detected a gas leak that costly, sophisticated equipment had missed. Though we'd simply been doing our jobs, Glimmer basked in the attention with typical doxie pride, preening for the cameras and taking theatrical bows. I couldn't bring myself to mention how absurd she looked in that neon outfit, though perhaps I should have. Her triumphant strut made it clear she intended to exploit her newfound fame shamelessly.

Her discovery offered genuine hope for a breakthrough. Only someone with mining industry knowledge and access to dental equipment would understand that the sensors would not detect this particular gas. While not conclusive, this insight narrowed the suspect pool considerably and opened an investigative avenue.

The moment we squeezed through the crowd, a reporter from the *Peak Examiner* cornered me. I praised Chili and his team and plugged my brother-in-law's dog training center for Glimmer's expertise.

At the risk of being rude, I cut the interview short the moment I realized both Gram's truck and my sister's vehicle had left the parking lot. What were they thinking? Running away solved nothing except avoiding me ....

I walked to my SUV to activate the FindMe app on my sister's phone—something I'd never done before today.

Intent on my mission, I didn't notice the mayor until she grabbed my arm. "Goodness, Hunter. Did the gas affect your hearing?" Her breathless voice suggested she'd been chasing me down in those fancy Ferragamo heels. Perhaps I really did need a pair after all.

"I'm sorry. I need to get Glimmer out of her suit," I took a calming breath. I needed to slow down, be more aware, and open to subtle clues.

"Don't let me stop you. With all her fur, the poor dear must be roasting."

I doubted that. I hadn't broken a sweat, and Glimmer loved to nap in the warm afternoon sun.

No response needed. The mayor kept talking. "You just missed your grandmother and sister."

Nice to know my family had confirmed I was still breathing before disappearing. Not that Hope needed confirmation—I'd felt her relief the moment we'd identified the laughing gas.

"Your niece, I'm not sure which one, was injured on the soccer field. Your grandmother and Hope drove over there to help her. She asked me to tell you to meet her at the ranch later this afternoon. Oh, what a day!" Ruby wailed.

I recognized the excuse for what it was. Hope out of the chief's reach bought us time.

"She also gave me this." The mayor looked furtively around, then palmed an organdy bag into my hand.

I recognized it as my fingers closed over a hard stone. Gram had ensured I had the tools to investigate. "When do you plan to tell the chief that the Peak has been stolen?" I asked.

Ruby shook her coiffured head. "Your grandmother asked me to wait until you left."

I nodded. Rockman would be furious about the timing, and I couldn't fault him for it. We were essentially restricting his access to evidence in an active investigation. "You need to call the insurance company," I said. "They'll have to officially retain me as an investigator. Otherwise, the chief won't cooperate."

"He'll cut you off in a New York minute," Ruby announced in uncharacteristic candor. "I would."

Had I underestimated Ruby's commitment to the letter of the law?

Her open palm stopped my rebuttal. "I will not be the mayor who lost the Peak Diamond. It needs to be found. You and your dog are our best hope."

She wouldn't keep her position much longer otherwise.

Without the diamond, Sunset Peak couldn't survive as an independent town. I kept that observation to myself. Ruby understood the political stakes well enough. "You weren't thrilled about paying my finder's fee either."

Ruby's half-smile confirmed that point. "No, I wasn't."

Fortunately, the mayor's mercenary tendencies could ultimately be counted on. So could Sterling & Sons, the company insuring the Peak Diamond. A minor issue like a conflict of interest would not deter them from hiring a proven recovery specialist.

"Do you really think the gas and the murder are related to the stolen diamond?" Ruby asked.

"There are no coincidences."

She nodded sadly.

"Make the call," I said.

I waited for Ruby to dial before dropping the Bronco's tailgate and depositing the fake diamond into my fingerprint-activated gun locker. I undressed Glimmer next. Free of the fitted rubberized suit, she puppy-shook from head to tail. The shiver corkscrewed its way to the tip of her tail before she yawned and not so subtly curled up into a crescent beside her breakfast cooler. She'd been promised filet mignon. Chicken and carrots didn't stand a chance today.

I ran my hand the length of her soft body instead. "You did well, girl. I'm proud of you."

Glimmer cracked one eye open and licked my hand. I smiled while peeling off the hazmat suit. The last thing I needed was a dog bouncing around, demanding attention. My occasionally stubborn dachshund had her own bossy way of keeping me focused. We were good together.

Her dismissive snort cut through my sentimental moment. I had a fake diamond to examine before the chief demanded I hand it over.

I tossed the clothing mounds into the back of the SUV and scooped up Glimmer. Cleaning protocols could wait. Gram may have thought she'd pulled a fast one on Rocky Rockman, but I'd learned the hard way that the man was worse than a dog with a bone. Ruby would cave to his unbending stare in no time.

Which meant I'd better use the time I had wisely. I waved to Ruby, still on the phone with the insurance company, as I pulled out of the parking lot.

I turned left onto Whiskey Row, passing the quiet tourist saloons, then made a right onto Peak Way. My stomach rumbled as I spotted the bright yellow awning with its black paw print trim. A plate of chicken and Waffles, drowning in honey-butter, was calling my name. Pure willpower kept me driving straight to Starlight Estate Jewelers. The open sign told me Sunny had come in to cover for Hope and me. Perfect. I'd need the help.

My phone rang as the garage door lifted. The familiar international area code made me smile. The mayor's call had quickly activated the insurance company's gem recovery protocols.

Of course, Sterling & Sons would assign their top recovery investigator, who happened to be a friend of mine. "What took you so long, Sophie?"

Her clipped, upper-crust British accent brought our long talks at our London flat to mind. "Still disrespecting my tea, I see."

"Tea?" Oh, yeah, it was five p.m. in the UK. Two years of monitoring De Beers site auctions together hadn't converted me. I still liked dinner in the evening.

"I rather knew you'd already be in the thick of this."

"The Peak is my hometown's lucky charm," I replied.

"Yes. Well, I suspect I should offer a bit less than your usual fee."

"Not unless you want to offend your best producer."

"Perish the thought. What do you need?" Sophie asked.

My own personal Watson. Sophie's knack for digging up crucial details made me a far better investigator. "Edward Blackwood's been murdered. I need a full package on him, including associates."

"I see." British efficiency at its best, she continued. "Do you need anyone else?"

I added two additional Gala attendees to the list. "Get ears out on buyers. My gut is telling me to look Russian."

""Russian." Her steady tone couldn't mask her concern. I'd wounded some serious Cossack pride during my last museum diamond recovery.

"The provenance on the Peak Diamond is going to come up," Sophie said.

I gritted my teeth. "Known charlatans have filed the claim who, I might add, so far haven't produced a shred of evidence to support their opinion."

"It is a government entity."

"A corrupt government agency. The stone's rough discovery has been well documented. There is even a photo of the original rough in the local newspaper dating back to 1922."

"There is a photo of something resembling rough. Worldwide, there are but a handful of fire diamonds. Yet a significant stone was unearthed in a failing copper mine in Arizona where, to date, no other diamond, orange or otherwise, has been discovered."

"I admit, it sounds impossible, but newspapers in Phoenix reported the find, too. So did period diaries. The stone's cutting was also well-documented."

"Meticulously documented," Sophie repeated, "... by a man who by all accounts cut corners, as you yanks say."

That was the strangest part of the tale. During a time when provenance wasn't even a vocabulary word, Grant Peak had painstakingly created a legend. "It's unusual but not unheard of for an orange diamond to be found in or around copper veins."

"The People's Commissariat of Finances claims the Peak belongs to the Imperial Russian collection," Sophie said.

Of course, those overzealous Russians would claim ownership.

"They say the Peak is the large orange stone worn by Czarina Alexandra in 1912."

"The information was miraculously discovered in a previously unknown diary," I shot back. Hope had checked the documentation and responded to the allegations two years ago when the claim first came to light. Shame on me for thinking it had gone away.

"Possession is nine-tenths of the truth," Sophie said.

Which was exactly why the Russians wanted the stone. Their claim brought nagging questions to the surface. Was the Peak Diamond's legend a hoax? Had our town's founder bought the stone in the aftermath of the Russian Revolution? If so, where had he acquired it, and how had he paid for it? No one, including the Russians, could establish a money trail.

"Do you need access to the copy of the stone?" Sophie asked.

"I happen to have it for now. I'll perform the usual tests and forward the results."

"I see." She didn't, and a long-winded explanation wasn't worth the time.

"I'll arrange bail." Sophie's deadpan dryness made me smile.

"Oh, ye of little faith." I explained Hope's situation.

Sophie's long pause affected my pulse rate. "You'll need me to run interference. I shall catch the next flight."

Although her presence invariably proved valuable, I declined. Something told me this problem was all mine. "I need you to turn up the heat on the diamond. Whoever Blackwood double-crossed has the stone. He'll be looking for a buyer."

"Quite sexist of you, Hunter."

"Hardly. Statistically, women prefer poison as a murder weapon." My sister's target practice accuracy came to mind. No. I'd know deep down if my twin had killed someone. Until I saw the autopsy report, I refused to speculate.

Determining the type of weapon used could narrow down my suspect list. The information would give me something with which to negotiate with Chief Rockman, assuming he kept the investigation in-house.

Chapter Five

WHAT YOU SEE IS NOT ALWAYS WHAT YOU GET— WISDOM FROM A JEWEL THIEF

SUNDAY, 12:00 NOON.

My right to investigate the Peak Diamond's disappearance now established, it was time to examine the duplicate diamond for clues.

I nudged my snoozing dog. Glimmer buried her head beneath her paws, refusing to move. Any wonder the doxie's whistle-like snoring irked me. A sneeze a block away woke me.

"Come on, sleepyhead. We have work to do." Glimmer yawned and stretched. I scooped her under my arm as I exited the vehicle.

I walked through the elegant back room and waved to Sunny in our retail store, offering a potential customer pieces from our extensive turquoise collection. No real surprise. Sales of the blue-green mineral set in hammered .925 silver paid the mortgage.

My stomach rumbled in tune with Glimmer's. A "hangry" dachshund did not add up to productivity. I detoured to the kitchenette.

Sunny Diaz joined me a few minutes later. "That turned out to be a good sale. I think you should pay me commission." A giant compared to me, standing 5'9" tall in flats, her curvy shape and the neon-red strip braided in her dark hair seemed to make her approachable. We had to be the only stodgy estate jewelry shop employing a Bohemian Latina who had a love affair with rainbow-colored locks.

"I'm all for paying you for what you sell. It eliminates salaries," I replied.

Sunny scrunched her nose. "Never mind. I, uh, bow to the conquering heroines." She removed an imaginary hat with a courtly flourish. "You totally deserve a reward."

The weiner dog thought so, too. Her excited woof-woof encouraged Sunny to push the dog food bag aside. "No lumpy vomit for you today, Princess." Sunny removed a butcher paper-wrapped sandwich from the refrigerator. With her crazy, painted fingernails, she picked off the bread and offered the doxie a chunk of her mother's famous carne asada. The dachshund gobbled it without chewing.

"You intend to eat Glimmer's breakfast?" I asked.

"Heck, no. You're buying lunch." The doxie's head toss agreed in solidarity.

I recognized defeat when I saw it and returned Sunny's grin. I couldn't resist her dimple, and she knew it. I handed her my credit card. "My usual pancakes. Get whatever you want."

Sunny's smile spread from ear to ear. "I'm on it."

Of course, she was—with my credit card in her hands. A hot minute later, Sunny said, "As I hear it, Glimmer found the smoking gun."

Sunset Peak's gossip network ran at full speed this morning. "Gas canister," I replied.

"Seriously? Not a mine thing?" She waited for my nod. "What kind of gas?"

"Laughing gas. Except I don't think anyone is chuckling."

"Like from the dentist's office?"

"Yup." Sunny drew her phone like an enthusiastic gunfighter from her skinny jean pocket. "There are two dentists in Sunset

Peak." She whistled. "A lot in Phoenix. Did you get a serial number?"

I forwarded her the photo Chili had taken. "The tag was a white paper barcoded label." Not a particularly unique point, but maybe something.

Her fingers flew across the screen. "I'm on it."

She was until I broke her concentration. "I'll be in the lab when brunch arrives."

"The lab?" her voice squeaked. "Has something happened to the Peak Diamond?"

"What? Where did you hear that?" I asked more sharply than I'd intended. So much for secrecy.

Sunny didn't seem to notice. "Hope asked me to give this to you." She handed me a tampered-with envelope. "It's the Peak's diamond plot. I peeked."

Not even a pretense at contriteness bothered me. Sunny's never-ending curiosity routinely got her into trouble. It went along with not being able to keep a secret.

I crossed my arms, not giving in.

Sunny turned on her most engaging smile. "There's no other reason you'd need it."

Our assistant really was too intuitive for her own good. I stopped myself just short of admission. "When were Gram and Hope here?"

"Thirty minutes ago. They kinda reminded me of Thelma and Louise."

Not a comforting thought. "What made you think that?"

"Your grandmother stood by the door like a lookout. She kept telling Hope to hurry."

Great. Guilt by admission. "You're watching too much TV again."

"They cleaned out the safe," Sunny added.

The bottom dropped from my stomach. My sister removed millions of dollars of consignment and store inventory? I refused to believe it. I spun on my booted heel and strode through our gem testing lab to our small office tucked into the building's southeast corner. Sunlight poured through the upper windows, illuminating the farmhouse-style office in a warm glow. I focused on the sealed envelope centered on the maple desktop. My heart pounded in my ears as I tore open the letter.

Come for us when the coast is clear. "How Bonny and Clyde!" I muttered to myself.

I approached the wall safe hidden behind a photograph of Hope and me competing in a 4-H barrel race. I pressed my thumb on the fingerprint-activated safe lock. The door clicked open with foreboding—the low-pitched suspense kind. I felt Sunny's breath on my neck as I peered inside.

The clear lidded trays glittered with precious jewelry. The loose stone gem envelope boxes lined the left side. Even the pile of cash looked untouched. I breathed easier. "It's all here. What exactly did you see?" I looked over my shoulder, forcing Sunny to back off.

"Hope stuffed a black velvet bag into her purse," she replied. "It looked large."

I reached back into the darkest corner of the safe, so far back I couldn't see it. I felt it, though. One velvet bag where once there had been two. The knot in my stomach tightened. This was serious. I closed and locked the safe and I sat in the nearest chair. Hope had taken her diamond cache—thirty-four IF, D color, 1 carat, brilliant cut, untraceable commodity diamonds that had arrived via courier every year on our birthday. No sender's card accompanied the devil's gifts, but we knew who had sent it. *Le Renard Argente* hadn't forgotten his daughters. Over the years he'd provided us with means, courtesy of his ill-gotten lifestyle.

Hope had broken our pact. How many times had we wanted to sell just one to expand our business or pay for Pop's medicines? We'd never touched the stash until now ...

I took a deep breath, reaching out in my twin way. *Why, Hope? What have you done?*

I heard her response as if she sat right beside me. *Protect your-self, Taylor. I had no choice.*

Not the words of an innocent woman. How was I supposed to defend her if I didn't know exactly what she'd done or thought she'd done? Which was likely the point. My sister was protecting someone. The realization didn't surprise me. Hope and Gram shared a deep maternal instinct I'd never quite developed.

I'd better figure it out if I intended to help. "Sunny, your imagination is working overtime," I said as lightly as I could manage. "Hope took my mother's diamonds to be reset for Amber and Kyan. Nothing more." Good thing my nieces had a birthday coming up.

I'm not sure Sunny believed me, but the privacy alarm rang announcing another shopper's arrival. Sunny scurried off. Glimmer's snort summed up my emotional state. I hated the unknown. Best I searched for answers.

"I know. I'll get to work." I closed the office behind me and settled in the gem testing lab. Satisfied I was on target, the dog curled in a crescent and sank into her squishy memory foam bed beside my wheeled desk chair. Located in a dark, unlit corner, the L-shaped testing area resembled a wonky dark room that met a high-budget science lab. I powered up the 15x magnification Gemolite microscope and the GIA iD100 diamond tester. Time to discover exactly what the damaged gemstone could tell me.

Redundant as the procedure seemed, I needed to follow protocol. First, I scanned the Peak Diamond's official GIA plot into the computer and displayed it up on one of the two computer screens. Next, I removed the two amber-colored stones from the carry bag with a jeweler's tweezers and visually examined each piece. The high color saturation met the criteria for a vivid orange, and the pear-shaped stone's light dispersion appeared genuine. I held the stone in front of Glimmer. "Find."

Her single bark confirmed that she sensed carbon, which, by definition, meant the stone was a diamond. Natural, treated, or lab-grown was the question.

I cleaned both stones with a well-used gem cloth before setting them in the black velvet viewing box. I turned on the fluorescent spectroscope and probed for microscopic lattice defects created during the stone's formation. Though not perfected for orange diamonds, a REFER result meant the diamond was not naturally formed and changed the next testing phase.

I checked the calibrations before touching the larger stone with the pinpoint probe. The two-second delay felt like an eternity. I didn't realize I'd held my breath until the computer voice said PASS, and I exhaled in a rush. The probe reported the stone real by most jewelers' standards. Had Gram been wrong? Was the Peak Diamond really damaged? My gut told me to keep looking. Man-made diamond manufacturing companies have always sought ways to circumvent the system.

I quarter-turned my chair to face the GIA photomicroscope. A true innovation for gem identification, this device would video every step of my findings. I turned on both the LED lighting and 6.3-megapixel camera and programmed the image to show on the second computer screen.

My eye went directly to the outer girdle. "No identifying inscription" didn't surprise me. The Peak Diamond didn't have an identifying number. It had been cut long before laser inscription existed. Not the case today. Although legitimate man-made diamonds were required to have serial numbers, an illegal copy of a world-renowned diamond would not have one either.

Good thing all diamond manufacturing houses left a mark of sorts—something unique about their process, if you knew where to look. Anticipation tingled in my fingers as I increased the magnification to 15x. I loved playing Sherlock Holmes.

No metallic inclusions, no straining, no Color zoning. I sent a copy to Sophie. She would be impressed. This copy was good, dare I say, the best I'd ever seen. I increased the magnification. The signature was there somewhere. I just needed to find it.

The Carbon pattern ... was that a wrinkle?

The hairs at my nape prickled a heartbeat before Glimmer

growled—not in danger precisely, but a warning. I tensed. My body blocking my hand movement, I reached beneath the desktop, palming my faithful 9mm Glock, ready for anything.

"I should charge you with impeding an investigation, Taylor."

Chief Rockman! I jerked as I released the weapon, banging my nose on the microscope's raised eyepieces. *Ouch.*

"I'm officially on the case." I rubbed my stinging bridge.

"We'll see about that." His gaze challenged mine. Coupled with his clipped tone, I dug in my heels, prepared to fight the battle I couldn't afford to lose. He was in my world now.

"You need me. My gem recovery record is unmatched." Appealing to his need to succeed made sense. Yet, the tactic didn't work. He still threw out an objection.

"You're personally involved."

A hard no in any investigative work. I knew that. I still didn't give an inch. My sister needed me on the inside. "I have the most advanced research and GIA set up in Arizona."

"I don't doubt it." Tension crackled like a live wire between us as he seemed to overwhelm the small space.

Even in boots, my cheek barely reached his chest, I still refused to back down. Intimidation wasn't going to break me despite my crooked neck. Glimmer ended the standoff. She planted her front paws on his pant leg and barked, vying for attention.

Her interruption worked. Rockman reached down to scratch her ears. "What did you find?"

Conciliation? Not a chance. He wanted to know what I knew. Was he testing or using me? "The diamond is lab-grown."

"Is it traceable?" He was direct. I hated to admit it, but I liked that about him.

"There's no ID number," I replied.

"Didn't expect one. Is the diamond traceable?" He'd interpreted my hesitation accurately. Geez. The man read me too well.

"Theoretically. Every manufacturing chamber has a unique carbon layering process."

"So, what type of diamond is it?"

"A lab-grown Chemical Vapor Deposition diamond." Baffling him with my brilliance failed—I saw his flash of recognition. Rockman had supposedly transferred from the Los Angeles PD. Not exactly the place where you'd pick up knowledge about diamonds. "You're familiar with CVD diamonds?"

"Yeah. I worked a few jewelry store robberies in the day."

No guile in his response. Was I imagining it? I eyed his swimmer's shoulders. My BS monitor fired. Note to self: Have Sophie check Chief Rockman out. The man had more than a patrolman's knowledge.

"How many places can make it?" he asked.

"There are only a handful of CVD manufacturers worldwide. Mostly in India," I replied.

His lazy-arm cross didn't faze me. I saw it coming. "I don't need your help."

"But you do. This signature in this stone is new." I had his attention now.

"How do you know that?"

I gestured toward the dual computer monitors beside the microscope. One showed a picture of the diamond's computerized plot and photos flashing like fingerprints beside it. "The computer is comparing the diamond against all known GIA and AGS plot files. So far, no matches."

He stroked his chin, drawing my eye to a lightness in the chiseled plane. I blinked. This man stood between me and protecting my twin.

Glimmer tapped my shin about the same time Rockman cleared his throat. "What do you see?"

Too much ... I'm sure I blushed. Was that amusement in his sharp gray eyes? "An innovative new player with technology equal to a carbon 3D printer. I've never seen anything this precise before. This diamond is a near-perfect replica," I pointed to the feather inclusion deep in the girdle. "Including exact placement of the feather on the Cleavage Plane."

"Adding inclusions isn't easy, but it has been done before," he said.

"It's more art than precision. Come look in the microscope."

He brushed by me, leaving a whiff of something intriguing in his wake. I steeled myself. "The truly remarkable part is the Cross-hatching strain pattern."

He adjusted the scope with the skill of a seasoned pro. "I don't see anything unusual."

"Increase the magnification and look closer."

"I still don't ... wait a minute." Silver flashed in his eyes. He had to be wearing colored contact lenses. How else could the riveting color be explained?

He'd found it. "Until now, only natural diamonds have had that carbon signature. CVD diamonds normally have a banded pattern. Unlike HPHT, high pressure and high heat, which has no patterns due to consistent pressure," I explained.

He backed away from the microscope and leaned against the entry. His gaze still locked with mine, but something had changed. His stance seemed less tense. "I don't trust you ..."

"I don't trust you either," I shot back with more feeling than I'd intended.

His raised brows questioned my outburst, but he stayed on subject. "We'll get to your issues later, right now you need to understand mine. Your twin sister is involved in this, and I don't trust you to be objective."

"I won't be. My sister is not involved, and I will prove it."

"How do you know she's not involved?" Suspicion again. Would he believe me?

I touched my heart. "It's not logical, but I know. It's a twin thing." His headshake gave me hope. "You understand."

"No, I don't." He ran his fingers through his dark hair. "Your involvement is a mistake, but you're right. You are the best in the business. We need each other to find the diamond."

He was more right about that than he knew. His words still

touched me in a weird, sensual kind of way. I was in. That's all that mattered, for now.

"Don't think I won't kick your butt off the case if I see anything unusual going on," Rockman warned.

I couldn't help myself. "Define unusual." Look at me stirring the proverbial pot.

"Don't try me."

I wisely said nothing more.

"That out of the way, can the manufacturing equipment be traced?" he asked again, all business.

"Maybe. The problem is, making a diamond isn't that complicated. All you need is a diamond seed, a vacuum chamber, and a way to introduce methane and hydrogen."

"Can I buy the parts at Grainger?"

"Easier than that." I held up my phone. "If you're a Prime member, Amazon will deliver everything you need in twenty-four hours. Industrial quality parts can be bought from food-equipment manufacturing companies. The trick is in the process." I'd surprised him. I was starting to recognize his tells. Everyone had them—some were more subtle than others. Rockman's was the ever-so-slight twitch just above his left brow.

"Was this diamond home grown?" he asked.

I shook my head. "This copy is too good. Whoever created it also had a copy of the GIA report."

"What aren't you telling me?"

Save me from open-ended questions. Was this a test? He couldn't possibly know about Hope's part yet? Heck, I didn't even know exactly what her part was. I chose the redirect. "Blackwood's buyers generally have museum-quality taste."

"Meaning?"

I'd just suggested that his murder was linked to the jewel theft, yet Rockman hadn't even blinked. "My gut tells me duplicating the Peak Diamond is only the beginning." I let my ominous words sink in. "Whoever has this technology can replace any diamond at will, and no one will know the difference."

"Except you."
Which likely made me the killer's next target.

Chapter Six

BEWARE OF THE DOUBLE-DOUBLE CROSS— WISDOM FROM A JEWEL THIEF

"What was the murder weapon used on Blackwood?" I brushed over the threat. I felt my handgun press against the small of my back. I knew how to take care of myself. Jewelry recovery and unsavory individuals went together.

Rockman referred to his phone. "No updates from the ME." His gaze held mine for a split second longer than seemed necessary. "Preliminary observation indicated a clean kill with a 9mm."

"Execution style?" I asked.

"No. No sign of struggle either."

"Blackwood knew his killer," I said. "Don't let Karo leave town. He and Blackwood were not-so-friendly competitors." We were done here for now. I tweezed the diamond pieces into a velvet pouch, switched off the microscope, and dropped on the protective black cover.

Glimmer stood, her nose airborne, ready to go.

Rockman filled the doorway in a deceptively lazy stretch. "That diamond belongs in evidence."

Although his word choice deserved praise, our clashing interests loomed in front of us. The fact that I needed Hope's opinion on the striation pattern weakened my position. My

"

sister's voice in my head reminded me to *compromise.* Not exactly my forte.

I removed a second velvet pouch from the drawer and placed the smaller piece inside. "I would argue that the diamond is more secure in my safe, but, in the interest of fairness, one for you and one for me. For further analysis." Which was true.

"Why? You've already recorded the diamond plot." Rockman's directness could be viewed as aggressive.

I took a deep breath. My need to win trumped pride in this case. "How do I put this?"

"How about the truth?" Coming from the man who called my   wouldn't-recognize-the-truth-if-it-hit-him-square-in-the-face ex-husband *friend*? I held back a scoff, barely.

"Careful what you ask, Chief. Deniability is an asset, and my rules of engagement are not under the same scrutiny as yours are."

He crossed his arms. He got it. "I will not allow you to compromise my murder investigation. Nor will I look the other way if you break the law."

A part of me actually believed him, which made no sense based on the way he'd supported my ex-husband's lies. No time to examine this inconsistency. "There's breaking the law, and then there's bending it." I saw that little tick in his brow again. A rule follower partnering with someone who lived in the proverbial gray area would be hard enough. Add our history ... My sister accused me of having an elephant's memory. Maybe I did. Like spots on a leopard, people did not change. Sure, some could hide it for a while, but, in the end, they reverted to who they were all along.

For my sister's sake, I needed to cooperate. "Whoever has the Peak Diamond is methodical, well-financed, and willing to get his hands dirty. He's also a ghost and isn't going to be easy to catch." I let that sink in before adding, "You need to build your case by determining when and how he switched the diamond. I'll find out who the buyer is, which may lead us to who stole it. Unless you have a better idea?"

"He? Do you know the thief was a man?"

Not the question I expected, unless he knew something about my sister's involvement. "The hypothetical 'he,'" I said quickly.

Rockman's stiff hand extended for his bag. He didn't like the plan. "Russian involvement? That's a big leap. The Peak Mine's response team includes six former special forces members."

Common practice in war-torn areas, but in small-town Arizona? Rockman's officers drew their pens to issue parking tickets, not their weapons. "What are your thoughts?"

"Don't know yet." His annoyance came through loud and clear.

"Redacted files?" His nod confirmed my fears. Former high-profile military personnel added a new dimension and additional suspects. A misdirect? "If you give me their names, I might be able to help."

He didn't believe me. He would after this demonstration. I turned my back on him in favor of my computer. "A similar MO came up in '20 in Palm Beach, Florida. An antique rose-cut diamond necklace displayed at a charity event was replaced with a CVD replica. The quality was visually good, but the switch was caught at the stone's reevaluation when it was transferred back to the owner." I didn't look up from my task. Glimmer did. Her throaty growl questioned my sanity. Sharing still seemed prudent. "Blackwood and Karo both attended the event. I'll send you the official file."

His breath tickled my neck as he looked over my shoulder. This awareness was getting irritating. "Your information is ..."

I forced myself not to notice. "MI6 quality. Yup. Don't ask." My warning invited a fight. "I'd give me a crack at those special forces guys."

He didn't take the bait. He handed me a handwritten list. The bold all-caps said a lot about his personality. I'd never put much store in the study of graphology, but Chief Rockman checked all the boxes. Upright-pointed letters indicated he was intense and aggressive. The heavy pressure added that he enjoyed being in charge.

"You worked this case?" Rockman asked.

"I assisted. We ultimately found the diamond in a local's possession."

"Glimmer found it?"

"Her mother did. It was stashed in plain sight." I smiled, remembering. "The dachshund leaped onto the entry table, toppled a crystal vase, and dug the stone out of the ornamental rocks at the bottom. What a mess. Flowers, water, and rocks all over the Italian marble floor."

"The owners must've been annoyed."

"They were. It was the first time we'd deployed a diamond dog. I was terrified the dachshund had thought up a new game. Fortunately, the dog was right, and the cliché proved true. The butler did it."

Not even a flicker of a smile from Rockman. Maybe you had to be there to appreciate the humor in the situation. I hadn't laughed until afterward.

"Why did he do it?" Rockman asked.

"Money. The butler's mother was ill."

"In that case ..."

"The second was in 2023 in London. We haven't recovered the stone yet, but a housekeeper admitted to sewing the diamond onto the pattern in a biker's jacket." I stopped his question with the one-minute sign. "What's important to note is that in both cases the stones were of Russian origin."

"And Karo's buyers tend to be Eastern European or Russian," Rockman replied. "How does Blackwood fit in?"

"His loyalty is to the highest bidder."

"Could Karo and Blackwood have been working together?"

I'd considered Rockman's suggestion, but ... "A double-double? More likely the buyer has a contract out and they are competing." I took a breath. "The Peak is unusual because it is rarely out of the vault. The window of opportunity for this theft indicates serious preplanning."

"Why?"

"The CVD replacement takes months to create. And the process seldom works on the first try. Even if it did, in this case, the Peak Diamond showing was only decided on three weeks ago."

"Was there talk of it being displayed before the announcement?" Rockman asked.

"The mayor has always said she wanted the stone to be part of the centennial celebration, but the city council vetoed the idea for safety reasons."

"What changed?"

He asked all the right questions. "Someone on the council changed their vote." I didn't add that Hope's support for the plan and lobbying alongside the mayor had swayed opinions.

"Is it possible someone created the diamond and waited for the stone to be put on display?" Rockman asked.

"I suppose. The copy wasn't easy to make or inexpensive. I keep coming back to the amount of planning that had to go into this. The location and set up of the jewel wasn't finalized until last week."

Rockman tapped a note on his phone. "I'll look into all this. Meanwhile, how is Blackwood's death related?"

Considering all the local incongruencies ... "Maybe it's not related at all."

"I don't believe in coincidences," Rockman admitted.

Of course, he didn't. On that, we agreed.

"The Peak is a valuable diamond, but you're right, this was no easy heist. The question is, why? What is the upside?" Said with a law enforcement professional's opinion, it did give me pause.

"The money." The obvious reason seemed the most probable.

"High degree of risk and planning on this one."

"The Russian claim for the Peak," I said.

"The claim is weak," Rockman stated.

Everyone had an opinion. "I agree."

I displayed the Gemology Today article discounting Sunset

Peak's provenance. He zoomed in on the grainy picture. "The photo is black and white. Impossible to confirm?"

"The diary entry provided a good visual description of the diamond. The Russian society's theory is that the Peak's discovery in Arizona was a hoax."

That tick in Rockman's brow again. "What do you think?"

Never expected that one. "I don't want to believe it, but there are some inconsistencies. The thing is that the law favors possession."

"Do you have any proof that the Russians are involved?"

I turned to face his skepticism with a broad smile. "The beauty is that I don't need proof. Just the diamond."

And there it was out in the open—the difference between my job and his. And the paycheck, of course. Rockman's shrug acknowledged his agreement.

It was time to confess Hope's involvement before he found out from someone else. My heart thumped. Getting along with him had felt oddly good. Glimmer's nose batted my calf. I got her point: take the opening or don't, but move on.

"I, uh." I'm sure I blushed.

Me at a loss for words?

"You, uh, what?" Rockman asked.

The words spilled out in a rush. "My sister graded the Peak Diamond last month for the insurance update. She was technically the last person to see the real diamond."

His slow smile perplexed me. "I was wondering when you'd get around to admitting that."

Of course, he'd known all along. No sense testing this truce any further at this stage. I needed him more than he needed me. I'm not sure he knew that yet. I'd better come clean with the rest. "Her fingerprints are at the crime scene."

"That's to be expected," Rockman replied easily. "She discovered the body." I'm sure I gaped at him.

"You didn't know?" Rockman asked.

"She must've told me when I was suiting up to enter the

museum to deal with the gas leak." Could I have been too distracted to catch her nonverbal cues? Or had she intentionally covered her tracks? Why hadn't she simply clarified her role when I'd accused her of infidelity? There had to be more. Why else would she have fled the scene?

"And your father's an international jewel thief."

My pulse jumped. "Y-you know that, too?"

"I have my own sources."

My ex-husband, no doubt. Whenever I thought that relationship was in my rearview mirror, it came back to bite me. "More of a sperm donor. I haven't seen the man since I was seven."

Rockman's scrutiny didn't faze me. I'd passed every lie detector test I'd ever taken for a reason. I had nothing to hide regarding *Le Renard Argente*. If I were ever unfortunate enough to meet him, not only did I have nothing to say to the man, but I'd turn him in for murder.

"Your baggage, Taylor Hunter, is the kind that gets people like me killed."

"You've got issues, too," I shot back defensively.

His short *yeah* summed it up. "I am the police chief in a tourist town with a murdered visitor and the principal financial resource missing."

And somehow my twin was involved. "I'd say we've both had better Sundays."

Chapter Seven

NO GHOST HAS EVER BEEN SEEN BY TWO PAIRS
OF EYES—WISDOM FROM A JEWEL THIEF

SUNDAY, 2:00 P.M.

So much had changed since my earlier drive through the springtime buds to the museum. This time, I turned left on Spring Street instead of continuing straight to the museum.

Hidden behind a thicket of vibrant bougainvillea and white moonstone roses, the territorial adobe-style buildings emerged like a mirage among lush oasis gardens. The two-story main building—housing reception, the historic bar once robbed by Jesse James himself, and the award-winning Mexican fusion restaurant—promised a memorable western experience. Casitas clustered around babbling water features, and meticulously designed Zen gardens created peaceful pathways leading to the spa nestled into the rugged hillside. Any wonder people journeyed from every corner of the globe to immerse themselves in the legendary healing powers of our mineral-rich mud and rejuvenating springs.

I parked my SUV alongside a wall draped in white climbing roses. Their scent lingered as I circled the imposing stucco and glass structure, taking inventory of the security system's blind spots. Unfortunately, except for the entry and exit doors, this place delivered on its privacy promise.

The casual elegance created by the supple leather sofas nestled in intimate alcoves, overlooking postcard-perfect mountain sunsets, added to the nature-meets-comfort vibe. Even the floral arrangement atop a mesquite table overflowed with local wild-flowers in deep amethyst hues.

Behind the matching live-edge reception desk stood Opal, a name she wore as both identity and accessory.

"Good almost afternoon. May I help you, uh?" The opalescent gems adorning her neck, ears, and woven through her bouncy blonde hair glistened like dewdrops.

"It's Hunter." Not an unusual explanation. Except for Gram and apparently Chief Rockman, no one could tell Hope and me apart.

Opal leaned across the desktop. "Oh, there's Glimmer. I missed her. Hi, sweetie."

Glimmer barked. Opal's bright smile seemed to outshine even her jacket's silver buttons and gave no indication anything out of the ordinary had occurred today.

"How are you holding up?" Notably high-strung, I'd expected Opal to have taken the rest of the day off.

Her dramatic inhale told me she wanted to talk. I settled in for what felt like forever before she began. "It's just awful. That nice man from Los Angeles."

"N-nice?" I almost choked. Narcissist better described Edward Blackwood. "How, uh, did you find him?"

"Not me. Your sister found him," Opal admitted. "I would've fainted dead away."

That, I believed. I rested my hands on hers. "Tell me what happened."

Opal freed her hands. Drawing on her high school drama training, she acted out her explanation. "Hope delivered his food order from the café."

I blinked. "What?" I couldn't have heard her right. My sister delivered food for Blackwood? Could this day get any odder?

"Yeah. She had one of those taped Canary Café delivery bags," Opal insisted. "I know. Crazy, right? Unless the dog training business is failing …" She let that supposition hang.

"No. I …" I'd better come up with a good reason, or gossip would have my sister destitute by dinner. "She was probably doing Crystal a favor."

"Well, that makes sense. Hope would help a friend who owns a café."

"Hope would help anyone," I added. Glad I escaped that pit. "You gave her Blackwood's room number?"

"No. I'm not allowed to give any guest information out. Come to think of it, she never asked for it." Opal brushed back her long hair, the opals twinkling in the midday light.

Then how had Hope known the room number?

"I knew something sinister was afoot there. There have been weird things happening. I told Mr. Blackwood I'd upgrade his room for his safety. He insisted he'd be fine. Look what happened. It's all my fault."

Blackwood, turn down a free upgrade? Never. He'd wanted that specific room for a reason. "What room?"

"I just told you I can't disclose …"

"He's not a guest any longer."

Opal considered my words. "I guess you're right. He was in Organ Pipe 4." Her voice cracked.

I scooted around the desk and reached up to embrace the taller woman. Not that Opal was a giant. Everyone was taller than I was. "You did all you could."

"The chief said the same thing." She blotted a tear.

Rockman, sensitive? Not the man I knew. Yet, he'd apparently comforted Opal.

"I still feel responsible. He seemed so thoughtful," Opal said.

Compared to the *Wizard of Oz*'s lion, maybe. Most people would question Blackwood having a heart at all. Israeli by birth, he'd grown up in the New York diamond district dealing the precious gems and who knew what else. A colored diamond expert, his long-standing interest in the famous orange Peak Diamond made his death extra suspicious.

"What strange things have been going on?" I asked.

Opal straightened, preparing for another stage performance. "The old miner is back. Two sightings in the past few days."

The Inn's Halloween ghost sighted in the spring? No wonder Rockman had scoffed at the witness statements. "Where has the ghost been seen?"

"Around the organ pipe garden."

Near Blackwood's room couldn't be a coincidence. He had been up to something. "Who saw the old miner?"

"Another guest reported seeing the bearded miner around midnight on Friday night. He was carrying the pick."

"Someone was digging?" Or burying something. Could finding the Peak Diamond be that easy?

Her slumped shoulders said dead end. "Naw. Luis found a couple of gopher holes on Saturday morning. You can ask him where."

No need for a consultation. I knew where and, with a diamond dog on the scene, she'd sniff out any diamonds on command.

Opal stopped my quick exit. "You know, the spa wasn't built until the late 1920s. The miners' shacks were in that spot at the turn of the century. I have an old map."

"I'd like to see that," I said.

Opal opened a file drawer beside her. "Do you think the old miner is back to help find the Peak Diamond?" she asked, her eyes the size of two-carat emeralds.

"I hope not. That's my job." If the Peak Diamond's discovery in Arizona really was a hoax, I didn't need a hundred-year-old thief on the loose.

"I guess I'd better get back to my job." Opal's shoulders sagged. "Breaking the news to clients that their spa bookings are cancelled breaks my heart. Some of these people have been waiting months for an opening in our restorative waters."

"The chief's forcing you to close?" The injustice of it rankled me.

"Not exactly." Opal's voice dropped to barely above a whisper. "Our springs are low. This drought has been merciless. We're only operating four of our nine treatment rooms."

Which meant securing a slot at the hot springs would become nearly impossible. Not to mention the financial burden. Odd that the mayor hadn't said anything, since she and her husband owned the property.

A guest approached the desk, offering me an opening to escape. Glimmer at my heels, I scooted out the door into the spa gardens. The dog jogged beside me as I hurried along the winding stone path, lined with native plants identified by both their scientific and common names. I paused at the old miners' fountain just long enough to toss a coin into the water exactly like I'd done a hundred times before. With any luck, my wish for my sister's safety would come true.

Flapping yellow police tape led me to a half-hidden casita far away from prying eyes. A large palo verde blanketed the single-story stucco cubical in bright yellow blossoms, turning the earth-toned building into a floral Chia Pet. Up close, the tape paled in comparison to nature's vibrant flowers.

Glimmer ignored the barrier, not breaking stride until she sat on what appeared to be a mini mound of fresh dirt beneath the bedroom window. Her arf alerted me to a find. I started to duck under the tape until Rockman's voice in my head stopped me with one toe in motion.

Don't push me.

Come on. I had every right to be here. But ... The pitfalls of self-justification up for debate, I caved. Instead, I motioned Glimmer to stay and circled to the casita's front entrance, where Officer Mason Pepper kept a handful of looky-loos, including the *Peak Examiner*'s reporter, at bay. No easy task when a once-in-alifetime story fell into a newbie's hands. Doubly so in Goldine Block's case. Her appearance on Phoenix network news had inspired the once laid-back human-interest columnist to go for the gold.

Me in the shadows seemed prudent. I ducked back behind the building and texted Rockman. No need to wait for his reply. He'd been advised. I ducked under the tape. The dachshund's tail swayed. "Find."

Glimmer's bark invited attention as she dove front paws first into the soft dirt. So much for stealth. Red dirt flew as those little feet burrowed with ancestral expedience. Her blond head disappeared in the dirt pile.

I closed the distance between us, avoiding two freshly filled holes. A minute later, Glimmer sneezed, sending red soil flying. She then backed away, sat at attention, and barked—a single I've-got-something bark.

My heart thumped. She'd found a diamond. The Peak? The rainbow twinkle in her mouth made it seem possible.

Blackwood bury a priceless diamond in an unsecured garden? It made no sense. Why didn't matter to me. Just recovering the stone did, I reminded myself. I crouched in front of the dog and extended my hand. Glimmer dropped the one-carat solitaire diamond earring into my hand. My breath caught. It wasn't the Peak Diamond, but recognition still registered. I touched my left ear and then my right to be sure. My stud earrings were in place. I rarely removed them since Gram had given them to me.

I turned the 18K basket setting upside down to inspect the prong. The repaired prong said it all. This was Hope's earring— the same one she'd worn to last night's gala.

Chapter Eight

PEOPLE SEE WHAT THEY WANT TO SEE—
WISDOM FROM A JEWEL THIEF

Escape my only option, I pocketed the incriminating diamond, scooped up my weiner dog, and jogged to my car. Rockman's words—*I don't trust you to be objective*—played back with annoying clarity.

That he'd been right irritated me. Although I'd never technically agreed to be objective, I never expected to be suppressing evidence in less than an hour. I had no choice. This diamond earring put my sister at the murder scene.

Was my faith in her misplaced? Hope had been the last person to handle the Peak Diamond and admitted to a connection with the unscrupulous diamond acquirer. Anyone else, I'd be demanding an arrest.

My gut knotted. Despite the evidence, I'd still bet my life on her innocence. I needed answers before I ended up in jail on obstruction charges.

I dialed Hope's cellphone number. Of course, the call went directly to voicemail. Next, I tried Gram's number with the same result. Perfect. I knew they hadn't left town though. I could feel them both watching and waiting for answers that I didn't have. I massaged my temples in a gentle circular motion. Gram did her best thinking on horseback. Hope hiked.

I exited the spa and turned left on Miners Road, bypassing downtown, as I drove toward the foothills and a veritable plethora of desert trails. My sister would choose a relatively unused path for solitude. In twin fashion, Hope's voice popped into my head. *Malachite Trail.*

Malachite? The stone represented the pain of a broken heart. Not for Blackwood. Could her boring, homebody husband have been having an affair? That made about as much sense as her pre-teen daughters being in trouble.

I turned off-road at the trailhead marker, jostling Glimmer in the passenger seat. Her low growl was a reminder not to interrupt her beauty sleep. "Get over it. Hope needs us."

The dachshund snorted and curled into another crescent on the leather seat. I slowed to a more respectful pace, mitigating the bouncing until I parked beside Hope's soccer mom SUV, aptly named for the accompanying bumper stickers. I climbed out of my vehicle. I'd need to go the rest of the way on foot, and without GPS since the cell phone flashed the no-service warning. What did I expect out here in the wild desert?

Glancing down at my impractical high-heeled boots, I detoured to the liftgate. Though scuffed and desperately in need of a professional shine, my well-worn riding boots would at least provide some comfort. They'd carry me a couple of miles along the uneven path, but I couldn't promise more than that. Given my sister's tendencies, I might be facing a trek just short of forever. I'd also pay the price for no hat in the bright afternoon sun.

I grimaced. I don't hate hiking, but I couldn't comprehend why anyone would walk anywhere with a perfectly good horse nearby.

Since Glimmer liked to hike about as much as I did, I'd also grabbed her carry pack, figuring I'd be lugging her for most of this ill-fated adventure. I gave her an extra minute to wake up before lifting her from the SUV and setting her on the ground. To my surprise, the dog barked twice and took off in a squirrel-chasing cloud of dust.

I shaded my eyes from the glare. "Glimmer. Heel!" Not even a break in her stride. So much for her exhaustive training. A weiner dog on a mission could not be deterred.

I cursed under my breath. Snakes, bobcats, and coyotes prowled this undeveloped area. I sprinted after her. Despite her short stature requiring two steps for each of mine, I only managed fleeting glimpses as I rounded each curve in the trail. Though horseback riding, power yoga, and doubles pickleball weren't exactly prime cardio training, the stitch stabbing my side at the very first bend seemed particularly unfair.

While keeping my gaze fixed on the scattered rocks littering the path, I couldn't help but notice the vibrant splashes of yellow, orange, and magenta that brightened the otherwise earth-toned landscape. The barrel, cholla, and prickly pear cacti interspersed among palo verde and mesquite trees were all decked out in their springtime glory. Even the majestic saguaro cacti stood sentinel-like, their upstretched arms crowned with what resembled Easter bonnets ready to bloom.

Perspiration trickled down my lower back as I pressed on with my chase until a hawk soaring in circles above a distinctive saguaro —the one Hope had nicknamed the torpedo arm—and the sound of flowing water reached my ears. The Verde Creek Watering Hole, as Pop referred to it, was a spot for quiet contemplation. Hopefully, my sister was there pondering her transgressions.

As I ducked beneath the rock arch, I found my twin lying on her back facing the clouds, and my dog licking guilty tears off Hope's cheeks. That moment, I knew Hope had been pulled into this mess.

"I don't know if I should hug you or strangle you," I said in sheer relief.

"Remember when we used to come out here and stare at the clouds?" Hope's wistful tone sparked a nostalgic glance.

"Yeah." The shapes of those wispy sky balls had sparked true debate. "I saw cumulus clouds."

"And I, horses or dogs."

"Don't forget the flying pigs."

She sat up on the flat boulder. "I was right then, and I am now. You can't be here." My sister wiped the moisture from her cheek with the heel of her hand. "You need to protect yourself."

The dog's brown-eyed glare dared me to agree. I didn't. Like it or not, my twin and I were two parts of a whole. There'd be time later to reaffirm that. Right now, I needed information and took the opening. "Did you go to Blackwood's room last night?"

Hope nodded stiffly. "I didn't murder him. He was alive when I left at midnight."

A clandestine, late-night rendezvous within the murder window looked bad. "Glimmer found your diamond earring outside the back patio door."

Hope gasped and reached for her right ear, then the left. Real fear replaced her quasi-peaceful acceptance. She hadn't known it had been missing. Odd, I hadn't noticed the earring missing when I'd seen her earlier either. In my defense, I had been facing a gas leak.

"You'd better start at the beginning." I removed a water bottle from her bulging blue backpack, cupped a handful for Glimmer, and leaned against one of the towering boulders protecting us from prying eyes to finish the bottle.

"You need deniability. You must find the Peak Diamond," Hope insisted.

Typical Hope, always looking out for everyone but herself. "Cut the crap. You're my sister, and I know you didn't do anything illegal."

"But I did, and I'm prepared to pay the price."

A fresh sheen of sweat beaded on my forehead. Hope, stubborn? I felt like I faced myself versus my let's-all-get-along sister. Time to lay down reality. "I'm not raising your kids or looking out for your husband."

Hope jumped off the bench-height boulder she'd been sitting on and paced the length of the area. "What? I'll lose my GIA grading job. I knew the risks. I'm prepared for that."

"The penalty for murder is twenty-five to life. Add special circumstances, and the circuit hanging judge will …" I let that threat linger. My sister watched enough western movies to get my point.

Hope gulped and stretched her neck. "I-I didn't kill Blackwood. I gave him two GIA diamond reports. That's all. I swear."

I believed her. Passing proprietary information was a crime, but vastly different than first-degree murder. "The Peak's?"

"No. No. I would never …" Her horror appeared real.

Good to know she had limits.

"Blackwood wanted the diamond plot for a specific 20-carat D Flawless Cartier drop necklace and an art deco 15-carat Van Cleef & Arpels Duette brooch," Hope explained.

The bottom dropped out of my stomach. I'd called it. Someone with access to a near-perfect CVD duplicator only needed final GIA reports to replace any gem effectively. "Who owns the jewels?" Pieces of that caliber couldn't be called jewelry. It was like calling Secretariat just a horse.

"I don't know. I can tell you Sterling & Sons insures both pieces."

Sterling & Sons Limited, London! The company I now worked for also insured the Peak Diamond.

My sister, the master of the obvious, added, "I'd say someone is after both of us or Sterling & Sons. Which begs the question: Who did we upset? I can't think of anyone."

Her innocent look hurt. I could name more than a few. Was this whole mess about me, courtesy of the unforgiving jewel thieves I'd thwarted over the years? Was my sister just caught in the middle? My mind reeling, it took me a hot second to ask, "How much does Gram know?"

"With her weak heart? Are you serious? I've told her nothing."

Good old perceptive Gram. "I have news for you: Gram knows." Maybe not all the details, but enough to know her girls were in trouble. "We'd be better off looping her in lest she goes rogue."

Hope knew it, too. She bowed her head and nodded.

"Start at the beginning." I needed to know exactly what we faced.

"My husband ..." Hope trailed off.

Of course, he'd been involved. My sister stopped my why-didn't-you-tell-me complaint with a schoolmarmish finger shake. "... sold a bomb dog to Phoenix Security. Their background checked out. I made the calls myself. When Hank delivered the dog, the security team took him out for a celebratory drink at a cardroom. As you can imagine, my card-counting husband couldn't help himself."

The bigger question was why hadn't my twin radar sensed it? "I take it the cardroom didn't toss him out."

"I wish they had. According to him, he won big for a while," Hope admitted.

"How much did he lose?" I asked. The scam was all too predictable.

"$250,000."

I whistled. "He lost that much playing poker in a single evening?"

"Not exactly. It happened over a few weeks. I knew something was off. I never imagined he'd break his word."

His dishonesty had hurt her more than the consequences. I got that. Trust ranked number one on my list as well. "He did pay his way through UNLV at the tables," I reminded her.

"Yeah. It got him banned from the Vegas strip casinos for life," Hope said.

"There's more going on here."

"No kidding. He claims he was expertly set up."

A quarter of a million dollars was a good chunk of money, but not enough to bankrupt us. "Why didn't you take the money from the office safe?" But I knew, because in a similar situation I'd have done the same. Not that I expected to get away with it.

"Because I'd have to listen to you tell me I told you so for the rest of my life. Besides, I had a plan."

Pollyanna Hope dealing with card sharks? This ought to be good. I waited.

"They promised to erase the debt if I appraised two pieces that clients wanted to reinsure."

"You saw the red flags, right?" I asked. This had disaster written all over it.

"Yes. I'm not stupid. I expected to be asked to fudge the values. I still couldn't pass up doing an easy appraisal to get Hank out of trouble. It seemed like a miracle. I ordered the GIA reports and showed up at the Amethyst Inn to appraise the physical diamonds as instructed."

"There's nothing illegal about that. You are a certified appraiser." What could the end game be?

"That was my justification."

"Except Blackwood was the client?" I knew what happened next.

"Yup. I recognized him despite the wig. I can't believe he thought I wouldn't know him with that wavy gray hair."

I couldn't picture it at all. The man had been bald for as long as I'd known him.

Her admission continued. "I knew something was wrong the minute I walked into the suite. My mistake was not leaving right away. Call it stupid pride. I wanted to be you, like we did in high school, taking tests for each other."

A smile curved my pressed lips. Hope hadn't taken a social studies test in junior or senior year. "Me? Why would you want to be me?"

"Your life is so exciting and fulfilling. Mine is boring. You make a difference. I don't."

"Me, make a difference? I deal with thieves and liars. I consider every case I walk away from a win. Your kids are the real deal." I got it. On the surface, being single and traveling to your heart's content sounded like a dream job. The reality wasn't so glamorous. Lonely nights in sometimes sketchy hotels, unrecognizable food when you could get it, and oftentimes hostile local law enforcement. The bad guys never paused for inclement weather or family events either. I'd made my choice. So Hope didn't have to.

"Tell me about the jewelry you appraised," I said.

"Cut, Color, Clarity, and Carat weight matched the GIA report. The wear to the platinum settings was era-appropriate. The plotted imperfections were slightly off. Not too unusual for a 1920s art deco piece. The piece hadn't been graded since the 1970s. Technology has improved since then."

The Peak Diamond seemed to warm my hip pocket. "Could the diamonds have been manmade CVD?"

Hope chewed her lip while considering my suggestion. "I thought about it after the Peak Diamond fiasco, but I saw faint cross-hatch strain patterns at 30x. No CVD standard bands. I had no reason not to certify the diamonds as natural."

"I didn't see the patterns on the duplicate Peak until 50x on the Gemolite microscope," I replied.

"The handheld grading device maxes at 30X."

"Blackwood knew that's what you would bring to an off-site appraisal," I said, suddenly getting it.

"If he knew the magnification limits, I suppose it's possible." She didn't sound convinced. "It's a lot of ifs, though."

No doubt exactly what Rockman would say to any warrant-granting judge. "I'll ask Rockman for the stones out of evidence. We can examine them under the stationary Gemolite microscope to be sure."

"I don't know if the police have the jewels. Someone pounded on Blackwood's front door, demanding entry about the time I started packing up. Blackwood told the visitor to wait and rushed me out the back door. I practically ran through the curtains to get out. That must've been when I lost my earring."

A shiver shimmied down my spine. Blackwood's rudeness had likely saved Hope's life. "Did you see Blackwood's other late-night visitor?"

"Only a silhouette through the curtain's crack. I think the man was shorter than Blackwood and thinner. I didn't see his face, but his hair was a striking silver."

"Like a fox," I muttered. Don't ask me why the comparison came to mind.

Hope's gasp concurred. She'd been thinking the same. "*Le Renard Argenté*. The Peak Diamond would be in his catalogue, but killing Blackwood doesn't fit our father's reputation."

But it did. If Blackwood got in his way like our mother had …

"Blackwood was a nervous wreck and in a rush for me to leave," Hope added. "He agreed I'd completed my end of the bargain. I didn't know how well until I turned on my computer this morning and nothing happened."

"Nothing?" I asked, confused.

"Yup. The screen was blank. My techy daughter said my computer had been wiped. She thinks Blackwood did it to cover up copying my hard drive." Hope twisted her hair around her forefinger. "I don't know how he did it. The computer never left my sight, but Amber says it can be done from a few feet away."

Technology scared me sometimes. If I lost all my data, I'd be in big trouble. "What information was on your computer?"

"Other than pictures of my kids?"

I shot her the "focus" look. She sobered immediately. "Notes on the all the diamonds I've graded."

Free proprietary diamond information. "You think your visit was all about Blackwood getting your data files?" That seemed high-tech for an acquirer like Blackwood. He must have an accomplice. "What else do you have on your hard drive?"

"Nothing important."

I took her at her word. "You need to tell the Chief what you saw."

Hope gulped. In her shoes, I would, too. "He'll never believe me. Not with Hank's debts and all the circumstantial evidence."

"Living on the run isn't a life. He'll eventually find out everything anyway."

"You have that much faith in him? I did purposely mess up the crime scene," Hope said.

I'd figured as much. "His skills are fine. There's something off about him."

"I agree. He's too perceptive for a small-town police chief."

My sister sensed it, too. I felt more than saw Hope's resignation. "You get to convince Gram."

"Me!" I'd rather face Rockman, and she knew it.

"Rock, paper, scissors." My sister readied her right hand.

Resolving adult issues with a child's game? What were we thinking? I readied my hand. "On three. One. Two. Three."

I went for the power rock. Hope covered me with paper. Of course, she won. "Two out of three?" I asked.

"Not a chance." Hope smiled in pure relief. "You handle Gram better anyway."

True, but ...

My sister changed the subject. "Any updates on the laughing gas's origin?"

Solving the case was our best defense. I automatically checked my phone. No service meant no news, which wasn't helpful at the moment. "I need to get back to civilization. The first forty-eight hours are critical."

I'd already wasted two hours of it chasing down answers from my sister. None of which got us closer to finding the killer or the missing Peak Diamond. My action items remained unchanged. Who had placed the laughing gas canisters at the museum gala and why? Why did the mine need a response team populated with retired special forces personnel? Why frame my sister?

Chapter Nine

SUNDAY, 4:00 P.M.

I limped into the shop, favoring what promised to be a killer blister on my baby toe. Sunny locking up well over an hour after closing couldn't be good news.

"Everything …?"

"Geez. Glimmer!" Sunny's exclamation cut off my question. "What have you dragged in?"

The dachshund's arf and agreeable tail wag smacked of disloyalty. "This is your fault. You're the lazy butt I had to carry for three miles."

The dog's cocked head and slow blink claimed innocence.

"Don't even go there." The weiner dog ignored my warning and slinked through my legs. Of course, I tripped. My right hand snaked out, grabbing the glass case. I stopped my fall but got a good look at my reflection. Yikes. Glimmer had a point. Sonoran Desert dust coated my hair and streaked my face, while my once-white top had a tan tinge. Even my lips looked pale and thin.

"You hiked to the Verde River Watering Hole?" Sunny asked.

She said it like she didn't believe it. "Yeah. What's the big deal?" Seriously, I wasn't that wimpy.

"You hate to walk. You drive to the Canary Café, and that's across the street."

True, but I always did what I had to do. "How'd you know I went to the Watering Hole?"

"The red dust on your boots. It's also like the best place to go to think."

So much for a secret rendezvous. I jerked my fingers through my flyaway lion's mane of hair, catching the split ends with a painful jerk. "Does everyone know about that place?"

"Just the locals. Don't tell me you hiked in those sissy riding boots." No need to answer. Sunny shook her head. "No wonder you're limping. How bad are the blisters?"

"One blister on my baby toe." It hurt like crazy, too. I couldn't remember the last time I'd gotten one.

"Ouch. Granny swore soaking in Epson salt helped," Sunny replied.

"My gram says the same thing. Must be a generational thing," I replied. "Why are you still here?"

"Our last client took forever." Sunny's grin offered cautious optimism.

"Good sale?" I asked.

She nodded. The gentle pull on her red braid suggested a big sale. "Oh. Chili stopped by with a filet for the princess."

I swear that dog knew her beef cuts. Glimmer jumped to her feet and trotted toward the kitchenette.

"Also, a courier dropped off an envelope for you. I left it on your desk."

I glanced at my iWatch. Ten minutes to six p.m. PST. Guess we'd call Sophie Sleepless in South Kensington. It was still the middle of the night in London. Wait a minute. We communicated electronically because, between the time difference and travel time, the earliest a package could arrive from London was Monday night. "What time did it arrive?"

"A little after five. The guy said the package was important and he had to have your signature."

A Sunday special delivery? How last century.

"I told him you weren't here, but you'd be back to feed Glimmer."

"How did you know ..."

"She's not the patient sort either." The dog tapped her paw in the doorway, proving it. "I didn't think you took her food with you. Anyway. I told him he could come back tomorrow, or, if it was important, like a Sunday special delivery should be, I could be trusted to give it to you."

Who could resist her dimpled smile? "I guess he gave in."

"Yup. He asked for my phone number, too."

Of course, he did. "What company did he work for?"

"I don't know. The bill of lading was generic. Now that I think about it, he didn't wear a real uniform either." Sunny scratched her chin. "He said he was a contractor. I never found out who he worked for. The late customer arrived and took over. Next thing I knew, the delivery guy was gone. I found the envelope tucked behind the counter when I rang up the sale."

A red flag? I wasn't sure. "What did he look like?"

"Average ..." Her long pause shocked her as much as it shocked me.

"Height? Weight?" I asked.

Sunny chewed her lip. "Not tall. He wore a hat, so I didn't see his hair color."

"Eyebrow color?" People colored their hair, but their brows tended to remain true.

"Light. I-I don't remember exactly."

Super observant Sunny? The customer must've been consuming. I made a mental note to check the entry surveillance video. "Who was the client?" The timeline bothered me.

"An older woman from the East Coast, decked out in one of those southwestern blanket jackets. She had a honking rock on her hand, too. She was all over the turquoise. She tried on like every bracelet. She picked out two pendants for her granddaughters and bought the oval, three-stone piece."

"The bridge. My favorite," I remarked, oddly wary. An unusual delivery and a late weekend client? Could it all be related to the missing Peak Diamond?

"I thought you'd be happier about the thousand-dollar sale," Sunny said.

Was I obsessing? "I am. Too much on my mind."

Sunny smiled. "On that note. I reached out to my dentist about the laughing gas. Her gas tanks have silver plates, but she told me to call Dentist Depot. I left an emergency message with their answering service." Sunny checked her phone. "No return call. That's weird. They advertise same-day emergency service. I'll stop by their office on my way home."

My pulse reacted. Hope and her family used that dentist. "No. Don't do that. I'll check in with the chief. He should do the drive-by."

Sunny crossed her arms. "You buddies with the Rock Man now?"

My emphatic no stopped further conjecture. Sunny gathered her backpack. Unable to stop herself, she added, "Thou doth protest ... Anyway, I saw him changing a flat tire last week. He's got some great pecs."

A shirtless, sweaty ... I swallowed. Glimmer barked, ending the trip down that rabbit hole.

"You'd better feed the beast," Sunny said. "Tah. I'm outta here." She waved as she exited the front door.

Maybe she hadn't noticed my digression. Who was I kidding? Sunny noticed everything. Except today's delivery guy? I turned the open sign to closed, deadbolted the front door, and turned off the showroom lights. Much as I wanted to check out the package, Glimmer's feed-me routine wouldn't allow for dallying.

She sat on her hind legs, her front paws raised like an Easter rabbit, drooling as I opened the refrigerator door. She squeezed by me, placed her front paws on the second shelf, and nudged the red-bowed Tupperware with her nose. As if I'd miss the gift.

"Okay. Down." The doxie obeyed. She circled my feet as I

carried the container to the table. Beef for two meals in one day? Her sensitive stomach would rebel. Like I could deny her. I dished half of the meat into her bowl and placed it on the floor.

Glimmer dove in, tipping the porcelain dish and spilling the diced meat onto the stone floor. I turned away. No need to clean up, the weiner dog would lick the floor clean.

A shower could wait, too. The special delivery packaging called me as I headed to my office. True to Sunny's words, a 10x14 manila envelope occupied the center of my desk. The computer-generated address label told me nothing. No return label? My heart thumped. An envelope from an unknown sender, delivered by a mysterious courier hours after laughing gas had been pumped into the site of a significant diamond theft couldn't be random luck.

Calling Chief Rockman crossed my mind for about a second. Whatever this envelope contained, someone wanted me to get it. Caution overrode my impatience. Best I follow the unknown package protocol.

Paranoid? Maybe. I still slipped on rubber gloves and carried the envelope to the kitchenette sink. The envelope was light and flexible, indicating that a heavier-grade paper or a photo was inside.

I cut the envelope across the top. Nothing jumped or spilled out. I relaxed and removed a single sheet of paper and a photo. Four men stood among kimberlite rubble at twilight, dressed in fur-edged hats and miners' insulated jumpsuits. My heart skipped a beat. I recognized two of the four men. Blackwood, twenty-odd years ago, stood in the center beside a noticeably younger Jasper Washburn. The third man looked familiar. I removed a magnifying glass from my desk drawer for a closer look.

The shape and color of the unknown man's eyes triggered a memory—the kind I couldn't ignore. No wonder Rockman knew about diamonds. The stones were in his blood. And he'd questioned my past ....

I unfolded the typed paper. Nikolai Volkov.

The name of the other unknown man? The photo connected Jasper Washburn to Blackwood years ago. I checked the time. 3 a.m. in London. I didn't dare wake Sophie. I quickly scanned the photo and sent it to her electronically with a short explanation instead. She'd see it as soon as she turned on her computer early in the morning. With any luck, I'd also have the Peak Mine's personnel information in six or so hours.

The big question was: who sent the photo and why?

More curious than ever to identify the secretive courier, I signed in to the shop's security footage. Clicking back to this afternoon took no time. Neither did watching the footage. Not one identifiable picture of the courier showed on the inside or outside cameras. Either he was the luckiest man alive or the smartest. I'd bet money on the latter.

I owed Chief Rockman a call. I texted instead and headed to the shower. I'd rather not advertise my transgressions when I needed answers from him. At the bottom of the stairs, I scooped up a growling Glimmer. She wasn't getting the balance of the filet tonight, no matter how badly she behaved. I finally put the squirming dog on the ground in front of my apartment door as I fumbled for my keys. I recoiled as the weiner dog nosed the door open. *What the ...?* The bomb-went-off disaster inside sucked the breath right out of me.

I caught the dog with one hand, pulled the door shut with the other, and sprinted down the stairs, not feeling my blistered toe until I locked myself in my office. I limped to the safe. The last recorded entry was mine a few hours ago. I opened it anyway, just to be sure. Nothing appeared to be missing.

Breathing easier, I downloaded the alley-facing security footage. No one entered or exited the back alley leading to my apartment all afternoon. On a Sunday? That alley connected the church to the downtown restaurants. That meant ...

This time, I dialed Rockman's cellphone. He answered on the second ring. "I got your text."

I ignored his annoyance. "I got a bigger problem now. Someone broke into my apartment."

A chair squeaked in the background. "The diamond ...?"

"Is safe. The business safe wasn't touched." Or was it? Suddenly, I wasn't a hundred percent sure. I didn't tell him that the diamond hadn't been locked up at all. He'd find out Hope had seen it soon enough.

"Send CSU. Though I doubt they'll find anything."

"Why is that?"

"Whoever broke in overrode my security camera feed."

His curse deserved an amen. "I also received a special delivery photograph," I added. "Why didn't you tell me your father was a diamond miner?"

Chapter Ten

HONOR AMONG THIEVES IS AN OXYMORON—
WISDOM FROM A JEWEL THIEF

I expected hesitation or denial. Not a quick response. "My uncle was a miner." Rockman's growl indicated a better-left-unsaid kind of story.

I refused to back down. The familial relationship explained his diamond knowledge. I still needed more information about him. "What was your uncle's association with Blackwood and Jasper Washburn?"

"What?" I'm pretty sure I heard a metal chair hit the tile floor. "What are you talking about?"

"I have a photo," I added. "You're not going to like it."

"I'll be right over."

"Send someone by the Dentist Depot. They aren't responding to emergency calls." I disconnected before he could accuse me of overstepping. Maybe he had a point. The break-in brought this case too close to home for me.

I shivered, unable to unsee some silhouette ruffling through my underwear drawer. Maybe it was time to listen to Gram and Hope and move.

Glimmer's bark and head butt on my shin refocused me. I had minutes before Rockman arrived. No time to change my clothing, but I managed to rinse the trail dust off my face in the kitchenette sink and pull my flyaway hair into a ponytail before the screaming sirens surrounded the shop. I let Rockman and two deputies in the front door. Both officers headed to my apartment while the chief remained at my side, his silver eyes an eerie reminder of his secrets.

"What happened to you?" he asked.

He should talk. His uniform, once crisp and pressed, showed a long day's wear. The red stain on his left cuff caught my eye—marinara sauce, maybe? Blood would look darker against that poly-blend fabric. I smoothed down my hair self-consciously. "I walked my dog."

"To the Watering Hole?"

Of course, he knew about the location. "So? What's so odd about that?"

"You went hiking in the middle of an investigation?" The arch of his eyebrow was razor-sharp—too perceptive by half. He'd spotted my evasion immediately.

I flushed, realizing two things: never underestimate his observation skills, and his expectation of honesty unnerved me.

"Where's your part of the diamond?" I asked, more to change the subject than out of genuine curiosity.

"You think that's what the intruders were looking for?"

I gestured around me. "Nothing was taken from the store." With easily fenced items all around us, the break-in was not about turning a quick buck.

"Who knew you had the diamond?" Rockman asked.

"You, the mayor, my grandmother ..." Gram could easily bypass the security system. She'd made a game of it when we'd upgraded the system. No. Gram wouldn't undermine my investigation. "... and Sunny."

"You told your salesclerk?" Rockman's accusation stung.

"Office manager. No, she figured it out on her own. Don't worry. Sunny is trustworthy."

His neutral tone lacked conviction. "Sunny was on site all afternoon."

"Yes. How'd you ... You've been spying on me?" I should be annoyed. Not today. Something dangerous was going on.

"I was watching a priceless diamond."

Of course, he was. Why it hurt made no sense. Not even a pretense of trust existed between us. No need to reaffirm his suspicions by admitting I hadn't locked the manmade diamond in the store safe anyway.

I redirected the conversation instead. "Who knew about the diamond in evidence?" The information leak had to have been from his side.

"No one." He patted his pocket.

Interesting. He'd bent the rules and kept the diamond close as well.

That limited the list to someone I'd trusted or ... "The mayor," I said, suddenly awash with a sense of betrayal.

"Keeping the Peak's theft quiet is in her best interests," Rockman pointed out.

"True, but the leak may not have been entirely her fault. She had to inform the bank president that the stone would not be returned to the vault, who must've advised his assistant. I know she told her husband."

"Everyone knows," Rockman filled in the silence. The realization didn't help my peace of mind any.

The chief's either, if I interpreted his clenched jaw correctly. "Show me this photo you have."

I motioned for him to follow me to my office. Glimmer trotted along beside us, surprisingly amiable. She'd even settled into her dog bed at my feet instead of demanding up into my lap when I sat in my desk chair.

Rockman stopped me from handing him the photo until he put on blue evidence-gathering gloves. Something I should've done. Too late now, I handed him the photo and waited.

His cuss confirmed my conclusion. "That is Uncle Richie standing next to Blackwood and Jasper Washburn. I don't know the fourth man. Do you have the envelope it arrived in?"

I handed him the generic manila envelope. Rockman glanced at it quickly and refocused on the photo.

"It says 1994 on the back in a nondescript scrawl. It could have been developed anywhere," I said.

Rockman scratched his chin. "Uncle Richie's receding hairline suggests the picture was taken in the mid 90s, which would put him in Russia."

My pulse jumped. The connection couldn't be a coincidence. "The Lomonosov Mine?" I leaned over my desk for a better view of the photo. "That mine's practically in the Arctic Circle."

"Northwest Russia to be precise. Uncle Richie complained loudly about the cold. He only stayed in Russia for two years before moving on to the Argyle Mine."

"Both Lomonosov and Argyle are fancy-colored diamond producers," I stated. "I get Blackwood's involvement. How was Jasper Washburn involved?"

Rockman shrugged. "I will ask him. Mind if I borrow the photo? This should get him to talk."

I shook my head. I'd already scanned it. The chief dropped the photo into a red-topped evidence bag.

"You might want to wait until tomorrow. I should have the report back on Washburn and his team ..." I glanced at the wall clock. "... in six or so hours." I waited for his nod before handing him the typed sheet. "Who is Nikolai Volkov?"

An ever-so-slight tick above his eye happened so fast, I would've missed it if I'd blinked. Recognition? I wasn't sure. "I don't know."

"I wonder who took the photo."

"I'd like to know who sent the photo to you and why," Rockman said.

I didn't flinch. The reason was evident. "Someone who doesn't want us working together." Why else incriminate Rockman? Unless this was a test of my loyalty.

"We both have baggage. Who would benefit from putting a wedge between us?" The chief's lineman's shoulders overwhelmed

Hope's desk chair. Something about him sitting across from me felt right.

"Other than my ex-husband?"

His jaw tightened. "He has nothing to do with this."

I wanted to believe him, but I'd experienced the law enforcement brotherhood's code of silence firsthand. "Tell me about your Uncle Richie," I said.

His half-smile had to be real. "He was a character. Showed up around Christmas time every year with great presents and even better stories. I'll never forget the six Matryoshka dolls he brought back for my sister."

"Russia, Australia, and Africa." I could see a child's hero worship. I got it. I hoped my nieces remembered me as fondly.

"He taught me about diamonds. My mom doted on him. She pretty much raised him."

"He could do no wrong," I stated the obvious.

"Something like that. She still swears Uncle Richie was innocent in the Argyle diamond heist. Despite him being caught red-handed with the pink rough," Rockman admitted.

The reports had been light on details, presumably underplaying the extent of the theft. "How'd you find it?"

"He'd mixed the rough in aquatic gravel."

"Ingenious." Criminal creativity always amazed me. Imagine what they could accomplish if they focused on law-abiding pursuits.

Suddenly, that diamond surveillance detail Rockman had spoken about had a new angle. "You arrested him?"

"I was responsible for his arrest, yes."

I sat back in my chair. Integrity versus loyalty. I doubted I'd pass that test. "I'm betting your mother hasn't forgiven you." This said a lot about his character—more than I cared to know. "I forwarded Volkov's name to my contact. Hopefully, we'll know more about him in the morning."

His exhale lacked patience. "You can't stay here tonight."

"I'm going to Gram's." No escaping updating her anyway.

"We'll keep an eye on the place." His phone rang before I could thank him.

A moment's pause, followed by another curse and a gruff, "I'll be right there." He disconnected the call and immediately dialed another number. "Call the MEO."

My gasp escaped. "The Medical Examiner's Office! Another dead body? At Dentist Depot?"

His curt nod confirmed. Thankfully, Sunny hadn't driven by for a look. "When?" I asked, hardly recognizing my squeak of a voice.

"The coroner will need to determine the exact time, but the paramedic thinks twelve hours or so."

"After Blackwood's murder. Same MO?"

"Gunshot to chest. Some indication of struggle." Rockman's expression hardened.

"Torture?" My forefinger tingled. "Why kill the guy you stole the laughing gas from?"

"The dentist caught the thief in the act?" Rockman suggested. "Or this murderer doesn't leave loose ends."

That bit of criminal psychology hit me hard. A sudden irrational fear crushed into my chest, making breathing a challenge. "Hope is next."

To his credit, Rockman didn't ask why. He simply dispatched a patrol car to Hope's home.

I grabbed my purse, ready to run.

"What did your sister see?" The chief's calmness caught me flatfooted.

"I, uh." A flip answer would not pass his intense scrutiny. "Not what. Who. She might have seen Blackwood's killer."

"Hope can identify Blackwood's killer?" Annoyance showed in his precise enunciation and that ever-so-slight tick above his eye again.

I swallowed hard. "Not exactly. But the killer doesn't know that." Which puts her in danger. "It's not my story to tell."

"Yet you know it."

No denying that truth. "She'll be in tomorrow morning to give you her statement."

"I see. She asked for time to calm down after finding Blackwood's body." He raked his fingers through his hair. "You met her at the Watering Hole."

Rockman had cut Hope a break? A side of him I'd never seen before. Too quickly, I added, "We're talking about the same thing."

We weren't, and he knew it. "Hunter, I know you're used to running an investigation your way, and, so far, you've been successful. But this is bigger than you."

Alarms fired. I'd sensed it since the beginning. "How much bigger?"

He never answered. An officer appeared in the doorway, calling him away. Watching his hurried and, dare I say, relieved exit, one thing became clear: Rocky Rockman had secrets, and I had a bad feeling they could get my sister and me killed.

Chapter Eleven

NEVER LEAVE LOOSE ENDS—WISDOM FROM A
JEWEL THIEF

SUNDAY, 8:00 P.M.

I snapped the magazine into my Glock and tucked the barrel into my concealed holster just behind my left hip. I'd equipped this handgun with a target laser, more to scare away potential attackers than for actual use. Whoever kept coming at me with a red dot homed in on a vital organ was a crazy S.O.B. and needed to be stopped anyway.

Pop had taught me to shoot at twelve after a run-in with a territorial rattler in the back barn. Looking back, the dogs barking had warned me the snake was there. My bad that I hadn't listened. I'd learned that lesson—like so many others—the hard way.

Although Gram lived on a ranch surrounded by no less than a dozen future police and government detection dogs, I still tucked a safe second against my ankle beneath my jeans. Over-prepared worked for me, especially when people with what appeared to be only a peripheral association with the missing diamond turned up dead.

I managed to drive the entire twelve miles to Gram's house without waking Sophie, thanks to Glimmer. The dog stood on the center console in a wolfish pose, her nose pointing skyward, and howling at the full moon. An omen of what was yet to come for sure.

I waved to the officer in the marked SUV tucked beneath a palo verde tree carpeted in wind-tossed yellow flowers outside the security gate. That Rockman delivered assistance as promised gave me hope that he could be trusted.

I punched in the security code and waited for the Aztec-inspired iron gate to roll open. Homesteaded during the Peak Mine's heyday, Gram's great-grandpa had raised cattle on the four-hundred-acre spread he'd named the Sunset Ranch. Over the years, the land had been parceled and sold off. Today, the remaining ten acres were home to domestic animals rather than livestock.

I drove past the recently renovated ranch-style home I'd grown up in, now occupied by Hope and her family. Except for lights glowing in my niece's bedrooms, the house was dark. My sister wasn't asleep. She paced the hallway. I felt her worry. It matched my own.

I had a plan. We'd execute after I spoke to Gram.

Of course, she was waiting on the porch of her Craftsman cottage, half-hidden in shadow as she rocked back and forth. The bright living room lights silhouetted her figure, and each rhythmic creak of the floorboards ratcheted up my tension.

Keeping her in the dark to protect her had been a mistake. Worry etched her brow. Even Glimmer's doxie-bounce up the stone path and wiggle-lick didn't break the line of her pressed lips.

"Rock always loses to paper," Gram remarked drily. "But you know that."

I ignored her inference. She knew I'd protected my sister. "Hope is in danger," I announced. I stood before her, facing her wrath with the same ease I had the day we'd argued over my De Beers assignment in Angola. It never got easier.

Gram exhaled. "Hank is an imbecile. I told her not to marry him."

She'd ordered me not to marry Chad, too. "Hope's heart follows a different path."

Gram harrumphed. Reasoning with her in this mood tended not to be worth the effort. I tried anyway. "I'm not sure it's entirely his fault."

"He's gambling again." That sin trumped them all. He'd broken his promise.

Agreeing allowed me to deflect some of the blame. Reluctantly, I admitted, "This could be about me."

The rocking paused. "Explain."

"I, uh, repossessed a necklace from a certain Russian collector."

"Revenge for bringing thieves to justice. Bah, we fight together." Gram always said exactly what I needed to hear.

"I know Chad recommended Rockman for the chief's position. Was he the only reference?"

Gram's emphatic "no" made me feel better. Gram had seen through my ex-husband from the start. She'd called him Chad the cad under her breath until the divorce. Afterwards, she voiced her opinion with gusto. "Despite his association with The Cad, the glowing recommendations from a number of high-ranking Los Angeles police officers were all the city council needed to hear."

Of course, Rockman had been hired. "Rockman's uncle was an associate of Blackwood's."

"Blast it!" The rocking commenced. "Your London friend's information?"

"An anonymous photo."

"You're serious? Are you telling me we've got a fox watching the chicken coop?" Gram asked.

"I'm not sure. When I called him on it, he didn't deny anything. He admitted to putting his uncle in jail for the Argyle Mine thefts."

"You're telling me his uncle was a ..."

"... diamond thief." I finished her thought.

Gram whistled, the rocking pausing. "Small world."

"More like a stunning coincidence. Two of them." I let my words sink in before adding, "Someone doesn't want us working together—"

"Or is warning you not to trust him." Gram kicked up her tempo. "What's your gut telling you? It's not let you down before."

If only I knew. "I'm not exactly unbiased."

She scratched her chin before answering. "That you see it, is half the battle."

Her words of wisdom didn't help. With a killer on the loose, I needed all my senses to be focused, not mired in perceived betrayals, which caused me to see conspiracy where one may or may not exist. My problem to deal with.

I moved on. "There's a chance Blackwood's murderer thinks Hope can identify him."

Gram's reach for her shotgun propped against the shadowed wall behind her didn't surprise me. When it came to family, she'd never quite left frontier justice behind.

I motioned for her to move inside. No one needed to hear my plan, and who knew how far our words would carry in the clear star-studded night? She stumbled as she rose; her creaky knees betrayed her age as I followed her inside.

The smell of beeswax and chocolate chip cookies greeted me like a warm hug. Gram's stress baking had advantages. I didn't ask how many dozen she'd made this time. Over the years, my grandfather's expanding waistline had confirmed her worrywart nature. I fell into my spot on the leather sofa, reenergized for the fight. "Rockman dispatched an officer at the gate. I'd prefer you post a guard dog."

Gram positioned her rifle at an arm's length and sat in her broken-in La-Z-Boy. "Agreed. I have a Shepherd in mind. The girls love him. They'll be happy to stay home until this blows over."

I nodded. "You'll need to run interference."

Gram rolled her eyes. "The twins are just a little spirited. Not unlike the two girls I raised."

I chose to change the subject. Second-guessing Hope's over-protectiveness seemed counterproductive today. "Have you heard of Nikolai Volkov?"

Gram shook her head. The possibility I'd overlooked something faded.

Glimmer's bark announced my sister's presence before she strolled in, carrying a plate of Gram's cookies. "Only five dozen? The twins bet you'd be closer to ten by now." She handed me the plate and chose two for herself.

I helped myself to a pair as well. The gooey chocolate melted in my mouth.

"I ran out of sugar," Gram snapped.

Hope slid into the seat beside me, suddenly serious. "I was at Blackwood's, but your home was ransacked. Are you sure the killer doesn't think they saw you—instead of me?"

I patted my cross-body bag, hidden beneath my puffy vest. "I think they were looking for the Peak Diamond copy."

"That could mean they think there is something to be found," Hope stated.

I nodded. "I need you to look at it under 50x and track it to its origins."

"That will require the Gemolite microscope at the shop," Hope said.

I handed her my car keys and Glimmer's leash. "Since you can't leave the ranch, it's back to high school, Sis. No one can tell us apart anyway. With my dog at your side, everyone will assume you're me."

Gram directed her remark at Hope. "The antics never end."

Hope missed Gram's point. Instead, she returned the leash, mischief in her grin. "I have a better plan. Dee, come."

Two barks? A moment later, an identical long-haired blond doxie bound through the doorway. I blinked to be sure I wasn't seeing double. There were two of them. I pointed to my foot. "Glimmer, come."

Both dogs scooted to my feet. I crouched for a closer look. The coloring, even the slight cowlick on the back of their necks, matched. The difference was in their eyes. Glimmer looked bewildered, the other weiner dog openly curious. Wearing identical collars, from a distance, no one else would be able to tell them apart.

"Meet Dee, short for Decoy," Hope said. "She is not a trained diamond dog yet, but we have great hopes for her."

"How is she related to Glimmer?" This dachshund was too close a match not to be a relative.

"They are technically full sisters. Both dogs share a mother and a father since Pops froze Glimmer's dad's sperm before he passed. She's my project. I wanted to duplicate your dog's amazing qualities," Hope explained.

More like clone her. I didn't say a word about Glimmer's numerous faults. I didn't need to. My dog displayed them all in a doxie-attitude huff. Gram and I shared a questioning glance. "Another diamond dog would be—"

"Incredible, right?" Hope's excitement bubbled over.

"Yeah," I finally agreed. "For this subterfuge to work, Dee can't be seen with Glimmer, ever."

"No problem. I'll take Dee with me. You can keep Glimmer here with you."

Not sure that was a good idea, I said, "Dee's a lowly WIP until her training is completed."

"If she makes the cut," Gram added. "Only 45% do."

The cold reality didn't discourage Hope. "She will."

Not sure if the way the decoy dachshund held her head high convinced me or something else did, but I agreed.

Gram and Hope chatted through logistical details while I rechecked my phone. I expected information from Sophie to start arriving in a few hours. Now, I'd better get some sleep.

I yawned as I followed Glimmer down the picture-lined

hallway to the guest room. Both twin beds made up with fresh linens meant Gram had known I'd be staying here all along. Too tired to contemplate my grandmother's ever-accurate ESP, I crawled under the spring-scented sheets, moving to the edge as the doxie brushed my back when she burrowed to my feet.

I might not know what was going on yet, but my family was safe. For now.

Chapter Twelve

OBSERVATION IS 9/10THS EXPECTATION—
WISDOM FROM A JEWEL THIEF

MONDAY, 6:30 A.M.

Pretending to be Hope always turned out to be more challenging than anticipated. Her preferred racer-back workout tops required sports bras that always pinched my sensitive underarms. I liked her new lightweight SPF 50 foundation enough to order my own, though.

Papers piled in my special I-know-where-it-is order spread across Gram's speckled gray and black granite kitchen countertop. I kitty-stretched in the warm morning sun, careful not to tip my steaming tea mug onto my laptop before I read Jasper Washburn's dossier.

The air shift behind me interrupted the cactus wren's morning song. Something warm and wet brushed my neck. What the ...?

I flew out of the chair, reacting with one swift, entirely defensive martial arts move I'd learned in hostage escape training.

Before I knew it, Hank, Hope's husband, lay flat on his back on the tile floor, fumbling for his inhaler with my foot pressed into his solar plexus and the dorsal side of my hand a hair's breadth from his throat.

The commotion brought the two dachshunds, as well as Hope and Gram, scurrying in. "Oh, Han-key." My soft-hearted sister hip-bumped me aside to cradle her gasping husband.

"Oh, sh …" Hope's glare made me choke. "… oot."

"Do I need to wash your mouth out with soap?" Hope demanded.

"I said shoot." I gagged. One whiff of that green stuff she called punishment soap did me in every time.

Her lips pressed into a scary scold. "Everyone knows what you meant."

"We're all adults." What was it with me and losing battles? "Your daughters aren't even here."

"Pop always said curse words were a sign of a poor vocabulary," Hope insisted.

Said the four-letter detective. According to his coworkers, Pop could make a Marine platoon blush. Not that I'd convince Hope of that. I changed the subject.

"I'm sorry, Hank. I've told you a hundred times not to sneak up on me." My justification sounded remarkably ordinary. Maybe this time he'd learn his lesson.

Gram said nothing. Instead, she handed me a flour sack towel. I wiped my neck. Pop had to be turning over in his grave. In his era, women of my size didn't overpower men. Rockman came to mind. With his feline reflexes, I wondered if I'd have budged him. I beat back that thought. Finding out tested my self-control.

"I-I thought you were my wife," Hank coughed with what seemed like a theatrical flair, a boyish strand of sandy hair falling across his forehead.

Hope melted. Her sympathetic cooing and protective embrace made me nauseous. Gram clearly felt the same. Even the dachshunds synchronized their disapproving head tosses. No accounting for taste. Another big twin difference.

I suppose I did need to concede that I was wearing her clothing. The good news was that we'd fooled Hope's husband up close and personal. I needed to make sure that incident never happened again, though.

"Imbecile," Gram muttered under her breath as she huffed past me.

I chose neutrality. Hank's not recognizing his wife bothered me more than a little. Rockman hardly knew me, and he saw the difference between us. My frustration came out in my question, "Why are you here?"

Sitting on his butt on the kitchen floor, Hank readjusted his Poindexter glasses. "Artemis is watching over the girls." He gestured toward the main house.

Named for the fiercest of Greek protectors, I had to believe he and Gram had chosen the right dog for the task. I shared a glance with Hope. Time for her to inspect the fake diamond. She backed away from her husband. "Hunter will be here if you need something. I'll be back as soon as I can." She scooped up Dee and darted out the kitchen door so fast that it slammed shut behind her.

Hank didn't try to stop her. He brushed something off his pant leg and stood. Head bent, looking everywhere but at me, he said, "I need to help. I know this is my fault."

About the most insightful thing he'd said all day. Maybe there was hope for him. "Tell me about the infamous cardroom."

Hank swallowed. He reminded me of a feral cat about to bolt. "It's behind a cinderblock building out on the reservation."

Of course, it was. Not only was snooping impossible on tribal land, but law enforcement followed its own rules. "Do you think you could find this place again?"

Hank raked his fingers through his thinning hair. "I don't know. The SUV had tinted windows. It's gonna sound crazy. I swear, I didn't drink anything either. All I remember is knowing I was going to win."

My hot coincidence alarm fired. He explained that same euphoric feeling I'd experienced after inhaling the laughing gas at the gala. "Would you recognize the driver if you saw him again?"

"He wore a mask. One of the white ones with a filter like we wore during COVID. I figured he had a cold or something."

More like he didn't want to breathe the gas. An interesting development. Could the dentist have been part of the gang? "Who else was there?"

"I was alone in the SUV. At the cardroom, five men and a dealer played five-card stud at my table." He closed his eyes, clearly visualizing the scheme. "I counted three guys in on the scam."

"How did you know?"

"You can't cheat a cheater," Hank announced.

An interesting admission from the guy who'd sworn he'd done nothing wrong. "Yet you lost big."

"I know," he exhaled miserably. "I can't believe I didn't see it. They shared hands. The team was good." Hank explained the con in detail. Respect edged his frustration. "I need to fix this."

"You need to go on with your routine as if nothing has happened. The twins' safety is the most important thing."

"Yes, of course, but I need to do something. You and your sister aren't invincible Amazons."

A compliment or criticism coming from a Greek scholar? Hope and I were strong and capable women raised by a grandfather who'd blamed himself for his own daughter's weaknesses. Was that training somehow the cause of our constant power struggles with men?

Begrudgingly, I saw his point. Maybe there was something he could do. "Have your clothes from that evening of playing cards been washed?"

"Yeah. Why?"

"I'd like Glimmer to sniff them for gas residue." Proving the link to the diamond heist might help.

"You think I might've been drugged?" His shoulders straightened.

"I don't know. It doesn't matter if you don't have ..."

"My shoes and socks are in the barn. I'd stepped in something.

Hope would've killed me if I'd tracked it through the house. I haven't gotten around to cleaning them yet."

"Procrastination pays off," I murmured.

He responded to my flip comment with an ear-to-ear smile. "About time. Come on, Glimmer. Let's have a go at it."

The doxie looked to me for approval. I gave it. The spark in Hank's step showed purpose as he hurried out of Gram's kitchen. In a crisis, everyone needed a job, I realized. A lesson for both Hope and me to remember.

Although his explanations demanded further exploration, my phone alerted me to call Sophie on the secured line. Anxious to get the reports I'd requested, I dialed in, one hip on the counter stool in front of my laptop. The first connection beeped, and I typed in the authenticator code displayed on my cellphone. The next spy craft security protocol demanded two passwords and a thumbprint. It took another minute before Sophie's familiar voice came across the line. "Good afternoon."

The steam curling above my teacup begged to differ, but who was I to argue? "What do you have?"

"Nikolai Volkov graduated with an advanced degree in chemical engineering from Mendeleev University of Chemical Technology in Moscow. His research focused on harnessing carbon under pressure."

"Exactly what is needed to create perfect manmade diamonds." The pieces were starting to come together. "He must be the brains of the new CVD process."

"Not likely. He was killed in a Mirny Mine accident in 2001."

"That was two years after the photo had been taken."

"Precisely. A league of scoundrels?"

"How did he die?" I asked. The person who took the photo had to be in on the plan.

"The helicopter he was travelling in was drawn down into the mine's 1200-metre open pit."

Of all the possible hazards in a mine, dying in a black hole seemed like a long shot. "I thought that was a myth." Theoretically, the changes in air weight caused by the pit's size and scope could affect the aerodynamics of a helicopter, but the chances had to be minuscule.

"Myths are generally based on truth." Sophie's remark begged questioning.

"I suppose that someone always knows what really happened."

"Yes, quite so, but, in this instance, the Russian government suppressed the incident. The mine closed a few months later."

I whistled. "That's some seriously bad karma."

"Indeed. It is possible someone has resurrected Nikolai's research."

"Twenty-five years ago, manmade diamonds were in their infancy. Whatever Nikolai discovered had to be obsolete."

Sophie's silence caused me to ask, "How did the four men meet? The two mines are located in the middle-of-nowhere Russia, and thousands of miles apart."

"I rather suspect Washburn is the connection. After completing four years of service with the British Army, he returned to South Africa, where he took employment with a private mine security company. His records are neither publicly available nor complete. I did come across numerous references to altercations. I'm afraid I cannot provide a concrete timeline of his whereabouts. He founded his own mine security company in 2013."

"No wonder his mine emergency team includes retired special forces men," I replied.

"Black operations personnel. Their records are decidedly more black than white. All hailed from competing companies. I'd venture that Washburn collaborated with them all at some stage in his security work."

"What are their specialties?" My curiosity piqued, I wanted to know. Their presence seemed so out of place.

"That is a curiosity. Two are sharpshooters. One is a demolition expert."

The bomb guy made some sense ... "Makes me wonder what they've been hired to protect in an old Arizona silver mine."

"Yes, quite. There are some questions regarding the validity of the revolutionary silver extraction process in which the new mining company is using at the Peak Mine," Sophie added.

My butt slipped off the stool. "International Mine Explorations must believe in it. They're not novices in the mining world. They own Colorado and Canadian mining companies." I knew that after attending the Sunset Peak community forums discussing the mine reopening.

"International Mine Explorations, LLC is underfinanced."

I felt as if the rug had been jerked from beneath my feet. "How bad?" But I knew. Following the money trail never lied.

"They need a win, as you yanks call it."

"Equipment has been arriving at the Peak Mine for weeks now." The semis rattling down the road beside our jewelry shop indicated as much. "Can you get the delivery manifests?"

"Certainly. But a paper trail may not tell the full story."

Agreed. Arranging an up-close look may not be so easy either.

"An interesting tidbit: Washburn is a voting stockholder in the international mining company."

The art of British understatement fired my coincidence alarm. "How did he finance that purchase?"

"A question I cannot yet answer."

Washburn's overprotective response to the gas leak potentially took on a new meaning, too. "Someone with Washburn's experience would know that laughing gas wouldn't trigger the mine's gas alarms. He could easily have set up canisters and stolen the Peak Diamond."

"Possibly, but if the Peak Diamond had not been grabbed, we would not have looked into the mine and learned of the man's connection."

"True. That's what doesn't track. The status quo is in Washburn's best interests."

"I fear this is far more complicated than a rogue minority stockholder."

I didn't need an MI6 dossier to tell me that. The Peak Diamond's role confused and concerned me.

"Your Chief Rockman is another curious case. He reads like an ordinary fellow."

Denial flared. Rockman ordinary? The thought of his penetrating gaze sent a chill down the length of my spine.

"He graduated in the middle of his class from the police academy. Unremarkable reviews as a patrolman at the LAPD. His first showing was on an FBI task force."

"Where he caught his uncle smuggling."

"Precisely. Quite a bit of the Irish, I'd say."

More like he'd been recruited. Begging the question, what were the chances he'd end up as police chief, involved in another diamond heist? "Can you get a copy of his graduating class picture?"

"Ah, so you are doubting his good looks and winning personality."

"I don't know yet. Something feels wrong."

"Your ex-husband vouched for him," Sophie added.

She didn't need to voice the appearance of impropriety here. I got it. "Who else would kill to get the diamond?"

"That is the question. I have no confirmed buyers. Karo was seen at the Carrousel du Louvre in Paris last week."

Sophie's croissants and brie accent reminded me of her multilingual European upbringing. "So?"

"It was fashion week."

Should I have known that? I glanced at the tips of my sister's dusty western boots. Karo and high fashion hardly fit. The man was a walking advertisement for Brooks Brothers. "A new woman?"

"Perhaps ... or a clandestine meeting."

A good thing to ask him. I checked the time. Hope should be at the shop by now, leaving me two hours before I needed to head to town so she could give Chief Rockman her statement. As much as I wanted to continue the investigation and speak with Karo and Sunny, I needed to "be" Hope, which meant following her routine. Since my sister did, on occasion, enjoy a morning horseback ride, I could check something off my list and visit the backside of the Peak Mine.

Hank interrupted my plan. He caught me as I entered the barn. "Come see, Glimmer is guarding my boots." The sparkle in his eyes told me all I needed to know.

He'd trained Glimmer. He knew her responses. Sure enough, my doxie lay in the barn dust, her body blocking the boots.

I motioned the dog aside and picked up the dusty, leather footwear. She growled when I tried to remove the socks. That made sense. The cotton would hold the odor longer. I rubbed the dark dirt off the heel and rolled the gritty material between my fingers. "Where did you step in this?"

"At the cardroom, I think." Hank dropped his readers over his eyes and looked closer. "What is it?"

"Could be anything," I said quickly. "Think back. Where did you go that day?"

"I visited Phoenix Security for the bomb dog's last follow-up." He stretched his neck. "Got into it with the guys and took the SUV to the cardroom."

"You said the cardroom was in a cinderblock building. Was it a business?" I pictured the structure, like so many on the reservation, on the side of the road, surrounded by desert, with no power or water service; some were occupied, most were abandoned, their intended use unknown.

"Yeah. I think so. It looked like a geode cutting place. There were totes filled with rocks out front."

Which would generate rock dust and coarse mineral residue ... "I'll have this officially tested for the gas."

"It links Phoenix Security and the cardroom to the Peak's theft, right?"

I nodded at Hank's triumphant smile. Of course, I couldn't

tell Rockman. The socks' origin opened a line of questioning that I couldn't reveal yet. The truth had a way of coming out eventually, but, for now, Hope needed to be protected, and that meant Hank's involvement, too.

Insistent barking drew my brother-in-law's attention. He lunged toward the exit. I didn't stop him as he disappeared into the training area.

I bagged the boots and stashed them inside a stall, ordering Glimmer to stay. She couldn't come riding with me anyway. Sophie could arrange the testing. A horse's whinny interrupted my crazy thoughts. I'd recognize the dirt on Hank's shoes anywhere. Wars had been fought over it, and empires crumbled. People coveted and died for it. It was kimberlite, the host rock for natural diamonds.

In Arizona? The last significant find had been the Peak Diamond a hundred years ago. Another discovery in the area could explain Washburn buying up land. It did not explain Blackwood's death or what part the man-made Peak Diamond played.

Chapter Thirteen

CHAOS IS YOUR FRIEND—WISDOM FROM A
JEWEL THIEF

MONDAY, 7:30 A.M.

The familiar scents of aged leather and saddle soap brought trail rides and horse shows to mind as I cinched the saddle on my sister's champion barrel-racing mare, Marvel. In the barnyard, the working dogs barked as their trainers ran them through obedience and protection drills. But it wasn't the dogs causing the commotion—it was my own mount, clearly miffed that I was not my sister. Ironic, really, how animals always knew, their senses far more in tune than humans, the supposed superior race.

Marvel twisted her gray head, ears pinned as she took aim at my shoulder. I shifted just in time, narrowly avoiding the nip and hopping back to save my foot from her stomp. When I finally mounted, the horse went wild, bucking hard enough to test even my experienced seat. More amused than annoyed, I jiggled the bit in her mouth until she acknowledged me. I then shortened the reins, and I pulled her head toward me, meeting her dark eye with unwavering determination. "Get over it."

The horse let out a defiant snort, her black mane flying as she tossed her head one final time before accepting. The dispute

96

resolved, I guided us through the gate and onto the winding, government-managed trails to start our ride.

It felt weird to be on horseback without my trusty dachshund companion riding beside me in her saddlebag attached to the pommel. Today, we needed to keep up the pretense that I was Hope out for a ride. Glimmer understood. For all her attitude, she always did her job.

Marvel did, too, eventually. The horse walked a short distance, barely stretching her legs, before her ears twitched in warning. Someone was watching us. I palmed my Glock strapped to my hip as I scanned the sun-soaked hills. Overhead, a turkey vulture spiraled lazily, likely tracking a morning rabbit. Nothing else moved in the stillness.

I patted the horse's neck. "It's okay, girl." We were both getting paranoid.

Dotted with granite boulders and tall saguaro cacti separated by patches of twisted mesquite trees, prickly pear, and cholla, this land was anything but desolate. Especially in the spring, when the brilliant wash of yellow, purple, and orange wildflowers transformed the rugged terrain into living art.

I nudged the horse into a slow lope. We stayed in the sandy wash, Marvel's hooves kicking up clouds of dirt and lightweight debris until it swirled around us in a miniature dust devil. Desert grit coated my teeth by the time the horse eased to a walk and carefully picked her way up the rocky mesquite-lined arroyo trail where ocotillo blooms crowned the spindly stalks, their feathering orange tips softening the plant's thorny appearance. Another turkey vulture soared overhead.

That crawling sensation at my nape returned. Someone was out there. Closer than they'd been earlier. I lifted my binoculars, scanning the ancient rock piles and the stick markers that denoted long-dead miners' claims and unfulfilled dreams. The desert appeared still, but ...

There. A metallic glint.

I adjusted the magnification and spotted an ATV's frame

painted tan, camouflaged to blend in, its rider nothing more than a dark silhouette topped with a distinctive flash of silver. A helmet or a hat? I couldn't be sure. Then they melted back into the background.

I steered Marvel toward the vacated lookout. We arrived in a cloud of desert dust a few minutes later. I dismounted. On inspection, my hope for an identifying clue vanished. Not even a flattened shrub greeted me.

My pulse hammered in my ears. This guy was good—a ghost trained to be invisible. If I hadn't been on alert, I'd have missed that momentary flash in the sunlight. What was he doing up here?

I turned my field glasses toward the adjacent hillside and the new Peak Mine's entrance. This was the best observation point to get eyes on the mine, begging the question: was I the one being watched after all?

I pointed my binoculars toward the blur of activity surrounding the mine's entrance. Two security guards I recognized from yesterday's confrontation with Jasper Washburn appeared to be inspecting an outbound package. A common practice in Africa where conflict diamonds funded all sorts of violence, but in an Arizona silver mine? The exact process repeated a few minutes later.

"What are you looking for?" I asked no one in particular.

Marvel whinnied a response. I patted her neck, my unease unaffected by the desert stillness around me. It was hard to get answers when you had no idea what questions to ask.

I watched the mine for another thirty minutes before I gave the speed demon Appaloosa her head to race back to the barn. Time to become me again and learn what Chief Rockman had uncovered.

Chapter Fourteen

KEEP YOUR EYE ON THE PRIZE—WISDOM FROM A JEWEL THIEF

MONDAY, 10:00 A.M.

Hope and I arrived at police headquarters together. Dressed in identical Starlight Estate Jewelers button-down blouses and jeans, we turned heads on entry. It felt like high school again. How many teachers had we played the *Parent Trap* game on?

Of course, Chief Rockman wasn't fooled. He picked up Glimmer, who trotted a few feet ahead of us to greet him, and handed her to me without missing a beat. "Karo is in the conference room. He came in to see you."

"Me?" Karo tended to be easy to read. Since he hadn't disappeared like the wind, he hadn't stolen the Peak Diamond. The only reason he'd still be in town meant there was a chance it would show up.

"I figured you'd like a go at him." Rockman didn't wait for my agreement before neatly ushering me to the nearest office and closing the door behind me.

Admirably handled, I admitted. He'd separated me from my sister and controlled my access to Karo in one move. I made a mental note not to challenge him at chess.

Glimmer's growl trilled deep in her throat. She'd taken a bite out of Karo's ankle on our last meeting. I doubted he'd forgiven her or me, for that matter. I'd cost him a nice commission. I wasn't afraid he'd take revenge here. It wasn't his style.

The light-haired Slavic remained casually leaning against the far wall, his tailored suit accenting his height and muscular build. He reminded me of Cary Grant. Not in looks, but in his continental mannerisms that starkly contrasted with the utilitarian interrogation room.

"We meet again, Miss Hunter." Annoyance underscored his innocuous words. I heard it beneath his practiced British undertones.

"You are like a bad penny." I smiled at his furrowed brow. Like most Europeans, his fluent English lacked an understanding of American sayings. "You do keep turning up at the most annoying times."

"On that we agree."

At least twenty years my senior, I'd come to expect brusque annoyance from him. This thoughtful regard intrigued me. What was his game? "Was the Peak Diamond exhibition all you thought it would be?"

"The diamond lacked fire."

Acknowledgment that the stone was a fake? "At least now you have one less rival."

"Rival?" He scoffed. "Blackwood catered to the masses."

"And you to criminals," I shot back.

His hazel eyes flashed. "Patriots."

"Forgive me if I disagree." The same old cat-and-mouse game.

Karo straightened his cuffs. "We are destined to be at odds."

A nice way to put it.

"For the record ... I did not murder Blackwood." Karo twirled his diamond pinky ring, which was permanently placed by an enlarged knuckle. "I prefer a more personal persuasion."

I inclined my head. A one-time Olympic boxer, shooting

someone in the back didn't fit Karo's persona. "Double-crossing the wrong guy ..." I let him fill in the blank.

Karo shrugged. "When you play with fire ..."

The Peak Diamond was a fire diamond. Had he slipped or was that intentional? "How much is the Fire Diamond going for these days?"

Karo's intense stare cut into me. "An eye for an eye." He sought and held my gaze for what felt like forever before standing. "Do pass the word on, child." Glimmer separated us, her crouch defensive, her teeth bared.

Karo smiled—a scary, I-dare-you-to-try look that made the protective weiner dog bark.

"I didn't know you were a fashion connoisseur," I remarked. "I hear fashion week can be quite competitive."

His slow regard seemed to find me lacking. "A wonderful place to people watch."

No denial. "A particular lady?"

He smirked and said, "A gentleman never kisses and tells."

The mystery of Karo's unnamed lady friend intrigued me, and clearly Glimmer too. She lunged toward him—her way of demanding answers—but the leash caught her just short of contact.

"I believe I shall enjoy my coffee in peace." With no authority to stop him, I stepped aside as he brushed by me, every bit the cocky Cossack I'd come to know. His deliberate message made no sense. Who did he expect me to pass the word to?

Rockman entered a few minutes later, changing the energy in the room so that even Glimmer curled up beneath her chair, resting her head on her paws, diligent but unconcerned.

"It's best when a suspect comes in on his own that you don't chase him away," Rockman remarked.

"Good advice." What else could I say? I knew the interrogation protocol rules. I'd failed the implementation this time. Guilt raised its ugly head. "He knows something."

"I suspected as much. Karo showed up thirty minutes ago and insisted on speaking with you. Only you."

"He came to deliver a message."

I had his full attention. "What did he tell you?"

"I asked how much a fire diamond went for these days."

"And his response?" Rockman asked.

"An eye-for-an-eye."

I expected confusion, not a dark look. My certainty that he knew more solidified. What was I missing? "What haven't you told me?" Disappointment snuck into my tone. I couldn't help it. We'd agreed to work together—to share information. Apparently, that went one way.

Rockman crossed his arms, visibly annoyed. "Don't look at me like that."

"Like what?" I couldn't meet his gaze.

"Like you expected me to disappoint you. I haven't seen you since last night. The bullets that killed the dentist and Blackwood were not fired from the same weapon."

"That doesn't mean the murders aren't—"

"Connected. I agree. Blackwood's murder is connected to the Peak's theft."

I exhaled. Being right didn't answer who had stolen the Peak Diamond. "Karo didn't steal the diamond. He'd be long gone if he had. He doesn't know who did either, or he'd have acquired it already."

"He knows the diamond is a fake?" Rockman asked.

I nodded. "He said the stone lacked fire."

"And that's code for?"

"He didn't steal it either," I replied. "Trust me on this. I know the man."

I expected more questions. Rockman's literal mind had to be having fits with my intuition-based conclusions.

"Did you meet with Washburn yesterday?"

"No. He's in Colorado. He's expected back tomorrow morning. I have a nine o'clock appointment."

"Is that an invitation?"

He nodded. Finally, he said, "I don't appreciate you coaching your sister. She sounds guilty trying to follow your advice on what not to say."

This couldn't be good. "I didn't coach her. I told her to tell you the truth." Minus a few incriminating details.

"Except the part about her husband's gambling debt and the diamond plots Blackwood expected as payment."

My stomach dropped. "You know about that?"

Rockman's even tone didn't sound particularly annoyed. His eye tic said otherwise. "I'm a good investigator. I do my homework, I follow leads, and I use my sources, which are different from yours. You filtering information because it doesn't fit your agenda is exactly what I was afraid you'd do."

I tempered my denial. I'd been caught, but I needed to keep this connection. "Hope will always be my top priority," I admitted simply, oddly bereft.

His long exhale could go either way. Would we end our association here?

"I don't think she murdered Blackwood," Rockman said.

Relief shot through me, lifting the fear-fog that had been hanging over my head. That he was right about information-sharing hit me next. He hadn't determined Hope's innocence based only on my recommendation though. He knew something.

"Point taken. No excuses, but I normally work alone. Collaborating—"

"Will take time. I get it," Rockman said. "We both need answers. Together we can solve this case."

In theory, I agreed. Relieved he hadn't ended our partnership, I didn't dig deeper. It was time to test the information-sharing part of our agreement. Since Hope would never give her husband up, the question was: how did Rockman know about the gambling? "Who else has been taken in by the ring?" A larger conspiracy was the only scenario that made sense.

Rockman confirmed nothing. "You know I can't share information from ongoing investigations."

"Gambling is legal on the Indian reservation. Extortion is not." Since it had happened on an Indian reservation, the case fell under Indian and possibly federal jurisdiction. He must have some good "friends" for information to be shared with a local police chief. "How deep are you into Phoenix Security?"

Another tic along his brow line. I checked my phone. Something to share regarding the company would help me now. Sophie's email popped up just in time. I read the first line. "Phoenix Security is owned by a Cayman Island shell company." I looked up from the screen. "How is that even possible? Doesn't a security company need federal approvals?"

Another pause.

I tapped my foot.

He relented. "No. It's surprisingly easy to operate in Arizona. The company only needs an Arizona Department of Public Safety license, which requires personal information and public background checks of all owners, partners, and corporate officers. And verifiable insurance," Rockman explained.

"Phoenix Security passed the basics. Hope checked before she agreed to sell them a bomb dog. What are they fronting?"

"I can't say."

"I can help. You know I can." I held up my phone. "I'll know in thirty minutes."

His scowl indicated indecision. Finally, he relented. "Money laundering."

The metal interrogation chair screeched on the tile floor as I flopped into it. "Karo acquires collectibles for the *Sindikat Krasnogo Medvedya*." The man's cryptic comment, an eye for an eye, came to mind. "Your undercover operative could be in jeopardy."

Rockman's jaw tightened. He typed something on his phone before looking at me. "Why would Karo give you the message?"

"I don't know. I'm not on the top of his I-love-you-the-most list. Glimmer bit him the last time we saw each other." The weiner dog's head raised in acknowledgement.

"You've got good instincts, girl," Rockman said.

"I could be misinterpreting everything," I admitted. But I knew I wasn't. Karo's message was clear. Someone was going to pay for the Peak Diamond to be returned. I needed to figure out who.

Chapter Fifteen

ANONYMITY IS CRITICAL—WISDOM FROM A JEWEL THIEF

MONDAY, 12:30 P.M.

Lunch at the Canary Café offered down-home comfort food served in a whimsical setting and a chance to catch up on local gossip—the kind I needed to start connecting the seemingly unrelated information.

Hope sat across from me at our usual square table tucked into the corner beneath a painting of an oversized birdcage containing plump canaries sipping from tiny teacups. All around us, vintage cartoon posters lined the walls between cages that double as light fixtures.

Call it spending too much time in dark places, but I felt more comfortable sitting with my back against the wall. I appreciated my unobstructed view of the cartoon's eternal chase scenes coming to life all around us.

All appeared normal, including my sister, who methodically ate each ingredient from her cobb salad. I picked out some chicken, fed it to Glimmer, and mixed the rest, combining all the flavors and eating it as a salad was intended to be eaten. Another twin difference I couldn't quite figure out.

"I didn't tell the chief anything he didn't already know,"

Hope insisted. She glanced over her shoulder and lowered her voice. "It was creepy. He told me things about the gambling place Hank never mentioned."

"Like what?" I asked.

"It's nothing." She forked a tomato.

"It was something," I replied. Not sure where she was going with her comment.

Hope stabbed another tomato. "I'm not sure what's worse. If my husband didn't tell me to avoid hurting me or because he hadn't noticed."

Her fork, aimed at my heart this time, could only mean one thing. "There were girls there?" I bit my lip not to laugh. Of course, there were. Likely scantily clad, sexy women hanging all over the high rollers.

"Yeah." She crushed the tomatoes into the salad. "How'd you know?"

I ignored her question. Hope worried about everything. When she started to obsess about it, I needed to get to the root cause fast. "You think Hank—"

She cut me off. "No. No. He's a gambler. Not a cheater. That's the problem." No doubt in her words.

I thought about my ex-husband's philandering. Was my judgment clouded? After Hank's behavior, my confidence wasn't in his favor. "What exactly are you concerned about? He's horrified about gambling."

"He's horrified he got hooked by scammers."

She was right about that. "I don't think he'll go down that road again."

Hope frowned. "Gambling is like being an alcoholic. It's an addiction. You can't take one drink."

I'm not sure I believed that. Hank was a lot of things. Stupid was not one of them. For all his faults, he loved my sister, and I doubted he'd test her again anytime soon. I changed the subject. "What did the chief say?"

Hope half-smiled. She knew what I'd done. "It was like he'd been there, the way he talked about it."

No wonder he'd reacted to my speculative statement about an undercover operative. Was he the inside man? I never considered that the gambling ring had manipulated him. No one coerced Rocky Rockman into anything he didn't want to do. I admired that. Begrudgingly.

"I'm shocked I'm not wearing orange right now," Hope admitted.

I concurred. Overwhelming evidence incriminated her, yet Rockman hadn't charged her. My insistence on her innocence hadn't swayed him. He trusted me about as much as I trusted him. He either knew something more or had another agenda. At the very least, he knew what the gambling ring was capable of.

I stirred a hard-boiled egg around in my salad bowl. "Did you see anything remarkable in the fake diamond?"

Hope's expression lit up like a festive holiday decoration. "The wrinkle pattern you found had a squiggle along the culet, which could have resulted from a graphic overlap."

Her technical terms made me smile. "A programming defect in the CVD machine?" Probably correctable if the programmers knew it was there.

"Maybe. CVD diamond processing varies by machine and operator. In this case, creating the feather likely caused the issue and ..."

My bestie, Crystal, slipped into the chair to my left, stopping Hope's explanation mid-speech. A statuesque 5'10" in boots, her jeans covered by a yellow apron with black bow ties, she fit the theme perfectly. A year ahead of Hope and me in school, I'd been looking up to her since high school.

"Holy canaries. I feel like Sylvester staring into an empty cage." Dressed in a cheery yellow polo shirt with her dark hair pulled back in a canary-printed scrunchie, she gave the café a happy-face feel. So did the steaming lemon drop oatmeal cookies she'd placed in front of us.

Hope and I responded in unison. "Amen."

Crystal glanced at Glimmer, chewing chicken on the floor between us. Salad fork in her right hand, Hope reached for a cookie with her left.

"Ha! Got you." She grabbed Hope's hand. "A wedding band tan line? You can't be Hope. She never takes off her wedding ring. Unless ..." Her dark eyes narrowed. "You two are up to something again. I know it."

Hope's chuckle stopped the lecture. "We're adults now."

"Sometimes I wonder." Crystal had participated in enough of our twin antics to recognize the signs.

I didn't flinch under her stare. She shook her head. "Will you two wear name tags or something? This who's who makes me crazy."

And give away our advantage? Never. "I'm Hunter." I flashed my ring finger. No telltale wedding ring mark remained. At least that part of my life was over. Why did a vision of Rockman hit me? I cleared my throat. "Whose last-minute order did you have to fix?"

She'd been rushing around the kitchen ever since we walked in. The question answered itself when Dale's assistant burst through the front door—Dale being our bank president, of course.

"Poor woman," Crystal said, watching the frazzled assistant. "She kept apologizing for the mix-up, but I suspect he's the one who changed his mind. He's been scattered ever since his wife walked out."

"That was three years ago," Hope pointed out. "Lucky for him he found Kathy."

"She handles everything. He'd be smarter to put a ring on her finger," Crystal added. "Man's hopeless on his own."

"Why would he do that?" I asked. "He's got the perfect setup as it is." Not that I had anything against marriage, but the disapproving looks from both women told me I'd better shift gears.

"Speaking of new faces, have either of you met those mining contractors?"

Crystal nodded. "Sort of. I cater six meals, 3 or 4 times a week."

"They are good for business." Hope pushed away the salad in favor of the sweet treat.

"Who picks the orders up?" I asked.

"Usually the computer guy. I think the other guys bully him. He's kinda shy. Doesn't say much, but his gray eyes are sweet."

Sweet gray eyes? Sunny had said the same thing about the man who'd delivered the photo of Washburn, Nikolai, Blackwood and Rockman's uncle. "Do you know his name?"

"R. Lobo is the name on his credit card." Her little smile said why she didn't need to look up the information.

"No first name? Who uses an initial on a credit card?" Hope asked.

"Apparently, he does. He told me to call him Lobo."

I texted Sophie. Why didn't I know anything about the computer guy? "You like him."

Crystal's smile grew. "He's cute. Not my type, though." She added quickly, "He's a little old for my taste."

"How old is too old?" Hope's voice jumped an octave.

Deep breath, Sis.

My warning worked. Hope polished off the cookie.

"Mid-forties, I'd guess," Crystal replied.

Hope relaxed. I didn't. Dad could easily pass for a younger man. "You looking for a sugar daddy?"

Mischief danced in Crystal's eyes. "Maybe."

I wanted to pry for more information, but too many eyes seemed to be focused on us. I dropped my voice to a whisper. "What else can you tell me about Lobo?"

"He loves my gluten-free meatloaf. He says it's nice to not get sick enjoying his favorite meal."

"I can attest to that. I'll never forget not being able to breathe after eating shrimp." Hope shuddered.

That memory still haunted me. Of course, I don't eat shellfish either. Why chance it? "R. Lobo is an American?" I asked.

"He's got a Texas drawl." Crystal should know. She'd spent too many years in Waco. "You two worked with the dead guy at the Amethyst Inn, right?"

We nodded in unison. "He was a bad man," Hope said.

Crystal huffed. "So was the dentist."

Of course, Crystal knew about that murder. Secrets rarely remained such at the Canary Café.

"Nobody likes dentists," Hope added.

"This guy, especially. He charged more than the insurance paid and demanded that patients pay the balances."

Not an illegal practice, provided he disclosed the rules in advance of services. I noted Hope's narrowed gaze focused on no one in particular. The same dentist treated her family differently, and my gut answered the why. "Hank knew him?" It wasn't really a question, but rather an opening for an admission.

"Hank knew him from college," Hope replied.

No need to say more. The guy's student loan debt likely topped six figures. Not that it excused his billing practices.

"Poor Hank. The dentist was a sleaze," Crystal said. "It was only a matter of time before he annoyed the wrong person."

"Or got involved with the wrong people," I suggested. "Was he a card player?"

"Yeah. His receptionist works my weekend breakfast shift. She says he's a bear when he's on a losing streak. Which is often on Fridays," Crystal said.

"Where does he play?" My heart thumped in my chest, awaiting Crystal's response. Did we just catch a break?

"At the Indian casino, I think. I can find out, though." Crystal's natural Nancy Drew curiosity paid off. She had even more information to share. "Recently, I heard a rumor about a card game on the Indian reservation."

"Who did you hear it from?" I asked.

"Hmm. I'll need to think on it. I don't remember. Is it important?"

"Yes." Hope's quick response said way too much. She also motivated Crystal to dig for the answers.

"It'll come to me," Crystal said. "What else do you need to know?"

"Anyone else playing cards around town?"

"Pepper."

"The fire chief?" No. Chili had been as shocked as me discovering the laughing gas. I refused to believe he could be involved.

"Mason Pepper, his son. The kid is involved in too much garbage. Go figure how he qualified to be a cop," Crystal said.

"Friends in ..."

"... low places," Hope finished my thought.

A great asset for the gambling ring. Not only had Mason been assigned to secure Blackwood's crime scene, but he'd also been guarding the Peak Diamond last night. He could easily have switched the stone. What was the chance that all those events would line up for that opportunity?

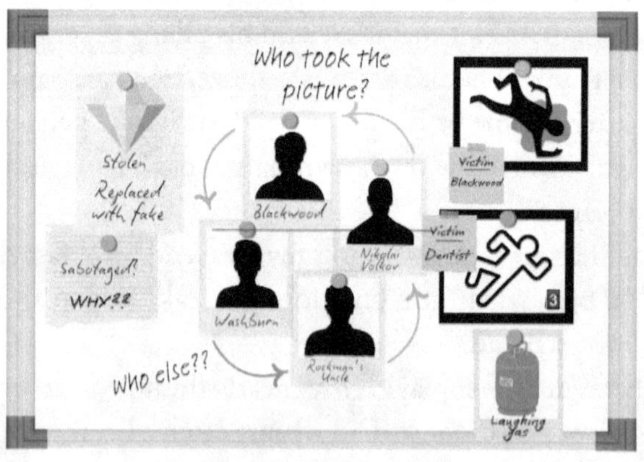

Also, if the gambling ring had hooked the dentist, why kill him or Blackwood, who had to be the fence? Even more confusing was the discovery of the fake diamond. The odds that the fake Peak Diamond would be dropped and discovered so quickly after leaving the vault had to be infinitesimal ... unless the stone had been sabotaged. That conclusion made even less sense than thieves with the worst luck in creation.

I'd solved complex crime puzzles before, but this one stumped me. While some clues made intuitive sense, the randomness of others supported multiple crimes.

The mine crew had to have something to do with this. A conversation with the computer guy might help improve my insight. And I knew exactly how to arrange it.

"Tonight's meatloaf special includes delivery," I said.

"I'll let Mr. Lobo know I'm testing a delivery service tonight." Crystal didn't say a word about the pot roast special sign. "The order will be ready for pickup at 5:15."

I nodded. That gave me enough time to review the personnel files and speak to Rockman. He needed to know that he might have a spy in his ranks.

Chapter Sixteen

ANTICIPATE YOUR MARKS NEXT MOVE—
WISDOM FROM A JEWEL THIEF

MONDAY, 2:40 P.M.

Finding Rockman proved more difficult than anticipated. The dispatcher recalled him leaving the building around noon. A patrol officer noted his vehicle heading west on Miners Road at 12:10. After that, no one had seen or heard from him. The question was, why was I the only one concerned about him?

I dialed his cellphone number. It went straight to voicemail. I asked to speak with Officer Pepper. No luck. He wasn't on site either. My alarm bells went off when his phone went directly to voicemail, too.

Rockman MIA in the middle of a double murder investigation? "Please track the chief's patrol car," I requested. "Something feels wrong."

"Chief's been on call for the last two days. I'd hate to interrupt his, uh, quiet time." A couple of shared looks between colleagues didn't deter me.

Of course, Rockman had a preferred place to disappear to. An odd annoyance toyed with my unease, solidified with the reminder that wherever that place was, it was none of my business. I needed his help to find the Peak Diamond. The end.

If I mobilized a search party to find him snoozing somewhere indiscreet, he would not be happy. Not that his happiness concerned me. I know every patrol car is equipped with a location finder. I'd tapped into that database during my divorce proceedings.

"You really think he might be in jeopardy?" the dispatcher asked.

I pressed his indecision. "I'd like to be sure. I don't need to know where he is. Can you just confirm he's in a safe location?"

"I guess that's okay." He typed something into his computer. "The satellite GPS is 99 point something percent reliable. What the ...?"

My gut reacted. That unheard of point-something percentage dominated this disconnected investigation.

The dispatcher jerked his fingers through his hair. "This is impossible." He reentered his request. "The GPS unit isn't responding."

Of course, it wasn't. My concern ticked up another notch. Disabling the mobile device didn't require a PhD, but it did prove intent. Was Rockman hiding from or for someone?

I left the police station, unwilling to waste time debating when the proper time was to sound the alarm. With Rockman and Officer Pepper out of contact, the mayor was technically in charge. Although Ruby's legal career included prosecuting criminals, I doubted she knew how to find them.

I checked the time as I clipped Glimmer into her car seat and climbed into the vehicle. 10 p.m. in London. Interrupting Sophie's nightly beauty routine came at a high price. I dialed anyway. No time to analyze my motivations, my gut cried foul.

"This had best be life or death." Her strained voice indicated I'd caught her wearing a pore-tightening mask.

"Chief Rockman is missing. His cellphone is turned off."

"Perhaps he chooses not to be found."

Maybe, but I needed answers, not testy practicality. "I'm not imagining this. Mason Pepper is unaccounted for as well."

"I see." Water splashed in the background before her normally clear tones responded. "I will activate the phone. A minute." Rapid typing followed. Each click felt like an eternity. "Coordinates on your phone."

I mapped the longitude and latitude. A topical map popped up on my vehicle's screen. "He's on the Indian reservation." Which made no sense. His jurisdiction ended at the city line, unless he was investigating the card room in conjunction with the Tribal Police or FBI. He'd said there was more going on than I knew.

"Can you locate the chief's vehicle?" Why had he gone in without backup?

"Good heavens. That GPS isn't working either?" No need to respond. Sophie muttered her stalking opinion. "Rather seems to me the man doesn't wish to be found."

"He could be in over his head." Though I doubted a situation existed that he couldn't handle. High praise from me. "He has no idea what Blackwood's associates are capable of."

A few keystrokes later, Sophie whistled. "You're not going to like this. I'm sending through coordinates for Chief Rockman's motor."

Concern escalated when I recognized the address. "I stop at Arrowhead Coffee every time I go to the reservation to buy turquoise." His vehicle miles from his cellphone didn't bode well.

I hit the gas. My tires squealed as my Bronco shot out of the parking lot, jumping a curb. I missed side-swiping a silver pickup parked on the street by a hair before my hostage-driving training took over. I righted the wheel and raced toward the coordinates. "Do you have satellite images?" It would be helpful to know what I was facing.

"Ninety-seven minutes."

"Too late." My adrenaline pumped. I hated to go into a

potentially dangerous situation blind. Was Rockman caught up in the gambling ring himself or tailing Officer Pepper? Either way, his vehicle shouldn't be miles away from his cellphone's location, unless the thugs had captured him.

"Charging in with all guns blazing, as you yanks are fond of saying, on an Indian reservation will require federal support," Sophie stated the obvious.

"I know."

"But you intend to go in regardless." I ignored Sophie's long-suffering sigh. "Need I remind you that your objective is to recover the Peak Diamond? The cowboy chief is rather on his own, I'm afraid."

Rockman a cowboy? Not exactly how I'd characterize that lone wolf. "I can't let the chief fall prey to an international conspiracy."

"I'll alert the FBI."

"Not yet. Let me see what's going on first." My ETA is fifteen minutes. I changed the subject. "What do you have on the mine's IT guy?" I'd only sent the request an hour ago, but Sophie never quit, despite her protests of being overworked.

"Not much. He has an MIT computer science degree despite a juvenile hacking record."

"What kind of hacking?"

"The record is sealed," Sophie replied.

"When has that ever stopped you?"

"I'll need until morning."

I'd give her that one. "Where is he from?"

"Texas. He worked as a rodeo clown." Sophie hummed. "Help me understand the clown bit. Getting gored by a two-thousand-pound Brahman bull doesn't strike me as particularly amusing."

"The clowns provide safety for the bull riders. Pound for pound, those clowns have more guts than the riders. They distract angry eight-hundred-pound bulls. It's not a job for the meek." Yet that's exactly how Crystal had described him.

"How does a computer specialist stare down charging bulls?" Sophie asked.

A good question. "One look from his unflinching, steely gray eyes."

"Brown eyes."

"Brown eyes?" Crystal had said the IT guy's eyes were gray. I doubted she'd miss that.

"Indeed. According to Rico Lobo's birth certificate, his father was a Mexican national and his mother a blue-eyed blonde."

The eye color mismatch bothered me. Why would someone pretend to be part of the miners' team to pick up food at the Canary Café? Add another unconnected incident to the long list.

I glanced at my GPS. "I'm four minutes out." And a world away from the biodiversity in Sunset Peak's higher elevation canyon grasslands. Here, the dusty Sonoran Desert blew tumbleweeds across miles of tired roads, its monotony broken by the occasional weathered shack, its occupancy determined by the number of pitted vehicles in the yard.

I pulled into the adobe-style strip mall, its tan stucco walls blending into the desert landscape barely a mile from the Indian reservation. Besides the coffee shop with its hand-painted sign, the complex housed a family-run Mexican restaurant, a neon-lit payday loan office promising quick cash, and a cluttered dollar store. Half a dozen battered pickup trucks, their original paint covered beneath layers of red dust and desert grime, clustered around the restaurant's entrance, while several minivans occupied the cracked asphalt spaces nearest the dollar store.

No marked police vehicles in sight, "I don't see his SUV."

"The motor's positioned at the eastern end of the building," Sophie replied.

I turned my back toward the sun and drove around behind the businesses. I found Rockman's SUV exactly where Sophie had directed me, parked beneath a branchy palo verde tree, its police markings obscured by a layer of yellow blooms. An abduction or a rendezvous?

I set Glimmer down and began searching for evidence. Nothing caught my attention until the dachshund guided me to a second set of tire tracks several feet away, preserved in hardened mud no doubt the result of a broken sprinkler. It might mean nothing, but I photographed the impressions and sent them to Sophie anyway. Identifying Rockman's getaway vehicle could be the key to tracking him down.

Next, I popped his door lock in nine seconds. My how-to-steal-a-car-in-sixty-seconds instructor would be proud. Remnants of ice still floated in his Taco Bell Coke cup. In 96-degree heat, I estimated he'd left here less than an hour ago. In his trunk, I found his uniform shirt neatly folded beside a gym bag. My thumb brushed his collar. He'd changed his clothing himself. This was looking more and more like an undercover op—or was Rockman heeding Karo's warning and getting his inside guy to safety?

My curiosity triggered, I loaded Glimmer back into the SUV and slid behind the wheel. Tracking the phone's GPS signal seemed straightforward until I noticed the movement indicator was active and closing in on my location. Less than a mile away, to be exact.

Shoot! No time to escape. I had maybe two minutes to hide lest Rockman catch me snooping—an explanation I did not want to make at this time.

Instinct took over. I stomped on the gas, causing my Bronco to leap forward. I drove past the overflowing dumpster, deciding not to chance it, instead backing into a parking spot in front of the coffee shop. Just in time. A flashy red Corvette entered the parking lot with Officer Pepper behind the wheel. I couldn't clearly make out his passenger, but I'd seen all I needed to.

I headed home before Rockman could leave. I woke Sophie, this time to run the Corvette's license. Her response didn't surprise me. Phoenix Security had been the original owner of the 'Vette. Mason Pepper had to be Rockman's undercover guy at the gambling ring.

Instant relief for Mason's dad changed to more questions. How had a local chief and officer gotten involved in an Indian reservation sting?

Good news for Hope. The chief knew she'd been set up. The question was: how widespread was the gambling problem, and how was a shady jewel acquirer like Blackwood involved? Another project for Sophie to untangle.

Chapter Seventeen

MAKE YOUR OWN RULES—WISDOM FROM A
JEWEL THIEF

MONDAY, 5:45 P.M.

Cracking any case meant fitting together what I called puzzle pieces. That included building a clear picture of the crime, identifying the perpetrator, and recovering whatever had gone missing. Sometimes, the pieces formed an imperfect image, blurred around the edges, but still sharp enough to point toward success. Other times, when evidence ran thin, I relied on informed hunches and calculated assumptions.

With the Peak Diamond case, I had a lot of clues. The trouble was, none of them made sense together. An hour after convening in Gram's living room to brainstorm, Hope and I had gotten nowhere.

"For the life of me, I can't figure out how sabotaging the fake Peak Diamond connects to an Indian gaming ring, a shady Israeli diamond dealer, and a murdered dentist." Hope threw her hands up in sheer frustration.

I didn't need to be a twin to empathize. I paced in front of my own version of a crime board—a grade school whiteboard I'd confiscated from my niece's playroom. Hope had propped it up against Gram's living room sofa to organize the information. Visual me loved the colorful connecting lines. In this case, the jumble looked more like a rat's nest, adding to my already pounding headache.

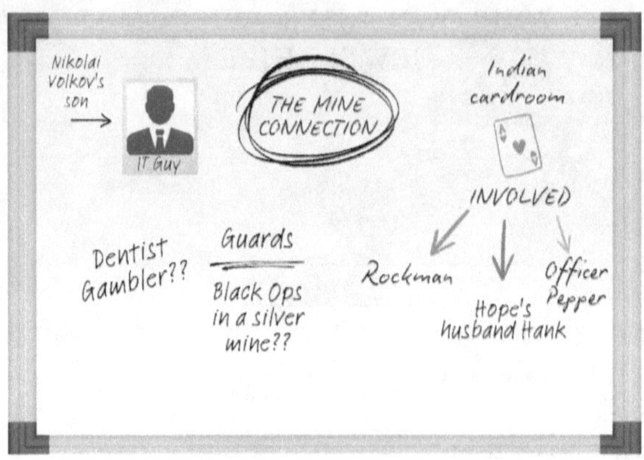

"I agree. It makes no sense that someone who has successfully replaced a priceless diamond would sabotage their own heist."

"I wouldn't put it past Karo because Blackwood got the diamond first," Hope suggested.

"Somehow, Karo would need to know the stone was a fake, which brings us back to: are the two of them working together?" I pointed out.

Hope's mutter said it all. "Not in this world. Those two are like oil and water."

No argument from me. "And why would Karo visit me with a warning promising an eye for an eye retaliation?" Pop's broken-in cowboy-leather easy chair groaned under my flop. "We're missing something." I'd felt that all along. There had to be a key element that connected everything.

Hope sat beside me in Gram's armchair. "I'd like to know how Blackwood discovered the gambling group."

So would I. For different reasons. I hadn't shared Rockman's involvement with anyone. First, I'd never jeopardize an investigation and, second, I didn't know exactly what role he played. "I'd like to know how the mine fits in. My gut is telling me Washburn is up to something."

"Which brings up another good point. If something is going on at the mine, stealing the Peak Diamond is the last thing they'd want to do."

Another question I had no answer to. Too many events contradicted reason. Glimmer jumped into my lap, her soft head rubbing against my hand. I scratched her ears. The silky feel of her fur reminded me of Mr. Teddy, my childhood bear, who knew secrets even my sister didn't.

My phone binged, alerting me to a text from Rockman.

Meet me at your shop in 30 minutes.

I glanced at my iWatch before responding, my thumbs flying across the touchpad. *90 minutes.* I had meatloaf sandwiches to deliver to the Peak Mine, but he didn't need to know that.

I left Gram's house no closer to answers than when I arrived and with no clear path to investigate. Sophie hadn't come up with anything new on the ownership of Phoenix Security or the root of the Peak Mine's financial woes either.

Twenty minutes later, I pulled my Bronco to the side of the gravel road a quarter of a mile from the new Peak Mine's compound. I left Glimmer in the SUV and hiked to an observation post concealed behind a thick rock formation. A believer in preparedness, I'd brought night vision goggles with me. Though daylight still streaked the sky, the long shadows of twilight tended to obscure details. Thanks to what had to be runway landing lights illuminating the entry area, my binoculars worked just fine.

The mine itself resembled a large, concrete portal built into the hillside. A vertical shaft house, constructed with a distinctive latticed steel design, stood to the right, hiding the all-important depth elevator.

The support buildings—more accurately, converted ocean containers and a single two-story office building—were clustered around the entrance. Some served as equipment storage sheds, and others barracks-style living quarters. Everything had a weathered, utilitarian appearance, built to withstand harsh mountain conditions, except what had to be the administrative building. It stood on the outer edge of the compound beside a waste rock pile, an angular gray heap that contrasted sharply with the surrounding mountain greenery.

Despite the late hour, the immediate area bustled with activity. Haul trucks, excavators, hoisting equipment, and ventilation fans for underground operations rumbled in front of me, bringing mining's golden age to mind.

I turned on my flashlight to review the dossiers of the four security guards. That all of their special forces' records were blackline redacted impressed me. Whatever Jasper Washburn's motives, he had assembled an impressive bunch—superhuman by most standards. Fortunately, however, manipulable thanks to the psychology of food. If I played my cards right, maybe I could get on site.

As I approached the twenty-foot chain-link fencing topped with coiled barbed wire, my early De Beers security training came to mind. The multi-checkpoint stops had a very South African diamond mine look to them. If the bold Private Property and No Trespassing signs didn't discourage looky-loos, the high-tech security cameras and electric fence warnings certainly would. Overkill to protect an underperforming Arizona silver mine.

I stopped in front of a neon striped arm blocking the entrance at the first guard gate. The man, dressed in a dark blue flight suit, approached, his left-hand hovering over his sidearm, his right carrying a glowing tablet. He motioned for me to open my window. "Miss Hunter, what is your business at the Peak Mine?"

Of course, the surveillance had run my license plate. I pointed to the Canary Café logoed bags on my front seat. "I am your Uber Eats driver today." The less said, the better. The guard's flinty stare could freeze molten lava.

"Where's our usual guy?" His southern twang gave away his Alabama origins.

I shrugged. "No idea. I'm doing Crystal a favor. She told me Lobo liked his meatloaf hot."

The guard bit back a smile. "Lobo likes a lot of things hot."

A man with a sense of humor. He had to be the guy who'd ordered the sandwich with potato chips tucked into the bread. I handed him his meal. I must've gotten it right because he thanked me with a smile and waved me to the next checkpoint, where another guard leading a German Shepherd walked the perimeter —the same dog my sister had sold to Phoenix Security? I wasn't sure until Glimmer's front paws reached for the window and she barked, her tail wagging. She definitely knew the dog. Good news or bad? Hard to tell.

The second guard, identically dressed, motioned me to pop my back hatch. I obeyed, making a point of shrinking from the big Aryan brute's superiority complex. In all fairness, the man's angry facial scar would make any duelist proud. The dog seemed to like him, though. A plus in my book. "I hear Lobo likes them hot," I joked.

Not even an acknowledgment in his pressed lips. "You need permission to enter."

A strict rule follower. I turned on my charm. "I'm just the driver. If you want to take the food and distribute it, be my guest." I reached for the order. "I have five meatloaf sandwiches left. One gluten-free with jalapenos that can't be contaminated by another sandwich. One with no tomato and potato chips." I shook my head. "Who eats their meatloaf with potato chips? Only one guy ordered the meatloaf the way the chef makes it. Really? The Canary Café's chef can cook. She knows what she's doing." I had to be the worst my-way culprit, but the guard didn't know that.

The guard's abruptness dropped a degree. "I agree."

His desire for order made him the only no-change order. I handed him his food bag. "I'll tell Crystal you have a dog. She has some great treats."

"No. He is a working dog." Like that explained his hardline.

Glimmer was, too, but she enjoyed an occasional treat. More than occasional. "I'm just trying to be nice. Anyway, do you want the rest of the order?" I lifted the grease-soaked bag.

The guard stepped back. "Take it to Lobo." He pointed to the two-story office building's steel door. I didn't argue. I'd gotten inside the perimeter. That was enough. He alerted Lobo as I drove inside.

If the thought of security at the dual gates was overkill, the heavy metal entry door looked bombproof. A speakeasy-style peephole slid open before my foot touched the step. "Where's my regular guy?" a raspy voice asked.

"You're the third guy to ask me that. I don't know. Crystal asked me to do her a favor and deliver to Lobo. Are you Lobo?" Silence stretched between us. Staring at two beady brown eyes didn't help my cause any. I needed to break down this barrier. "Look, if you don't want it ..." I turned, ready to go,

"No. I'm starving." The door groaned open. The dark-haired, lanky guy with thinning hair and a ferret-like look couldn't be the sexy older gentleman Crystal had the hots for.

"Are you Lobo, the IT guy?" I asked again to be sure.

"Yeah. Why?" The dark shadows on his teeth caught my eye. Bad dental hygiene? No wonder he chewed peppermint. The smell made my nose tingle.

"I-it's the gluten-free order. I can't give it to the wrong person," I said quickly.

His nod added one more enigma to this case. Who was the guy claiming to be Lobo at the Canary Café? And why lie about his identity?

"This is a cool setup," I gestured around me. "What's the big deal about protecting silver ore?"

"It's a precious metal." His practiced answer flopped. I'd found the weak link.

"Silver sells for $35.00, give or take an ounce. This kind of scrutiny is—"

"None of your business." He slammed the door in my face,

not before a layer of sweat glistened on his forehead. Was he the guy in charge? The guards deferring to him indicated as much. But did Washburn work for this guy? He added one strange dynamic.

Oh yeah, there was definitely something bigger going on here. Maybe Chief Rockman could tell me something.

Chapter Eighteen

BE CAREFUL WHAT YOU ASK FOR—WISDOM
FROM A JEWEL THIEF

MONDAY, 7:10 P.M.

My nape hairs tingled as I parked beneath the Starlight Estate Jewelers sign with a good five minutes to spare before Rockman arrived. Someone was watching me. I could feel it.

As I walked around the SUV to free Glimmer, I looked north then south on the shadowed street. Except for the sound of nighttime revelry emanating from the old mining bars, reminders of our town's less reputable roots, all appeared normal. The cool wind reminded me to grab a sweater from my office before I returned to Gram's guest room—my safe space until I carved out a new norm.

I'd crashed at the apartment above the shop after my divorce and never got around to finding a new place until now. Call it irrational, but my heart raced any time I thought about a shadowy figure rifling through my underwear drawer. I reached for the cold comfort of my Glock at my hip. It didn't help. I heard the nerve-wracking drip-drop of water, like a ticking clock deep in my subconscious.

My shrink called it PTSD. She was wrong. My dreams weren't

about Moscow. There was no hood blinding me in a damp underground bunker. I saw the golden eagle, her wings spread across iron gates, as clearly as the blood staining both of my hands and the tender yet stern voice that had plagued me for years. "*Ma chérie*, take care of your sister. In time, you will forget."

Hope, more dazed than alert and talking nonsense, leaned against me on the curb. "Papa." I felt the weight of the world on my seven-year-old shoulders.

The sedan door slammed shut, and my father sped away. Years later, I'd learned the truth. My mother had been murdered and my father fled Paris, pausing only long enough to drop my sister and me at the U.S. Embassy. Hope had been the lucky one, injured alongside Mama; she remembered nothing.

I hadn't forgotten. Not for a single minute. My safe spaces became my refuge, until those walls I'd built around me, too, were violated. Hope had tried to help. She'd completely disinfected and reorganized my tossed apartment. I told her to give everything away in the morning. I could never sleep peacefully there again.

Glimmer nudged my leg, forcing me to shake off my anxiety. I'd been tested before. I knew the drill. I just needed to put one foot in front of the other and keep moving ... Vulnerability was weakness.

I unlocked the front door and stepped inside. No alarm announcing my entry? I reached for my weapon.

"*Ma chérie*. Don't shoot."

That voice! It had been twenty-seven years. My heart pounded in my ears as I leveled the Glock. "Murderer."

Over the sight, I saw him. *Le Renard Argente*—Interpol's most daring jewel thief. Pictures depicted him as tall and elegant with a swath of silver hair and a flair for the exotic. The medium-built man dressed in a delivery uniform and wearing a baseball cap appeared so ordinary. My eye went right to the sliver of green, probably lettuce, wedged between his teeth. It took me a critical second to react.

"I am many things to many people, Taylor, but I am not a

murderer." His vehemence indicated innocence, but I knew the story. My mother died, and he'd run. He had to be guilty.

I held my gun steady. I'd envisioned this day for so long. Why didn't I feel vindicated? I'd dedicated my life to hunting thieves just like him. In a moment of raw honesty, I admitted to myself I had become a gem hunter to find him. My gut didn't even twinge. As much as I didn't want to, a part of me believed him. I responded in French. *"Je m'en souviens différemment.* I remember the story differently."

"Your memory is not complete," he said simply.

"Then prove it."

He responded in Russian, citing a common proverb. *Говорят, что кур доят. (Gavaryat, chto kur doyat.)* Hearsay played no part. I frowned. I'd researched and investigated.

He waited for my reaction before adding in English, "I read Ivan Krylov's fables to you and your sister at bedtime."

Of course, he had. Mom butchered the language of love with American arrogance. Speaking Russian far exceeded her linguistic abilities. Hope and I, however, were fluent. We also spoke French and German like locals. Our father had taught us from the cradle.

"Я помню. (Ya pomnyu.) I remember," I said.

"Your accent is perfect. Your great-grandmama would be proud. She was a code breaker with the French Resistance during the war."

His American accent was perfect, too—Midwestern, the accent preferred for newscasters. His attempt to build trust between us worked. Against my will, he'd drawn my interest.

He raised a silver martini shaker. "Beluga, Mariinsk. Shaken not stirred."

The iconic label with a beluga whale caught my eye. My favorite. I had a sneaking suspicion he knew that, too. And my fascination with James Bond.

He poured the classically-produced winter wheat grain alcohol into a frosted martini glass—no doubt from the lounge used for shop VIPs—and swirled the liquid. "Your taste is exquisite, *ma chérie*."

Fingernails scraping a blackboard bothered me less than when he called me that. He saw it. He raised his glass. "Let us toast to—"

"Answers." I holstered my weapon, as intrigued as he'd expected me to be.

"You will know the truth. It is, in part, why we are here today."

No sense wasting an excellent vodka martini. I accepted the glass and savored the crisp and super smooth taste.

A renowned jewel thief showing up after twenty-seven years on the run, when a priceless diamond had been stolen. It didn't take a brain surgeon to figure this one out. Suddenly, this nothing-adds-up case started making sense. "You stole the Peak Diamond."

"I did not steal the Peak Diamond," he replied without hesitation.

Not sure if his tone or his manner did it, but I believed him. "Yet, you're here in my town and involved in my case."

His slow smile somehow transformed his milquetoast appearance into someone familiar—the person I saw every day in the mirror. Like it or not, Hope and I had inherited his hazel eyes. The transformation shocked me.

"You have my mother's eyes. She still turns heads in a green dress."

The woman had to be in her mid-nineties. "Nice to know longevity runs in the family."

"Many things do. Your love of orchids, for example."

His words triggered a memory. My pulse leaped. "I remember you in Thailand in the hotel lobby." I'd stopped to admire an elegant display of dancing lady orchids when a Buddhist monk had whispered something about the language of flowers. My Chinese needed work back then, so I hadn't understood exactly. "It was you."

I'd tracked the Beeckman Diamond from Michigan to a cutting house in Thailand but lost the courier in Bangkok.

No denial. "The flowers caused you to rethink the puzzle. You went back to the ballet company, and you recovered the stone."

His nonchalance seemed hauntingly familiar. Where else had I seen him? I took a long look at him. Except for the distracting greenery in his teeth, there was nothing remarkable or memorable about his fair complexion or features. He looked ordinary, like the guy you grew up with next door. But I remembered ... "You were the artist on the Atlantic City boardwalk." The man's cloud paintings had changed my focus on the jewelry store heist I'd been investigating.

"Another case solved."

With his help. How many others had he been a part of? My confidence plummeted. Were my amazing gem hunting skills real or all him?

At that moment, I realized how crafty and clever he was. I'd "found" the important leads and the right people at the exact right time. Why hadn't I questioned my luck?

Because I hadn't wanted to. I'd gloried in my own cleverness, which had been a myth. For a moment, I almost understood my mother's fascination with him. He'd made her dreams come true, and she'd been happy turning a blind eye to everything else.

"I know many things about you and your sister and my beautiful granddaughters. You shall train them well. There is still time for you," he said.

My cheeks heated. "That ship sailed long ago." Rockman came to mind along with an irrational fear. If he caught my father here ...

"I sent the text from Chief Rockman," Dad said.

Relief gave way to shock. "You cloned his phone?" That meant he had been within ten feet of Rockman. Why chance capture with law enforcement? This just kept getting better and better.

"The chief is not what he pretends to be."

"And what is that?" My gut felt it, too, but Rockman had checked out—or had I been distracted by, um, other things. I stretched my neck.

He shrugged. "My *sixième sens* tells me to beware. I am rarely wrong."

A sixth sense? Did I get my gut feelings from him, too? I tried not to overreact. How alike were we? "Who are you really?"

"An illusionist. People see what I want them to see." No hesitation in his explanation, just truth.

I saw it then clearly as day. The lettuce between his teeth, designed to distract and disarm me. It had worked too well. He'd manipulated my curiosity and deep insecurities, or had I let him?

"What do you want *me* to see?" That had to be the point of this meeting. He needed something from me that he couldn't get on his own.

"Your father."

Laughter escaped as a croak. "Pop was my father."

"I will forever be in his debt."

Another piece clicked into place. I caught his tell—that barely perceptible glance to the left. He'd tried to conceal it behind a mask, but I'd spotted it at the gala. The mask hadn't been some COVID precaution; it was camouflage, and likely protection against the gas too. This man was neck-deep in the conspiracy. "You were working the bar at the centennial celebration."

No denial again. Was that pride in his smile?

I refused to fall for another mind game. He'd attended the Founders Day event. That put him in the middle of the theft and Blackwood's murder. Time for some answers. "If you didn't steal the Peak Diamond, then what did you do?"

"I sabotaged the fake stone."

"You? Why?" An answer followed by more questions.

"It was the only way I could protect you and Hope. The mine is the key."

Forget patience. My blood pressure spiked. "By setting Hope up as a murderer?"

"It's more complicated than that."

"No, it's not." I failed to rein in my temper.

"I did not set Hope up." His hazel eyes flashed right back at me. "The Peak was stolen to lure me out—to seek revenge against me."

Karo's warning came back with a vengeance. "An eye-for-an-eye."

"Who told you that?" His control slipped and, for a split second, I saw raw fear—the torturous kind.

"Karo. Why would the Peak Diamond ...?" But I knew. Hope and my connection to this stone forced him to step up.

"*Merde.*"

A break in his cool. I jumped on it. "Who did you piss off?" He was a jewel thief—the guy who stole from whoever got in his way. Would he even know? I'm sure the list was extensive.

"Sindikat Krasnogo Medvedya."

I fell back against the wall and slowly sank to the floor. The Red Bear Syndicate, the same organization I'd thwarted in Russia. A thousand images filled my mind. My miraculous escape from their clutches had been the stuff James Patterson wrote about. "You saved me in Moscow." Tears bit the back of my eyes. I should have died there.

"Of course, I did. You're my daughter. *Je mourrai pour toi.*"

That we both used the same cadence took a second to register before his words sunk in. He would die for me? I'm sure my jaw dropped. I believed him.

Had I truly been the catalyst for our current situation? My crazy need to right wrongs? Guilt racked me. This man I hardly knew had risked his life for me? How had he known? Was my feeling of being watched real after all? "What is going on?" I emphasized each word.

"I am a ghost. Dead to this world with no ties or loyalties—no leverage for someone seeking revenge."

"Revenge for what?" I asked.

"I helped Ivan Medved's wife, the head of the Sindikat Krasnogo Medvedya, escape from him."

"That was ten years ago." I could see why that would annoy the macho gangster. "Why now?"

"You and your sister were hidden until ..."

"Moscow." I finished his thought. Like Hope, he was in my head.

He nodded. "It was bad luck you crossed him."

I saw no regret. Another band of anger washed over me. "Medved is the enforcer for the People's Commissariat. He acquires what they cannot legally. If not, then it was only a matter of time before we crossed paths. Why did you mess with his wife?"

"I had no choice."

He wasn't getting off that easily. I'd had my fill of philanderers. "There's always a choice."

"Ivan Medved murdered your mother."

Chapter Nineteen

NEVER REVEAL EVERYTHING YOU KNOW— WISDOM FROM A JEWEL THIEF

MONDAY, 10:30 P.M.

"Our father was at our shop, and you didn't think to call me?" Hope's frustration elevated her whisper to a shout. She looked like a harridan waving her fist, wearing cactus pajamas and a headband. Even Dee, the decoy dog, had scooted out of her reach.

I'd been dreading this conversation since *Le Renard Argente* vanished into the night. "Shush. You'll wake Gram."

Our father was dead to Gram. Any mention of his name ended with her stomping out of the room. Childish, yeah, especially in the eyes of inquisitive teenagers, but Gram didn't abide by loyalty breaches. Pop had shared some things about the man, all in secret and at great personal risk.

"Too late." Her arms crossed, Gram stood in the doorway. Dressed in jeans and a puffy vest covering a plaid blouse, she appeared, like Joan of Arc, ready to take the world down. The fire in her eyes said she'd not only heard everything but had sensed it all along.

Of course, she had. Even I knew better than to question the woman's protective instincts.

I felt Hope's groan despite her best attempt to hide it. "It's late. You shouldn't be up. Your doctor said ..."

Gram cleared a place at the kitchen counter and sat down beside me. She directed her comment at Hope. "My girls in trouble affects my health worse than missing a few hours of shut-eye."

Hope bit back her rebuttal, instead pouring Gram a cup of decaf coffee. Good. She'd be the same way with her own girls.

Gram took a long sip. That she didn't stir in sugar indicated her head was someplace else. "Is he bald and fat?" Gram asked so softly, I barely heard her.

"That's your first question?" Hope paced between the counter and the oven. "What about, what is he doing here?"

"In due time." Gram turned to me. "Well, is he?"

My grandmother, the enigma. I tried not to laugh. "Sorry. He's trim and has all his hair."

Gram harrumphed. "Your mother always said he was 'a dream.'"

More like a nightmare—a disruptor of the status quo, the kind of man who flipped your world upside down. "How did they meet?"

Having survived one failed marriage, others' success interested me, especially when the couple came from different worlds.

Gram stirred her coffee, still without adding the sugar. "They met in Vegas. Your mother went there for a bachelorette party. Twenty-four hours later she came home with a husband."

"What? Why didn't you have it annulled?" Hope's pacing turned into a jog in place. "I would. After I shot the guy."

"Whoa. I do the shooting in the family." I turned to Gram. "And mom was nineteen. Legally ..."

"Old enough to get married." Gram focused on the twirling liquid. "I thought he wanted American citizenship and would leave her."

"It was love at first sight," I said. *Or so Dad had claimed.*

"First lie, you mean," Hope added.

I'd thought so, too. I wasn't so sure after a few hours with him. I'd never considered the possibility until today. "They met at his lounge show."

"He turned out to be a struggling French illusionist. They travelled around the U.S., holed up in one bad hotel after another until he landed a job in Europe. Your mother was pregnant by then. Your grandfather and I begged her to stay with us, but she refused to be away from him."

"Seriously?" Hope jerked her fingers through her already messed up hair. "You didn't stop her?"

"And how do you suggest I do that?"

"I don't know. Arrest him. Lock him up in jail if you had to. Pop was a cop. He had friends."

Far too many in questionable places if you asked me. Hope's overreaction portended real issues for my headstrong nieces. Dad was right about me being the voice of reason. Sometimes you had to let kids make mistakes. I repeated Dad's words. "*Говорят, что кур доят.*" (*Gavaryat, chto kur doyat.*)

Hope's jaw dropped. She remembered, too.

"English," Gram growled. "You know I hate it when you two do that. What does it mean?"

"Things are not always what they seem." Hope's suddenly haunted look emotionally charged the room. She remembered more than I'd thought.

I hid my shaking hand in Glimmer's fur. The beat of the dog's heart helped. Dee must've sensed my sister's mood, because she brushed Hope's leg until she picked the dog up to cuddle.

"Did he steal the Peak Diamond?" Gram's abruptness got us back on track.

"He claims no. He admits to sabotaging the fake."

"And you believed him?" Hope started pacing again, this time holding the dachshund like a security blanket.

I exhaled. "I don't know. His story is wild and so unbelievable that I keep thinking he couldn't possibly have made it up."

"He's a professional liar," Hope added.

"I know. He was incredibly convincing." I glanced at Gram.

Her harrumph summed up my opinion. The man had an agenda. I knew that for sure.

"And why did he single you out? We're twins. We share everything." There it was. Hope's hurt feelings coming out.

"Not everything," Gram said. She knew. I'd never entirely shared the Russian ordeal, but I wondered now if she'd always known, and that was why she'd begged me not to take the assignment.

I turned to Hope. "When I was in Russia, I was kidnapped by the Sindikat Krasnogo Medvedya." Tears filled my eyes, remembering too much. Dad had been under the radar, living a nomadic but safe life. "Dad broke me out. They're hunting him now." My voice broke. "I did this."

Gram came to her feet. "This isn't on you, Taylor. Your mother made a deal with the devil." The sweep of her arm knocked over the coffee cup, sending the steaming liquid across the granite countertop.

Hope grabbed the paper towels and lunged for the save. The distraction helped discharge the tension. Had Gram done it intentionally or was I seeing ulterior motives in everything?

The mess cleaned up, Gram finished her story. "The French authorities charged your father with your mother's murder, but your grandfather wasn't convinced. You know how he could get."

Like a dog with a bone.

"A friend of your grandfather's at the embassy looked into it and found the Russian connection. We begged your father not to pursue it."

"But he did. He used his tricks to steal jewels and mess with their smuggling shipments. He became an informer for Interpol until Ivan Medved's wife wanted out of the marriage," I explained.

"An eye for an eye," Gram muttered. "He helped her to fake her death."

"And his own. As long as he remained dead, we were safe," I explained. "He came out of hiding to save me."

Hope listened as quietly as I had. "Maybe all of that is true. Russia was over a year ago. Why is he here now? And what does the Peak Diamond have to do with it?"

Seventeen months and three days, but who was counting? "He thinks the Peak Diamond theft was a ruse to get him to come out of hiding."

"That's insane," Hope replied. "We never would've known the stone had been stolen if he hadn't sabotaged it."

"I agree. His action started a chain reaction that caused the dentist to be murdered and likely Blackwood," I said.

"So, who killed them?" Gram asked.

"Dad thinks whoever stole the stone to begin with. It appears that his disruption essentially stopped the diamond counterfeiters from setting up shop."

"My GIA reports?" Hope said.

"The evidence suggests that."

"Who does the evidence suggest has the diamond?" Trust Gram to keep us on target.

I shook my head. "The only thing that's been resolved is who sabotaged the diamond."

"How did Dad know the stone was a fake?" Hope asked.

"In one of his many, uh, thefts, Dad found the photo of Nikolai, Washburn, Blackwood, and Rockman's uncle in a file with Nikolai Volkov's name on it."

Hope whistled. "The Peak Diamond is just a small part of this. The case is really about criminals replacing natural diamonds with CVD manmade diamonds."

I couldn't have said it better myself. "The problem is that my proof is the word of an accused murderer and a thief. And even if Dad turns himself in, a connected smuggler is gunning for him. He won't make ten hours in holding, never mind through extradition." He'd put me in a no-win situation. I'd agreed to share information with Rockman, and I couldn't or wouldn't. Not now. Not ever.

Hope chewed her lip. She got my dilemma. "How are you going to prove any of this?"

"I don't know. Dad said that the mine was the key," I replied.

"Don't you have an interview with Jasper Washburn in the morning?" Hope asked.

"Yeah. With Chief Rockman."

"Isn't that good news?" Gram asked.

"I can't tell him any of this." Not that he'd believe it anyway. "Dad thinks Rockman's got another agenda." I agreed. I just hoped Sophie would deliver answers before the meeting.

Chapter Twenty

BEWARE OF THE HIDDEN AGENDA. IT WILL KILL
YOU—WISDOM FROM A JEWEL THIEF

TUESDAY, 5:20 A.M.

"Good morning, Hunter. I do hope I haven't disturbed you." Sophie's voice before my first cup of coffee couldn't be good news.

I tried not to growl. I'd been interrupting her sleep for days now. "What've you got?"

"You sound lovely this morning. A productive night?"

I opened one eye. "You might say that." Going over my visit with Dad again and again with Hope had tested my patience to its limits. How was I supposed to know what his favorite color was? Or if he preferred Turkish mud or café au lait? I got her disappointment that she hadn't met him, but we had bigger issues to deal with.

"Rockman does look rather cheeky in his Los Angeles police graduation photo. There is something about a man in uniform."

That image woke me up, most of me anyway. I squirmed, disturbing Glimmer. The dog grumbled on my behalf. Rockman really was a cop. Relief washed over me. Maybe he was what he claimed to be. Or not. "There's still something off about him."

"I hazard to say, your intuition might be spot on. I've

unearthed an internal affairs investigation involving Rockman in a case against Phoenix Security."

My gut reacted. "Phoenix Security?"

"Yes. Their Los Angeles office provides port-to-warehouse inbound shipment security. Key evidence against the company was misplaced."

"From the investigation involving his uncle?"

"Yes. Put down to an inside man. Never substantiated," Sophie explained.

It could mean nothing or everything. "Why did they suspect Rockman?"

"The chain of evidence was broken on his watch."

Currently, half of the fake Peak Diamond remained in my safe. Not exactly by-the-book protocol, but what internal affairs called evidence mishandling could simply be an attempt to solve the case gone awry. My more practical self played the devil's advocate by adding: or was he protecting his uncle? Or worse, working with the diamond smuggling ring. In which case, I might have unwittingly helped him.

I needed answers. "Did this evidence affect his uncle's case outcome?"

"Indeed. Rockman's uncle never revealed his partners."

Had I been played? Intuition warred with the case facts. I should be calling Phoenix PD's internal affairs, but we were missing something; we had to be.

Sophie sensed my hesitation. "First rule of a PI. You must follow the evidence."

"Except when it doesn't tell the whole story."

"Are you quite sure it's not your libido speaking?"

I'm sure my cheeks flushed. "Please. He's not my type." I pictured his lazy grin.

Sophie stated her opinion in a long-suffering sigh. "If you say so. I shall endeavor to dig deeper."

I'd owe her big time at the end of this case. I hoped Rockman was worth the effort. My father's warning about the man's "other" agenda suddenly bothered me.

"Who was Phoenix Security's customer in the mishandling case?" I asked.

"The more interesting information is the consignee." I pictured Sophie's knowing grin as I waited for her revelation. "The company that has supplied Sunset Mine's heavy equipment."

Dad had alluded to a link to the mine. Had I found it? I exhaled. What exactly was Rockman up to? "It appears recovering the Peak Diamond is only the tip of the proverbial iceberg." I bit my tongue too late.

Sophie cleared her throat. "Need I remind you the diamond is your sole interest?"

"I know. Get the stone. Get out. Simple," I replied quickly. But it wasn't. Not when Sunset Peak's safety potentially hung in the balance.

"Why don't I believe you?" Sophie paused before adding, "You were correct. Hank's socks tested positive for the laughing gas. They are connected to the diamond's theft."

Not surprising. Sophie's next statement was. "Something rather unpleasant popped up on your brother-in-law as well."

Oh, no. That bad sushi feeling tingled in my stomach. Did my sister know? Another possibility I didn't want to consider. "Does he owe more money?"

"It's not who he owes money to at present, but who he did," Sophie replied.

"I don't understand." But I did. Once a gambler, always a gambler, Gram had said. In this case, some obligations you never really got out from under. My father could attest to that.

"Let's just say he's on a good few people's 'favor' lists."

"Russian?" I asked.

"Da."

Of course, he was. How deeply involved mattered. Could I trust him to tell me the truth? My first loyalty would always be to my sister, nieces, and Gram—her kind of justice could get us all in trouble. "You're just the bearer of great news this morning."

"No trouble at all."

British understatement at its best. "Any chatter on the Peak Diamond?"

"Nothing. It's rather as if the diamond has vanished into thin air."

Which could mean whoever had the Peak Diamond intended to keep it, or didn't know how to unload it. Karo, still in town, made the latter a real possibility. The question that remained was who had stolen it and why? And what part did Rockman play? Something I'd better figure out before our meeting with Washburn in a couple of hours. I wasn't a good enough actress to pull off the status quo when meeting with someone.

Chapter Twenty-One

PEOPLE ARE RARELY WHAT THEY SEEM—
WISDOM FROM A JEWEL THIEF

I exited Gram's house determined to confront my brother-in-law before meeting Rockman at the mine. In the interest of time, I'd tracked Hank's cellphone to the dog training area. No surprise. He usually worked with the dogs in the early a.m. while Hope drove the twins to school. While he followed the normal routine, Hope and the twins remained behind closed doors in the ranch house with a guard dog on duty.

I shivered, the morning chill causing me to zip my puffy vest as I hurried along the rocky desert path toward the kennel, challenging Glimmer's little legs to keep pace with my purposeful stride. A peek at the sun's rays spreading over the two-story barn roof and I knew I'd be shedding a layer of clothing before noon. Spring in the desert made me want to sing. Even the cactus wren tweeted its native songs as it floated in the thermals.

My horse whinnied as I passed the barn and approached the white-planked kennel that created an L-shape. A mesquite log fence completed the enclosure on the remaining two sides, naturally forming a spacious central corral. Two aging SUVs now sat parked along the edges, divided by strips of artificial turf and a gravel pathway that had transformed the space into a makeshift park.

The area buzzed with focused energy as Hank, dressed in a desert camouflage jumpsuit, directed a canine trainee on the course—explosive detection, I guessed, if last night's scene at the mine checkpoint was any indication. A majestic tan and black German Shepherd moved methodically around one of the parked SUVs, its nose twitching along the undercarriage and wheel wells as Hank directed her actions. The dog obeyed, not deviating from the course until its focused body language shifted. It had caught the scent near the rear bumper. The Shepherd immediately sat and looked up at Hank with alert puppy eyes.

Hank praised her. "Good girl, Bisquet! Excellent find!" He immediately rewarded her with what I assumed was her favorite pull toy, along with additional enthusiastic praise. The Shepherd's tail could clear a coffee table with its enthusiasm. The man knew how to incite loyalty in a dog. I suppose that skill translated to people, too. My sister and his twin girls certainly adored him. Gram not so much. Me? I wasn't on the worship list either.

I approached as Hank scribbled notes on a clipboard. Alerted by the dog's single woof, he paused my arrival by flashing the one-minute sign and continued writing his report. I waited, surprised when he wiped sweat off his forehead before acknowledging me.

"What can I do for you?" he asked.

The crack in his voice gave me my opening. He was hiding something. I'd bet on it. "We can start with the truth about the Indian gambling group?"

"I told you what happened." Hank's gaze drifted everywhere but toward me.

"You told my sister and me a version of the truth." I paused for effect. "You do know that a lie of omission is still a lie."

His jaw slacked so quickly I'd have missed it in a blink. "H-how did you find out?"

I rolled my eyes. This man was not a career criminal. "That some sleazy dealers hold your markers?"

His shallow breathing confirmed everything. As usual, Sophie had been right. "What kind of favors are we talking about exactly?" I asked.

Hank stroked his bearded jaw. "It didn't seem like a big deal at first. I'd occasionally lure some big fish into a game."

"It never does." I crossed my arms. "You're still gambling."

His emphatic no had to be true. "I-I'm protecting my family." My sister would have a different take on that I'm sure. Hank added, "This goes back to when I was still in college. Long before I met your sister."

"If you weren't gambling then how did you lose the money Hope needed to repay?"

His long exhale gave me the answer. Of course, he hadn't lost the money. Hank's skill would've seen through any scam. There was more going on. "You better tell me everything."

Hank nodded. "Junior year, I hit a losing streak. I owed a lot of money. I was about to get kicked out of school. I worked a table where a couple of guys from Phoenix Security lost big. I saw the guys by chance later."

Chance? Not likely. They'd found their mark.

Hank wrung his hands. "They knew I'd been part of the scam. I couldn't spend three to five years in prison. When they offered me a 'get out of jail free' card to work a few games for them, I jumped at it. I never imagined it would go on this long."

My coincidence radar about exploded. "What are the odds you'd end up here?"

"Not so random." He flushed. "A guy from Phoenix Security sent me to meet Hope."

The big secret. "That was ten years ago." The magnitude of his confession struck me. Whatever was going on had been in the works for a long time.

Hank nodded.

"Who ordered you to set up Hope?"

He started to speak, then thought better of it. "I-I can't. They'll kill both of us."

"It's a little late to worry about that." I could take care of myself. Hank, I wasn't entirely sure. His confession did bring up a point. "Were you ordered to marry Hope?" My sister would love that. We had a traitor among us. We'd both missed it.

"No. No. It was love at first sight. I swear. I tried to break up with her before the wedding, but you know Hope ..."

I did. My sister was a sucker for a charity case and Hank defined that.

"... she wouldn't let me. Then the twins ..."

And he'd done the "right" thing, marrying my sister. Or was that part of the conspiracy and relevant to the Peak Diamond's theft? I mentally reviewed the timeline. The 1994 picture established Nikolai, Blackwood, Rockman's uncle, and Jasper Washburn's acquaintance. Thirty years later, Rockman's uncle was arrested for diamond smuggling. In 2019, the Peak Mining Company was reborn. "Who ordered you to set Hope up?" I repeated the question. This had to be the missing link.

"My usual contact." The words tumbled out faster than he'd intended, betrayal evident in his voice. "Rockman was there at the cardroom, too."

"Rockman! Chief Rockman?" My voice cracked with disbelief.

Hank's solemn nod hit me like a sucker punch. That dirty, hypocritical son of a... The rage that had been simmering beneath the surface threatened to boil over. He'd looked me straight in the eye and said my issues would get him killed! Had he been playing me from the very start, feeding me lies while working his own angle?

"What was he doing exactly?" I forced the words out through gritted teeth, my hands clenching into fists. Stay calm. Don't overreact. Not yet. I'd suspected he had someone on the inside at the cardroom, but this...

"He's part of the security team at the private high roller tables." Hank's voice dropped to barely above a whisper. "Rumor has it he worked for Phoenix Security in Los Angeles."

White-hot anger coiled deep in my chest. My gut reaction to

Rockman had been screaming warnings from day one, and I'd ignored it like a fool. The evidence was staring me in the face now, mocking me.

"He swaggers around like he owns the place," Hank continued, his own bitterness seeping through. "But some of the other guys say that he's been demoted." He paused, letting the implications sink in. "Why else would a man like that be banished to this godforsaken town?"

The insinuation hit like a lightning bolt. Why would a man with connections to diamonds—to Phoenix Security—be exiled to oversee a struggling silver mine in the middle of nowhere Arizona? It had to be about the Peak Mine. Everything always came back to that cursed hole in the ground. It had to be.

I'd deal with Rockman later. Now, I turned to face Hank, my stomach churning with a sickening realization. "You set up your own wife?"

Hank swallowed hard. "No. I refused. I wanted out. Whatever the price. I couldn't let Hope get involved."

"Your contact told you $250,000 would do it? And you believed him?" I stared at Hank in stunned disbelief. His naïveté didn't just amaze me—it infuriated me. How could someone be so gullible?

My brother-in-law's shoulders sagged as he nodded miserably. "Blackwood told me he only needed Hope to do a simple diamond appraisal. Nothing more." His voice cracked with regret. "I still said no. But Hope... she caught me transferring the money. I panicked. I told her I had it under control." He buried his face in his hands. "God help me, I had no idea she would go straight to Blackwood herself."

"You don't know your wife very well," I muttered bitterly, though even as the words left my mouth, I felt a stab of guilt. Recriminations weren't getting us anywhere. I forced myself to focus. "Was Karo part of the gambling scam?"

"I don't know." Hank's voice sounded hollow. "I only saw him once at the reservation card game—in the private room last week."

"The high stakes room?" The words came out sharper than I intended, alarm bells clanging in my head. "Was Rockman in the room?"

"No. He mostly showed up on weekends," Hank replied. "He was there yesterday, though. Rockman met with a guy I'd never seen before—someone kinda creepy looking. He had this burn scar ..." Hank's hand traced a path along his left jaw.

My pulse thumped. My illusionist father—the master of deception who'd been everything from a bartender to a delivery man to an IT specialist. How many faces did he have hidden up his sleeve? "Did the man have an accent?" I pressed.

Hank shook his head, frustration etched across his features. "No. I don't think so, anyway. I didn't notice anything unusual about how he talked."

"Could you describe him to a sketch artist?" I asked.

Hank scratched his head. "I-I don't know. I keep seeing the scar."

Definitely my father. The pieces clicked into place with terrifying clarity. Dad's belief that Blackwood had somehow lured him to Sunset Peak suddenly didn't seem so far-fetched. He'd taken an enormous risk meeting with Rockman, even hidden behind one of his elaborate disguises. One slip, one moment of recognition, and he could have blown everything.

"How much trouble am I in?" Hank's voice cracked with desperation.

"Legally or with your wife?" Hope's voice cut through the air like a blade as she materialized beside me. Her sudden appearance made my heart skip a beat—how long had she been listening? Her posture was rigid, every muscle coiled with barely contained fury toward her husband.

Hank's explosive curse made Glimmer cover her ears with her furry paws. I bit my lip hard, fighting back the urge to laugh despite the gravity of the situation. My brother-in-law had to be doing mental calculations right about now—wondering if three to five years in federal prison might actually be the easier road compared to facing the wrath of my sister.

Chapter Twenty-Two

KEEP YOUR ENEMIES CLOSE—WISDOM FROM A JEWEL THIEF

TUESDAY, 9:30 A.M.

I stepped away from Hope and Hank's escalating argument, but not before giving my sister a quick once-over for potential weapons. Armed with nothing more lethal than a nail file, I figured there was at least a fighting chance she might listen to reason instead of committing homicide.

The irony wasn't lost on me—I could only pray I'd show the same restraint when I finally came face-to-face with Rockman. Because right now, the urge to wrap my hands around his throat burned through my veins like acid.

While Hank's actions could be viewed as nobly misguided, Rockman had done the unforgivable. The fact that he'd deceived me so completely stung and made me doubt my usually reliable instincts. Yes, I'd been drawn to him, but I never ever allowed emotion to interfere with an investigation until now. I saw it clearly. The trouble was, even now, after everything I'd learned, something deep inside me still insisted I was reading him all wrong.

The drive on the winding mountain road to the new Peak

Mine usually took twenty minutes and should've helped me calm my racing thoughts. Today I made it in eleven. Glimmer's reproachful glare told me she hadn't appreciated the breakneck pace one bit.

The dog dismissed my apology with a head toss full of doxie attitude. Perfect. Glimmer would have to learn that life doesn't always go her way. I needed to rein in my anger.

Dad would say to swallow my pride and use Rockman to get what I needed—in this case, a one-on-one meeting with Jasper Washburn. But how could I pretend he wasn't a liar and thief? Further complicating matters, the chief read me like an open book. I considered sending Hope as a stand-in, but he'd spot that trick immediately. I was stuck. If I wanted to get the Peak Diamond back, I'd have to deliver an Oscar-worthy performance.

Even though I'd arrived early, Rockman's patrol car already occupied our meeting spot—the same boulder-protected vantage point where I'd stopped the night before. I wedged my SUV into the narrow space he'd left me, noting another diligent turkey vulture circling overhead. Was I the prey or Rockman? In his tan uniform with green epaulettes and gleaming chief's badge, he didn't look like the backstabbing snake I now knew him to be.

I clenched my teeth as I exited my SUV. This was going to be harder than I'd anticipated. My traitorous doxie solved that awkward first meeting by trotting past me to Rockman's outstretched hand, demanding a scratch.

Of course, he accommodated her, rubbing her ear until she rolled onto her back, exposing her full belly for a rub. Glimmer, the wary dachshund? Her character judging skills usually trumped mine. My uncertainty returned with a vengeance.

"What's wrong?" Rockman rose to tower over me. "You look like you're about to shoot me."

He wasn't far off. "Nothing."

"Sure." He crossed his arms. "Let me guess. This pertains to my absence yesterday?"

Of course, the dispatcher had told him about my concern and request. "Now that you mention it. Disabling a GPS tracker is ..."

"Necessary when you don't want anyone to know where you are." His quicksilver gaze bore into me.

No denial. He did have a way of saying exactly the right thing to disarm me. I swallowed. *Show no weakness*, I reminded myself. "So, what were you doing?"

"Following up on a lead."

"On the Indian reservation?" That allegation slipped out.

His knowing smile irked. He'd known. Had he seen me?

"This conversation can go no further." He waited for my nod. "I have a leak in my department."

Convenient excuse or for real? I couldn't tell. "Are you the undercover guy or Mason?"

That little twitch above his eye indicated that I'd hit a nerve. "You know I can't confirm or deny anything," he replied. "But I'm the good guy here."

Of course, he couldn't, which didn't help me one bit. Did I believe him? Evidence suggested otherwise—missing evidence in a criminal case, a suspicious association with the gambling group, and my father's warning—as if he was a reliable source.

The situation demanded a straightforward accusation. Except the cold steel of my Glock pressing against my back reminded me that I was alone with a man who also carried a gun. Retreat and regroup had to be the safest option. When had I ever taken the easy way out?

"You ordered Hank to set up Hope." My accusation hung between us.

For a split second, his mask fell, and I saw regret. "Hank has a big mouth. I promised him Hope would not be charged. I needed ..." Rockman's eye twitched.

"You set up Blackwood ..." I said.

Rockman closed the deal with another piercing I-know-you're-hiding-something look, too. "You're going to have to trust me. Just like I must trust you."

Trust? His sins far outweighed mine. I had no choice, and I knew it. "I've connected the laughing gas from the cardroom to the gas at the gala."

He started to speak but took a deep breath instead. "You need to let me do my job."

Whatever that was. Was he part of an operation tracking Blackwood and Washburn, or was he working for them to cover everything up? Dad's warning played back in my mind. Who could I trust? Both men had secrets. One would likely get me killed.

Bottom line, I needed more information. "What's the plan for the interview with Washburn?" I asked finally.

"I'll question him about his relationship with the deceased."

"And why his security team is all ex-special forces?"

Rockman shook his head. "Subtlety, Hunter. Don't make me regret inviting you to join this interview."

Like this was my first rodeo.

"Come on. We'll take my vehicle," he said.

The invitation wasn't really a suggestion. I scooped up Glimmer and followed him to his Police Interceptor. Essentially a law enforcement version of a Ford Explorer, I hadn't realized just how heavily customized the vehicle was until I peered inside. Beyond the standard driving controls, what looked like an airplane cockpit separated the passenger seat from the driver, complete with multiple rows of lights, switches, and buttons.

Rockman opened the passenger door for me. "Let me have your gun. I'll lock it in my ..."

"Not a prayer." Voluntarily relinquish my weapon? Never!

Rockman exhaled. "Do you honestly think the mine security team will allow you to enter the compound with a gun?"

I swallowed my retort. "Are you ...?"

He palmed his own handgun. "'No weapons' was part of Washburn's agreement to see me."

Much as I hated the idea, I had no choice and I knew it. For a quick second, I felt like the proverbial lamb being led to slaughter.

Who headed into enemy territory with no means to defend themself?

Me. Maybe I did have a death wish. I reached behind my hip and handed over my trusty Glock. No answers would be forthcoming without taking this risk. I needed to meet with the security chief, if only to shake it up a little. "I feel naked."

That little tic in his brow again. I bit back a smile. It felt good to get to him for a change and know that he wasn't completely immune to me either.

Clearing the mine security in a police vehicle turned out to be easy. The first checkpoint waved us through without even requesting ID. No bomb dog activity at secondary either, but the guard did scan both of our IDs with a tablet. "The meatloaf sandwich was excellent last night, ma'am," the guard said.

I'd hoped he wouldn't recognize me. No sense denying it. Rockman's inquisitive look demanded an explanation. "I'll tell Crystal you liked the new recipe."

"I'm in for any changes. You're right, the chef knows what he's doing."

"The chef is a she," I replied as he directed us to the same administrative building where I'd dropped off the delivery order the night before.

I preempted Rockman's questioning. "I delivered the Canary Café's dinner order last night."

"I'm sure Crystal will confirm this." Was that surprise or annoyance in his response?

"She will. I met Lobo, the IT guy; he's seriously gluten-free."

We pulled up in front of the two-story office building where the third guard—attired in a red jumpsuit—waited for us.

Just like the night before, the compound hummed with activity. Between the clanking hoisting equipment and rumbling ventilation fans, I felt the start of a headache. How did anyone work here?

This guard scanned Rockman and me with what looked like a Star Trek phaser with a small screen. Probably the metal detector device I'd seen used when I watched the mine from the desert hillside. At least I thought so until the device beeped as it passed my chest. I started. Perfect. Exactly who, I wondered, would they ask to pat down my underwire? "It must be my, uh, bra." I know I blushed. Rockman barely contained a grin until I kicked him in the shin.

"Naw. It's the dog's collar. Those real diamonds?" The guard stroked his scruffy beard.

"Yes. The collar was a gift from a friend." More like a satisfied customer, but no one needed to know that. Why would a **pavé** collar set off an alarm?

"For a dog?" The man shook his head.

"She's a special dog," I retorted. Had we been scanned with a diamond detector? I'd not seen one that compact before. The question was why was it deployed at an Arizona silver mine?

My gaze followed that circling turkey vulture as the guard walked us to the metal entry door. Tension tightened my gut. Something felt wrong, like I should run for cover. I didn't. Stoically, I stood beside Rockman, praying this didn't turn into a fiasco.

At the door, instead of waiting for someone to let us in, the guard released a hidden compartment. He pressed his thumb to a scanner and the door clicked open, revealing a long, white-tiled corridor. "First door on the right," the man said.

I motioned Rockman to silence as the door clicked shut behind us. My pulse jumped. The thumbprint, the oval-shaped cameras, and the solid door; I'd seen this security protocol before. The cameras recorded more than video; biometrics ran our identities the moment the door closed. No wonder Dad had sent me. He'd have been discovered instantly. Anger simmered in my gut. My own father had set me up. The Sindikat Krasnogo Medvedya knew exactly where I was now.

With Russian smugglers somehow connected to the Peak Mine, Dad's story not only seemed more plausible, but frighteningly probable. He had put me and Hope in the middle of a potentially deadly vendetta.

My hand shook as I placed Glimmer on the ground and glanced up at Rockman, who towered over me like a Herculean warrior. For the first time in my life, I questioned my ability to protect myself and my family. I needed to know: could I trust him or was he one of them?

Chapter Twenty-Three

WHEN CAPTURE LOOMS, DISAPPEAR—WISDOM FROM A JEWEL THIEF

TUESDAY, 10:00 A.M.

I pinched myself to be sure I wasn't dreaming. Washburn, the control freak who'd threatened violence over control of a gas leak, the embodiment of congeniality?

I wouldn't have believed it if I hadn't sat right across the coffee table from him. We'd gathered around the live-edge table, sitting in plush barrel chairs arranged in the far corner of a cavernous executive office. A full silver tea service occupied a silver tray between us. Although the bald man with the middle-aged paunch still looked like the same bulldog I'd met two days ago, his affable smile suggested otherwise.

"Ag, I want to thank you and your dog for tracking down those gas canisters." Washburn extended his hand. "That dachshund is something special. Word is he's a diamond detection dog, too?" Firm, yet tempered for a lady, his greeting felt sincere. "May I?"

Glimmer eyed his hand cautiously as he crouched to allow her to sniff him. The dog waited for my permission before approaching. My normally self-sufficient dachshund? She was trying to tell me something.

I understood the moment the doxie sniffed his hand and went rigid, nose pointed toward the ceiling. "Have you been handling gas?" I asked.

"Ja, indeed I have."

Discreetly, I motioned Glimmer to explore. The dachshund disappeared behind Washburn's desk and returned a moment later. She sneezed, a delicate little squeak that caused her long body to shake.

Washburn stepped back with a laugh. "He is something else."

"She," I corrected him. That odd enunciation in a few choice words made his South African accent feel strained. I wish I could place it.

Washburn's smile widened. "Right, so your family's outfit trained her?" He stressed the word 'her.' "I'm keen to get one myself. What's the delivery time looking like?"

An order for a unique, painstakingly trained dog? "It's not that easy."

"Isn't it just? I've already got one of your sniffer dogs—the bomb detection one. He's doing a proper job." Another long, measured look.

This guy was accustomed to getting his way. I refused to be intimidated and held my ground.

Washburn finally said, "I'll reach out to my usual contact. Sort it out through the proper channels."

My sister. Good luck with that. All compliments and an order for a dog? You'd think he was buying me off. Rockman thought so, too.

Washburn turned his attention toward the chief. "You didn't trek all the way out here to the mine to chat about dogs. So, what can I do for you today?"

I responded first. "Forgive me if I'm confused, but the last time we met you were—"

"A bear. My apologies. I'm not a morning person. Don't function properly before my morning cuppa." He directed his wink at me.

Something I could relate to and even half-understand.

An impatient Rockman spoke. "I am interested in hearing about your relationship with Edward Blackwood."

A momentary start—a clench, really. So fast, I'd have missed it if I hadn't been focused on his hands. "Veenie." Washburn sipped his tea. "We knew each other years back in SA. Those were the days." He faced me again. "What are the odds? Small world and all that. Right, Miss Hunter?"

"Not that small. It's curious how you both ended up at a party celebrating a silver mine in Arizona."

"Nothing curious about it. Just two diamond blokes checking out that legendary fire diamond."

He had a point. Washburn's down-to-earth commentary surprised me most. I'd never have called him likable until now. Had I misjudged him based on his morning monster persona? My guard dropped a degree.

Rockman stayed the course. "Did you two old buddies catch up while he was in town?"

The unyielding side of him intrigued me. Rockman could've been a lawyer. I'd hate to face his cross examination. Washburn's slow smile followed. "We had a quick chat at the gala on Sunday night. We were both flummoxed to bump into each other after all these years."

I remembered seeing them at the event. Not together. "How did a diamond guy end up mining silver?"

"I could ask you the very same thing."

"I'm a cowgirl with expensive tastes," I replied. Glimmer barked in solidarity.

Rockman's brow arched. "What's your story, Washburn?"

"I'm a miner. Born for the underground life."

"Including smuggling?" Rockman laid the photo of Nikolai, Washburn, Blackwood, and Rockman's uncle on the coffee table.

Washburn retrieved his readers and picked up the picture. "I haven't seen this one in ages."

"Thirty years," Rockman suggested.

"I reckon so. Look at us. Four young diggers with the fire in our eyes."

"Two are dead. Another in jail," I remarked.

"I am the last one standing," Washburn replied easily.

"Who took the photo?" My curiosity refused to wait.

"I remember it well. First day of sun we'd had in donkey's years—a whole month underground. Your uncle brought out that tripod of his to photograph the birds."

Washburn's hand jerked again. He was lying. The first rule of deception was to limit details. He'd already admitted to knowing Blackwood in South Africa. How close were they really?

Rockman cut off my question. "For the record, where were you between midnight and two a.m. Sunday morning?"

"Asleep in my bed alone. Security cameras will confirm. The bartender poured with a heavy hand at the gala."

"The gas enhanced the effects," I added. Washburn knew that. What was he up to?

"The bank president went wobbly early on. I imagine you had to give him a hand to get the Peak Diamond stashed away safely," Washburn said. Clearly, he knew about the retina security.

"Sounds like you've had issues with the vault," I said.

"The hours the bank keeps. A few weeks back I needed to get into my safety deposit box. Found Dale propping up the bar at Whiskey Jack's."

"Drinking?" I asked.

"Indeed. I drove him to the bank. His assistant had the paperwork prepared. A man's got to hold his liquor."

Dale's drinking problem was worse than I'd thought. I wonder if Ruby knew. "Your mine security is impressive. I haven't seen anything as thorough since the Congo," I said. Conflict diamond central, where one of every four stones was mined at the expense of others.

"From a De Beers insider, I'm chuffed. You impress me, Miss Hunter. Most women would decline that sort of assignment," Washburn replied.

I wish I had. Sophie and I had seen too much. We called surviving a win. I cleared my throat. "Do you have IT backup in this building or offsite?"

He responded with caution. "Onsite. Don't get many power cuts in Arizona."

Unlike the middle-of-nowhere Africa. "I'm curious about your metal scanning equipment. It reminded me of a diamond sensor."

"A little invention," he said, his chest puffing up with pride.

"Yours? Now, I am officially impressed," I said.

"Alas, no. My IT guy's sharp as a tack—a proper creative, and clever, too. Appreciate your delivering his dinner last night. The poor oke's got issues with his stomach. Chews charcoal like it's a sweet."

That would explain the dark residue on his teeth. "Charcoal?"

"Something his mother taught him. I suspect it makes him hangry, as you Americans call it."

My stomach growled in solidarity. "I can relate." I hadn't eaten since early either.

Washburn rose, signaling the meeting's end. I tried to stop him. I had a bunch more questions, like why were his guards all special forces trained, or, better yet, how did he become a mine stakeholder? And, of course, what he knew about the gambling ring. But Rockman overrode my objections by thanking Washburn for his time. We hadn't asked any of the hard questions, so why would he back down so soon? Unless Rockman really was protecting Washburn?

I had one last chance to get to Washburn. I took his hand in both of mine. "Is it possible to see the mine? I'd love to compare your processes to the diamond mines I've visited."

I felt his pulse pound through his veins before he pulled away. "Eish, that's not possible. Our methods are one-of-a-kind. Entirely proprietary."

He turned down my offer to sign an NDA and ushered us out of his office. I shaded my eyes in the high noon sunlight as we returned to Rockman's vehicle. I expected to be rescanned like the folks exiting the facility I'd seen from my hillside perch, but the security guard waved us through.

Rockman remained silent until we exited the final gate. "A mine tour? Did you really think he'd allow it?"

"No," I said. "He might have agreed to allow you to go though."

Rockman frowned. "Why is that?"

"Because I know mines, and they aren't mining silver in that hole in the ground." I brushed Glimmer's fur. Tiny dust particles fell into my hand. I rolled the dust around in my palm. "Do you have an evidence bag?"

"In the glove box." He reached across my lap, lightly brushing my breast. Sparks shot to my toes, the ripples awakening feelings I hadn't felt—ever. I jerked back. I couldn't help myself.

Glimmer nudged my neck, breaking the tension. At least he'd felt it, too. The quiver in his hand told me so when he finally handed me the red printed pouch.

I brushed the dust into the bag. "If I'm right, this is diamond dust. Legally attained, I might add."

"From a dog's fur? Don't see a single issue with the integrity there," Rockman said.

I frowned at his sarcasm. "A trained diamond dog signaled she found diamonds in Washburn's office."

"The defense will say he had a diamond ring in his desk. Look, I want this solved as badly as you do, but it needs to be done legally."

Said the man who'd been accused of evidence mishandling. Was he being ultra cautious or protecting Phoenix Security? I couldn't tell.

"Glimmer's collar fired the scanner. And why else would Washburn take such a hard line on my visiting the mine? I'd call it probable cause," I announced.

"For what? Misleading the company he's prospecting for? That's between Washburn and the parent company. Unless we can connect Blackwood's murder, which there is no evidence to, there's no crime."

Another reasonable denial. Maybe he had a point.

He must've seen me waver because his follow-up punch was a bulldozer. "Besides, what are the chances? The last known diamond discovered in this area was a hundred years ago."

"One of the finest fire diamonds in recorded history was found in the same mine they are exploring today." I chewed my nail. "What if Washburn found the original Peak Diamond's kimberlite pipe?" His blank look caused me to clarify. "They are the pipe-like formations created as a result of volcanic and tectonic activity millions of years ago. Ninety percent of all diamonds are found in kimberlite."

I caught his interest. "If what you say is true, and diamonds were discovered here, Sunset Peak would be overrun with treasure hunters."

"Exactly. It would be a boom to the town. Private claims seemingly worthless would now be worth millions. Can you check if anyone is buying up the surrounding land?" I asked. Could this elaborate set up be about greed? Why kill Blackwood and the dentist ... unless they had been victims of wrong time and wrong place? That didn't explain where the real Peak Diamond was or my father's role. None of the evidence fit together.

Rockman's nod seemed tentative. "This feels like a hoax. The rock formations in Arizona have never supported diamond production."

"Not natural ones." I let that thought hang for a hot minute before adding, "I need to get a look inside that mine."

"You'll never get past the security." That pulse in his brow again. He was hiding something.

"There may be another way ..." In retrospect, I should've kept that thought to myself.

Chapter Twenty-Four
KNOW ALL YOUR ESCAPE ROUTES—WISDOM
FROM A JEWEL THIEF

TUESDAY, 11:30 A.M.

I retrieved my weapon from Rockman's truck and checked the clip before holstering my trusty Glock. Better to be safe and prepared, I reasoned as I returned to my Bronco. I followed Rockman down Old Miners Trail to Quarry Road. He continued to police headquarters while I waved as I turned on Canary Trail and made a quick left, turning into the Sunset Peak Public Library lot. Considering his questionable loyalty, it was best that Rockman knew nothing about my next move.

A roadrunner darted past me as I walked to the front entrance, portending good fortune. I'd be sure to tell the librarian, Windy, that. With any luck, I was on to something.

Donated to the city around 1930-something by the madam herself, Scarlett's Social Parlor still dominated the corner of Quarry and Canary Trail. Once painted bright, inviting red, the two-story Victorian structure had weathered to a mellow, dusty pink, the gingerbread trim a comfortable beige. Contemporary wood shutters had replaced the burgundy velvet draping the tall windows, offering an air of genteel respectability to an establishment once frequented by the most successful miners.

Ninety years later, visitors of all ages entered to find mahogany-lined rows of educational and bestselling books, sophisticated gaming computers, and podcasting suites, all paid for by Scarlett's generous endowment. Some say she created the library to buy respectability in the afterlife. I like to think legends deserve eternity. All agreed that she watched over her legacy from her kitchen office, where the scent of lavender water still mingled with the aroma of cigar smoke.

Given the library's unusual beginnings, it made sense that the librarian would be equally distinctive. With her reputation for sweeping out tradition to make room for innovation, I figured Windy Dias—cousin to my office manager, Sunny—would have been exactly the kind of person Scarlett would have chosen.

Today, I found her hunched over one of the computer terminals, madly thumbing a gaming controller and chomping on gum. "Bless it! That dang dagger is going to be the death of me."

Glimmer pressed up close to my ankle, waiting for my reaction. "An educational challenge?"

"More like a patience test." Windy disconnected from the game. Glimmer, sensing peace, drifted toward the children's play area and a toybox overflowing with sticky-fingered plush animals. Another Windy addition that entertained both children and inquisitive dogs.

Windy wiped her palms on her strategically ripped jeans and straightened her puffy-sleeved peasant blouse. Unlike her cousin, who wore body art with pride, Windy preferred a natural look. She even tied back her curly dark locks with an old shoelace.

"You in these hallowed halls means trouble," Windy announced with conviction.

Perfect. Now, I had a reputation. "Hallowed? The ladies of the night have to be busting a gut about now."

Windy snapped her bubble gum. "I figured you'd be around eventually. I assembled every book, article, and diary containing references to the Peak Diamond." She gestured toward what had to be a three-foot Jenga-pile of hardcover books, ringed binders, and worn leather diaries. "Tell me why I'm always the last one invited to the dance?"

"Because you have two left feet," I suggested. "Thank you, anyway. What I really need today are the accounts from the two miners who survived the Peak Mine flood of '36."

"Ninety years ago?"

I nodded. Windy popped a fresh stick of gum and cow-chewed. "You do know the police concluded that the miners passed out in the desert and were never in the mine on the fateful day?"

"Yes, I know. They were called the luckiest drunks in town," I replied. "They also both swore on their deathbeds that they'd found another exit."

"Which no one has ever located. Not for lack of trying, I might add."

Windy's skepticism only added fuel to my theory. "What if those miners did tell the truth, and there is another way in?"

"That's a lot of ifs for a woman who survives on facts," Windy remarked. "Why are you so willing to believe?"

Windy did know me well. "I need to get into the mine."

Windy flopped into her swivel chair and spun a full revolution. "Is Washburn being a douche?"

"You'd think he had something to hide," I replied.

"They are hyper security conscious. A buddy of mine was detained for over an hour when he delivered some replacement generator parts."

"Why?"

"Because the unit broke down and needed a new compressor or something. I don't know. I can hardly put gas in my own car."

"You drive an electric car."

"Oh, yeah."

"Why was your friend detained?" I asked.

"He says he set off their metal detectors. Can you believe they made him strip down to his tighty-whities? A dang good thing he hadn't gone commando that day."

I swallowed. I had gotten away easy on my last visit. "Does his wedding ring have diamonds on it?"

"He's not married." She chewed her gum thoughtfully. "Come to think of it, he wears a St. Christopher medal. I think it has a diamond chip in it. You don't think ...?"

"I don't think anything," I said quickly. No sense testing Windy's ability to keep a secret. "I'd like to know where the lucky miners were found and where they said they'd escaped the mine."

Windy started to say something but changed her mind and transferred a pile of yellowed research material that had been stacked on the credenza behind her. She handed me a cracked leather book. "This is one of the miners' accounts. I also have two newspaper articles and fire rescue documents detailing injuries sustained by others who tried to find the entrance. The risk of rockslides is significant."

Only if you dug in the wrong place. The proximity of the information struck me. "Why do you have—?"

"The chief asked me to pull the same information about fifteen minutes ago."

He had believed me. He'd requested the information from his vehicle after we'd left the mine. To locate, conceal, or just stop me from finding the entrance?

"When will he be here to pick up the information?"

Windy checked her iWatch. "Any minute now."

I glanced toward the door. I didn't have a lot of time.

Windy's gaze locked on me. "What is the deal between you two?"

"Nothing," I replied too quickly.

She shook her head suddenly. "It's a competition, isn't it?"

"No," I replied, but she knew I'd lied.

"Goldine Block, that reporter from the *Peak Examiner*, is a step ahead of both of you. She asked for the same information yesterday. Plus, the map of the old mining village."

"The Amethyst Inn's predecessor. Did she say why?"

"She said the ghost was back, and she needed background information for her report."

Likely someone's idea of a joke, but worth a conversation. Nothing else was working out. "I'll take whatever you have on the old mining settlement as well." Extra information never hurt. I carefully extracted a map yellowed with age that had been tucked between the diary's pages and spread it across the nearby worktable. The prospector was clearly no cartographer—his sketches resembled some of my nieces' age-five works of art, complete with uneven lines and primitive symbols. "Can you help me match up landmarks with these markings?"

"Seriously? I can't find a gas station without Google maps," Windy announced.

My turn to stare. "What happens if the cell tower goes down?"

"I guess I'd stop at the nearest bar."

A comforting thought. "Great role model for children. What kind of librarian are you?"

"The computer genius kind." She removed a magnifying glass from her desk and handed it to me. "See the three circles with the X?"

I leaned closer, the magnifier to my right eye. "Is it a rock pile?"

"Possibly. The old claims were marked with rocks and desert debris ..."

I hated to squelch her enthusiasm. "There are a lot of abandoned claims in the surrounding area."

"Hundreds, to be exact. Some never even officially filed because the claimant never made it to the assessor's office." She stopped my objection with a shake of her forefinger. "Trust WWT."

"WWT what?" This ought to be good.

"Windy's Wonder Tool, guaranteed to blow you away."

Her enthusiasm drew my reluctant smile. "I bet you say that to all the kids."

"You know me well. In this case, it's a program that will compare the old miner's map and symbols to a current one and send directions to your phone."

"Impressive." Had to love spy craft gone mainstream. "How accurate is it?"

"I've seen the program detail historic tours all over Italy."

"Not exactly the same thing." Old roads and long-standing buildings were one thing. An open desert populated by tumbleweeds? Hardly a fair comparison.

Windy rhythmically chewed her gum. "Do you want me to try or not?"

"Do it. What do I have to lose?"

"My thoughts exactly. We start by entering the information into Google Earth." Windy snapped a photo of both maps and forwarded them to the computer at her desk. I pressed closer, leaning over her shoulder. Windy appeared to shrink before my eyes. "A little breathing room. Please."

I backed off a foot. Still close enough to watch Windy manipulate files. A few minutes later, a map popped up on her screen.

My pulse jumped. "X marks the spot?"

Windy leaned back in her chair. "Kind of. Assuming the miner's information is accurate. I mean, by today's standards, we'd call him dyslexic." She traced her finger across several entries where letters appeared reversed and symbols were mirror imaged. "That kind of processing difference would definitely impact his surveying accuracy, which might explain why this site has remained lost for so long."

My excitement wavered. "That's it? Just guesswork?"

"Not entirely. The mountain ridgelines have shifted over the decades, too—erosion, rockslides, that sort of thing. We're still looking at a search area spanning several hundred feet in any direction."

"Close enough to work with," I decided. "Can you send me the coordinates?"

As Windy did, she said, "You realize this is a long shot at best.

If there even is an entrance to be found, what makes you think you'll find it?"

"I have Glimmer, the best diamond dog in the world."

At the mention of her name, my doxie's head shot up in the middle of the pile of plush toys like a jack-in-the-box, her tongue lolling out as if she'd just devoured a jar of peanut butter. On second thought, I really didn't want to know what she'd been doing over there.

"If I can get Glimmer within 100 feet of the opening, she'll find it," I said more confidently than I felt.

Windy pushed her glasses to her crown. "You do realize that the Peak Mine is a silver mine, right?"

"So they say," I replied, more determined than ever to get inside the mysterious mine.

Chapter Twenty-Five
BEWARE WHEN THE VULTURES ARE CIRCLING—
WISDOM FROM A JEWEL THIEF

TUESDAY, 1:15 P.M.

Another turkey vulture circled overhead, portending who knew what, as Hope and I loped side-by-side through the high desert outside Sunset Peak, our horses jostling for the lead along a dry wash. Around us, the landscape shifted from boulder-strewn flats to scrubby ridges dotted with cactus, mesquite, and alligator juniper. We kicked up a stampede-worthy cloud of dust, and the clatter of a rockhound's shovel, pickaxe, and hammer packed on Hope's Appaloosa made any hope of stealth laughable as we raced toward the back side of the old Peak Mine.

Hope's horse bore the racket. Vaj, my palomino, carried the essentials: sloshing canteens strapped beside my western pommel, with Glimmer, the queen of the trail, secured in her custom suede pouch. The sack supported her hind legs while her front paws perched regally on my saddle horn. Her eyes were closed, but her nose lifted, catching every nuance in the desert breeze. With the sun warming her snout and the wind ruffling her ears, she looked like a seasoned scout, ready to pounce on danger or, more likely, demand a treat.

The turkey vulture vanished, hunting more interesting prey as we turned east at the base of the rocky incline. We continued for a good twenty minutes, with only the sound of our horses' hooves striking against the crumbled stone in a steady, deliberate rhythm. Each step tested our horse's balance as the desert trail narrowed into a jagged path flanked by barrel cactus and scrubby mesquite. The dust had abated once we left the wash, but still puffed beneath the horses' hooves and swirled in the dry air.

The scent of iron and sage filled the air. Higher up, the terrain leveled between two boulder-strewn ridges where we stopped for water and to rest the horses.

I removed my binoculars from the saddlebag beside Glimmer and scanned my surroundings. The rocky structure due east looked familiar. My pulse jumped as I referenced the map. I'd seen it yesterday from a different angle. The spot where someone had been watching me, or had they only been studying the Peak Mine's grounds?

The turkey vulture returned, this time circling the hillside directly in the GPS's path.

"That buzzard's making me nervous." Hope's beat-up Charlie 1 felt hat dropped down her back as she tilted her head to sip water.

I placed Glimmer's water on the ground beside her and took a swig of my own. I brushed the spillage away with my thumb. "I swear that bird's been tailing me." I'd seen it first on my last desert ride, then at the mine. No wonder I felt like someone was watching me.

Hope spewed her water. "Geez. We sound like a couple of whiny children."

Walking on eggshells did that to me. Setting the backbreaking pace to avoid discussing her husband had only delayed the inevitable confrontation. I stretched my neck. Uncomfortable as the truth was ... "The situation with Hank is your fault."

"Mine!" Hope shrieked.

"You knowingly married a man with a past." No sugar coating this one.

"But he never told me. He's kept secrets."

"That's a lie, and you know it." To give Hank credit, he had admitted his gambling problems before proposing to my sister. Probably hoping to scare her off, though the strategy had backfired.

Hope might have been looking for comfort, but the promise we'd made to always be honest with each other made that impossible in this case.

Hope's trembling bottom lip revealed something deeper than mere frustration. She opened her mouth to protest, then drew in a sharp breath instead.

"Why did you take matters into your own hands?" I asked.

Her cheeks flushed. "I didn't want ..."

"I get it." I hugged her stiff shoulders. "You thought you were protecting him and your family. I did the same thing with Chad ..."

"The cad," Hope interjected with a ghost of a smile.

The irony struck me. Not too long ago, she'd been the lecturer and I the recipient. Look at me now offering marital advice. "It takes two people to blow up a marriage." I'd never told her any of this before—anyone, actually.

"You're not condoning his cheating, are you?"

"No. That's on him. I started the cycle though. I stopped communicating with him." Time did offer perspective.

"We both have really bad taste in men," Hope admitted.

Chief Rockman came to mind. I'm sure I blushed.

"You really think Hank's right?" Hope asked.

"I think you need to decide if you can trust him again or not." My reply cut right to the core of the issue. In any relationship, trust mattered most.

"You don't trust him," Hope said.

"Trust isn't in my vocabulary," I said flatly.

"That's heartbreaking." She shook her head, pain flickering across her face. "You're shutting yourself off from everything good." But her words felt distant and hollow, like echoes in an empty cave. I'd watched her husband's betrayal tear her apart, felt every crack in her heart as if it were my own. Yet, somehow, Hope would find a way to forgive him. She always did.

"The cost is too high," I replied.

Glimmer's low growl interrupted Hope's response. The horses shifted restlessly, ears pricked forward. Every nerve in my body snapped to attention. We weren't alone. The way my dog's hackles rose told me whoever was out there was getting closer.

Hope sensed it, too. She pressed a finger to her lips, then quietly drew her knife from the saddle sheath. In one fluid motion, she disappeared behind the cluster of rocks to our right. My hand found the familiar weight of my Glock …

Like an apparition, Rockman materialized in front of me. "You're late." Dressed in tear-away khaki hiking pants, a camouflage shirt, and a vented Australian slouch hat, he looked like an out-of-town hiker.

"Late?" Hope slipped out from behind the boulder.

"We didn't plan to meet," I said.

The air crackled with unspoken tension. Had he been tracking me? How else would he have pinpointed my exact location? But deep down, I already knew the answer.

"Didn't we both get the same intel from Windy?" Rockman glanced at his watch. "You're thirty minutes late."

Hope's pointed look spoke volumes. *Too scared to face him alone?*

Our twin communication got on my nerves today. *Absolutely not.*

Well, maybe a little. Part of me had suspected he'd show up here. I'd been secretly racing to reach the mine's entrance first. "You hiked the whole way?" Even after three miles from the trailhead, he appeared fresh and alert.

"Left my ATV behind those rocks."

"That's not smart," Hope muttered.

I had to agree. "Might as well send up a flare to announce our presence." Then it hit me. "Wait—why didn't we hear the engine?"

He gave me a look that could have melted steel. "Ever heard of stealth mode?"

Hope ended our tiff. "You two don't need me." She turned to Rockman. "You can take my horse."

A good solution except, she hadn't cleared that with Marvel, who tossed her head and snorted. "I'll take your ATV home. You can come to the ranch to pick it up later."

His gape proved almost comical. Hope saved him. "Marvel is gentle. She's easy to ride."

"I can ride," he said quickly.

A cop from the big city? He's likely done a touristy trail ride. I bit back a smile. This could be video-worthy, the way Marvel shuffled from foot to foot, swishing her tail, contemplating how bad an idea this was.

"Okay then." Hope held out her hand. "Keys, please."

Rockman handed them to her. Her smile screamed conspiracy. "Be good, kids. Communicate. I hear it does wonders." She disappeared with a ta-ta and a silent *good luck, Sis.*

"Well, that was something," Rockman's amusement seemed genuine.

The certainty that I had been set up clouded mine. "I hope you really can ride. It's a long walk back to civilization."

"I'll be fine." He stroked Marvel's neck while he gathered her reins and inventoried our supplies. "You planning on digging my grave?"

"You figured me out," I shot back. "It's been ninety years since someone may have found this entry point. There will be vegetation to clear."

Rockman nodded. He evaded the Appaloosa's nip as he dropped the stirrups three notches.

"I'll hold her. She can be a little ..."

"Feisty? You don't say."

Was he talking about me or the horse? I wasn't sure. Before I decided, Rockman slipped his left foot in the stirrup and swung the right over the horse's back. Marvel objected with a quick side-step and buck.

I moved toward the horse's bridle, but Rockman gestured me away. He drew back on the reins—not harshly, but with firm, steady pressure that spoke of authority. The mare tossed her head defiantly, fighting the bit and trying to force him toward the jagged rocks. Rockman dodged both attempts, moving with an ease that could only be gained from experience. Marvel seemed to understand at the same moment I did. She let out a resigned snort and finally stilled. That battle had been over before it began.

"I was going to say that horse is a little brat," I said, still processing what I'd witnessed. The contradictions, the inconsistencies—what was I missing about this guy? Nothing added up. Or maybe everything did, and I just couldn't see the pattern.

"I like feisty better." His silver gaze swept over me like liquid light, intense and all-consuming. My breath caught, my pulse quickening to a wild rhythm. Glimmer's nose nudged me at just the right time.

I slipped my dog back into her pouch and mounted. "Where did you learn to ride like that?"

"My uncle taught me."

His mysterious, shady uncle again? How convenient. And a lie. "That's rodeo riding."

No movement above his eye. I'd read him completely wrong. Lobo had been a rodeo clown. Sophie had told me. That made Rockman part of this whole twisted web. I wheeled my horse around, hand flying to my weapon as I backed him against the rocks, cutting off any escape route. "Who are you?"

Looking back, trapping a potentially desperate man at gunpoint was probably my stupidest move yet. But he didn't go for his gun. Didn't even blink. His voice came out eerily calm: "Put the weapon down, Hunter."

Glimmer saw the red dot dancing across my chest before my brain processed what it meant. She exploded from the saddlebag in a blur, spooking Vaj into a sideways bolt that sent me flying.

I hit the ground with a bone-jarring crash that I knew would haunt me come morning—if there was a morning. I was about to pay the price for my bad judgment in men.

<h1 style="text-align:center">Chapter Twenty-Six</h1>

THE TRUTH DEPENDS ON YOUR POINT OF VIEW
—WISDOM FROM A JEWEL THIEF

TUESDAY, 3:45 P.M.

I'd experienced life-flashing-before-my-eyes moments before. So, when the only thing occupying my thoughts was the barrel cactus spine jabbing into my thigh, I figured this time I was either dead or carrying too much baggage to sort through in my dying breath.

Glimmer wasn't helping matters either. She alternated between frantic barking and slobbering all over my cheek. I was pretty sure the afterlife would be quieter than this.

I opened my eyes to find Rockman leaning over me. "Are you okay? You hit your head."

Genuine concern? Hadn't he just tried to kill me? "Yeah." I coughed, spitting out sand. The dust clung to every part of me. My shirt was full of it. I felt the grit grinding between my skin and the fabric. "What is going on?"

His hand appeared in front of me. I remained sprawled on the ground, my eyes scanning the barren landscape. The laser site on my chest had come from somewhere—but where? Nothing moved except that lone vulture circling overhead in the endless expanse.

"You're safe. Let me help you up." His calm voice cut through my fear. I believed him.

Forget pride. My skull felt like it was splitting in two, and I needed answers more than I needed dignity. His firm grip pulled me upright and guided me to a shady spot beside a boulder.

"Are you all right? You fell off your horse." He produced a cold water bottle from somewhere. I snatched it and pressed the chilled surface against my throbbing forehead.

"Like hell I fell. I dove for cover. Someone had me in their sight." I blinked, trying to clear my vision as I studied his face. "Why didn't they take a shot at you, too?"

"No one is shooting anybody," he said simply.

A loaded answer. My hand moved instinctively to my hip. Empty holster. Of course. My heart rate spiked. I wasn't safe— not by a long shot.

Glimmer pressed against my leg. I cupped a handful of water in my palm, keeping my eyes on the muscle jumping in Rockman's brow as she lapped it up. "You took my gun! Are you planning on killing me?"

His piercing silver gaze locked onto mine, unwavering and intense. "No. I'm one of the good guys."

Clarity struck. His sketchy background, the criminal connections, those dubious references. "FBI Criminal Investigation Division," I said. It had to be. This case went well beyond local jurisdiction. "How long have you been undercover?" And who else was? How had Sophie missed it? How had I?

Glimmer must've sensed my uncertainty because she curled up in a half-moon at my feet, her attention focused on Rockman.

"You're compromising a five-year operation," he said, his tone shifting to something harder, more professional.

"One that began in Los Angeles when they arrested your uncle." I watched his face carefully. "He is your uncle, right?"

Rockman's jaw tightened as he gave a barely perceptible nod. "Someday I'll tell you the whole story."

But not today. Despite everything, I found myself curious to hear it. "Your uncle sold out Phoenix Security." I didn't need his confirmation—the tension in his shoulders confirmed my theory. "So, how did you wind up in Sunset Peak?" Even as I asked, the pieces were falling into place. My father's warnings echoed in my mind. "The Red Bear Syndicate owns the new Peak Mine, don't they?"

"We can't prove it. But we know they're moving diamonds through a web of legitimate front companies."

"Including the Indian cardroom?" I asked.

Another nod. "Problem is, we couldn't trace the diamonds' origin point."

"Because there isn't one. They're not mined. They're manufactured."

His eyes sharpened. "We suspect that, thanks to you and your sister identifying that CVD signature. I hate to admit it was pure dumb luck that you stumbled onto it."

More like my father's interference, but I couldn't admit that. It did mean we were a long way from solving this one. "I'm a firm believer in luck versus skill."

"I find luck to be more a product of skill. However, in this case, I'll take whatever I can get."

There was a compliment in there somewhere. I'm sure. "Is Jasper Washburn—"

He answered before I finished my thought, eerily like Hope and me. "We think he's a lieutenant."

"For whom?" Washburn taking orders from anyone seemed unlikely with his ego. "Do you know where they're manufacturing the diamonds?"

Rockman's expression darkened as he shook his head. "That's what makes this whole thing so confusing. The Peak Diamond switch and those GIA reports Blackwood squeezed out of Hope—they all point to some elaborate scheme to replace priceless stones with fakes. But it makes no sense economically. Why kill the golden goose? They've got a profitable synthetic diamond operation running. Even stranger—

why would they sabotage their own product? The pieces don't fit."

Because this wasn't about profit, it was about settling old scores, and revenge rarely followed logical patterns. "We need to get inside that mine."

Rockman pushed his hat off his forehead. "We've been trying." He pointed toward the vulture, wings spread, soaring in the breeze.

A bird? I shaded my eyes to see. The vulture looked so real. "I don't understand." But I did. "You mean it's a drone?" I waited for his nod. "That's what had me in its sight?"

"The CSD isn't weapon-equipped. It's a live feed surveillance device."

"What does CSD mean?"

"Camouflage Surveillance Device."

Of course, it was. "Is that supposed to make me feel better?" It didn't. No wonder I'd felt spied on. That bird had been following me. "How many do you have?"

"Enough. The device is ..."

"A dangerous invasion of privacy." I'd never look at a bird the same again. "Don't tell my sister about this. She'd buy a cactus wren model in a minute to watch over her girls."

"The CSD is not for retail use."

"Give it time."

His frown disagreed. "The drone has been searching the area for the old mine entrance. So far, we've found nothing conclusive."

I refused to be discouraged. "Do you have sites worthy of investigation?"

I followed his gaze to Glimmer, drooling on my boots. "Yeah. But you need to rest."

"I need to find this entrance." My stomach dropped the instant his stare captured mine.

"You fell off ..."

"Jumped off." Misplaced as it was, his concern touched me. "I'm fine. We'll start with the possible sites and let Glimmer, the diamond dog, do her job."

My dachshund's head popped off her front paws on cue, proving her hearing, though selective, was good, too. She glanced from me to Rockman and kitty-stretched, the slow quiver working its way through the length of her elongated body.

Rockman remained unconvinced. "We're looking for a cave in solid rock."

"No problem. A dachshund is a scent hound. She's as effective a tracker as a bloodhound. Both breeds have 300 million olfactory receptors. Which means they can identify a single smell among thousands of aromas. The trick is for her to find what you want."

"I assume you have a command."

I nodded. "A search out here"—my gesture included the surrounding area—"is far easier than finding a specific diamond in a ballroom packed with fancy jewelry. In the African diamond mines, Glimmer has been accurate up to two hundred feet underground."

Rockman whistled, as impressed as he should be. "Why don't the mines use diamond dogs?"

"They did back in the 1980s. Technology offers more affordable options with reduced maintenance. Glimmer can be a handful." The dog snorted her agreement.

Rockman remained silent, instead focusing on a satellite phone. At least that's what I figured the handheld device he carried was, since cell service didn't exist out here.

While he scrolled, I rechecked the map Windy had provided. "I say we follow the original search coordinates. They are—"

"East," Rockman announced. His left hand pointed toward the bird-drone. "Five clicks."

I scooped Glimmer into her saddle pouch. Then walked to the left side to mount. Rockman stood between me and Vaj.

"The least I can do is help you mount." His voice was low, rough around the edges.

I should've declined. The desert heat suddenly had nothing on the warmth that spread through me at his words, at the way his hands settled on my waist to steady me. Every point of contact burned through the thin fabric of my shirt.

It had to be the relentless Arizona sun that made my skin flush and my pulse quicken. But when his fingers tightened slightly as he lifted me, when I caught the scent of leather and something uniquely him, I knew I was lying to myself. The saddle loomed above me, justifying the lingering pressure of his palms against my sides.

Glimmer's abrupt bark shattered the moment. Reality crashed back as I found the stirrup with my left foot and swept my right leg over in one fluid movement. The sharp pain that shot through my ribs—that had to be from my earlier tumble, nothing more.

He didn't step back right away. His hands hovered near my thigh for a heartbeat too long, and, when I glanced down, I caught something dark and hungry flickering in his gray eyes before he finally moved away. The air still hummed with whatever had just passed between us.

He swung up onto Marvel with practiced ease and took point. The fluid way he moved with his horse's gait, the play of muscle beneath his shirt with each stride—none of it did anything for my composure. Though I had to admit there was something absurdly amusing about Hope's saddle with its delicate floral trim looking so out of place beneath his rugged frame.

We picked our way carefully through the maze of weathered sandstone formations and ageless saguaro cacti, their arms raised in artistic angles against the cloudless sky.

The old-timers' map was a long shot at best—hand-drawn sketches marking landmarks that might have shifted or eroded over decades or were in a completely different locale. I referred to it anyway since every shadow between the rocks could easily conceal what we were searching for. I also watched for the telltale signs: the geometric lines of timber supports, the unnatural darkness of a shaft entrance, or the scatter of tailings that would betray human excavation.

The silence stretched between us, broken only by the crunch of gravel under our horses' hooves and the occasional rustle of a lizard darting between scrub bushes. With the temperature hovering in the mid-80s, sweat trickled down my back as we climbed over loose shale and navigated around barrel cacti bristling with needle-sharp spines as we climbed up the side of the hill.

My GPS beeped about the same time Rockman's did, and we stopped between two boulders almost directly beneath the remote controlled bird-drone. I noted several promising crevices surrounding us and Glimmer's skyward sniffing. Something had caught her interest.

"X marks the spot," I said as I dismounted. I tied cute, red Keds for dogs on Glimmer's paws before putting her on the ground. The shoes weren't only about protecting her feet from the heat. The rugged landscape and hazardous plants and animals that called the desert home could also harm her delicate paws.

I removed a flashlight and a small pickaxe from Rockman's saddlebag, careful to stay out of his way. The man was so focused on the map that I'm confident I could've knocked him over before he noticed. Glimmer sat in a mesquite tree's shade and watched us both.

"We're in the general area," Rockman finally announced. "Do you want to go right or left?"

I rolled my eyes. "Glimmer. Hunt."

The dachshund leaped to her feet and sniffed. She ran right, then left, sniffing. Suddenly, she darted west into the brush away from the map's suggested area.

I took off after her. A small dog alone in the desert had snack written all over it for the native eagles, coyotes, bobcats, and mountain lions. Rockman followed, leading both horses.

While the low-to-the-ground doxie easily slipped under brush or crossed over a rock pile, we could not, which left Glimmer tapping her foot waiting for us too many times to count and made me wonder exactly what we were chasing.

Twice, she paused at sites marked with the telltale signs—a line of rocks too straight to be natural. Wood fragments bleached silver by the sun and time. The subtle depression where countless boots had worn a path, now barely visible beneath years of wind-blown sand. After further investigation, we found no cave entrance.

At the second stop, I spotted a darkness that seemed to swallow our flashlight beam, tucked behind a screen of prickly pear and crumbling shale. The opening was smaller than I'd expected, partially collapsed but still passable. Cool air drifted from the gap, carrying with it the promise of secrets the desert had kept buried for generations.

Except the dog tossed her head and nudged me on. The shaft held nothing but empty rock. Another dead end. Now what?

Defeat settled over me like layers of dust. I hadn't really believed we'd stumble onto a ninety-year-old tunnel on our first try, but the crushing disappointment told me I'd been lying to myself. My track record had always been perfect—every clue led somewhere, every hunch paid off. Had my father truly been pulling strings behind the scenes all along? Maybe I wasn't the razor-sharp detective I'd convinced myself I was.

Rockman appeared with two water bottles. "Last of our supply. Time to head back and strategize."

Much as I wanted to protest, desert protocol allowed for no errors. Never let your water run dry. I gave a reluctant nod. He must have read the disappointment in my expression because his voice gentled. "Investigation work is all about chasing leads. Some pay off, others don't."

"This one definitely fizzled."

"We'll keep the drone deployed. It might spot something more promising by morning."

Or it might not. Every instinct screamed that finding the hidden entrance mattered. But what if Windy, the librarian, was right? If we were searching in the wrong area entirely, we'd never find it.

<h1 style="text-align:center">Chapter Twenty-Seven</h1>

BEWARE OF THE ULTERIOR MOTIVE—WISDOM FROM A JEWEL THIEF

TUESDAY, 6:00 P.M.

We returned to the ranch at an easier gait than our breakneck departure, sparing the horses more than ourselves. Rockman's resignation grated on my nerves. I understood his weariness—chasing this case for five years would drain anyone. But that was before the Peak Diamond vanished. Deep down, I knew that the clock ticked to recover it before it disappeared forever.

Hope waited by the ranch's gate, freshly showered and wearing clean jeans and a denim blouse. She backed away from the Pig-Pen dust cloud that followed me like a personal storm. "Good grief. Did Vaj drag you the whole way back?"

My irritated grunt didn't quiet her, though it did redirect her attention to Rockman. "How did Marvel behave herself out there?"

Rockman removed his hat. "Uh, the perfect lady."

I frowned at Rockman. "Liar," I whispered.

Rockman passed Hope the reins. "Nothing I couldn't handle."

That was true.

Hope beamed as she stroked the Appaloosa's neck. "That's my girl. I knew you had it in you." The mare pressed her muzzle affectionately against my sister's shoulder. The beast was definitely a one-woman horse.

"No point asking what you found. Your disappointment is a downer." Hope aimed that observation at me. "You two go get cleaned up. Gram has dinner waiting. The girls ..." Her pointed tone spelled trouble for the twins. "... have volunteered to groom your horses."

More like they'd been sentenced to punishment duty. I located two pairs of eyes watching me from one of the stall doors, looking anything but enthusiastic. I wasn't about to wade into that family drama. Besides, the feel of hot water washing away the day's grime overrode any desire to take on another one of my nieces' battles.

"Rockman, would you release Glimmer? She's overdue for dinner," I said.

He moved quickly, no doubt happy to escape Hope's scrutiny. He lifted the dachshund from her pouch and set her down. The little sausage dog bolted toward Gram without so much as a glance back. My doxie's stomach knew no loyalty.

I nodded my thanks to Hope and mock-saluted my nieces. "This way."

Rockman fell into step behind me, staying quiet until we were a comfortable distance out of earshot. "What was that all about?"

"Never come between my sister and parenting. Sometimes I think she's forgotten what hellions we were at their age."

"Still are," he added meaningfully.

He knew Hope and I had played identity swap. Not that it was any of his business. We hadn't broken any laws. The whole thing just put me on notice, which was likely the point. "Gram won't let you leave without a proper meal. She'll have towels and fresh clothing waiting for you in the guest bathroom. It's her version of Western hospitality."

"I can manage without ..."

"That's your battle with Gram." I stepped into the boot jack and worked off my first boot, then quickly shed the second. "I'm hitting the shower."

I left him standing at the kitchen door, gave Gram a quick wave, and headed for the promise of hot water and soap—lots of soap.

Twenty minutes later, my still-damp hair chilling my shoulders, I found him studying the murder board. I was far more curious than annoyed. Something had changed between us. Rockman looked different out of his uniform—younger somehow, with his hair dark and slicked back from the shower. The flannel shirt Gram had found for him was faded blue, sleeves rolled up over his muscular forearms. Drops of water caught the family room light as they tracked down his neck and disappeared beneath the collar. The borrowed jeans hung loose on his frame, cinched tight with a weathered leather belt. I'd have guessed the clothing had been Pop's, but Rockman stood five inches taller.

I didn't want to know. Somehow, he appeared one with his surroundings, though I'd never have pegged him vintage. "You saw reason," I remarked. Not at all surprised. Gram had that effect on people.

"Even I know a losing battle when I see it."

Was that a crack about this case?

Rockman continued. "I had a drill instructor less rigid."

I beat back a smile. Gram was a handful, but she meant well. He, on the other hand ... what were his motives and plans?

"This board is impressive." He turned to face me, his gray eyes bright with interest.

I spotted the longneck beer in his left hand and reached for the orange martini glass on the coffee table. Gram made the best Sunset Peak martinis. The first sip went down dangerously smooth. Despite wanting to unwind, I'd learned I couldn't entirely let my guard down around him. Was this a casual conversation or an interrogation in disguise? Until I figured out the rules of this uneasy partnership, I needed to remain sharp and in control.

"I have the information you requested about recent land purchases. Nothing particularly suspicious on the surface. In the past ninety days, the Amethyst Inn acquired two parcels adjacent to the mine from heirs to the claim."

"Did they obtain mineral rights as well?"

"Yes. Isn't that standard procedure in mining country?" he asked.

"Yeah." My instincts stirred. "Exactly where is the land?"

Rockman consulted his phone, then picked up a grease marker and jotted down two sets of coordinates on the board. "Both lots appear to extend to the eastern boundary of the property."

"That's near the springs." I massaged my temples, thinking. "Makes sense, I suppose. Opal says they've been dealing with water shortages from the drought."

I made a mental note to talk with Ruby. Despite being mayor, she still played an active role running the Inn. "What about power consumption? CVD diamond production requires massive amounts of electricity."

"We checked that angle. The mine has two generators. Combined, they couldn't handle the amount needed for industrial production."

"Has anyone seen the generators personally? Beside the mining folks?"

"No. My first visit was yesterday with you. I'm working off the city inspectors' report."

"What about on the reservation?"

"No unusual demand spikes." He eyed me. "What do you know?"

"Windy said she had a friend who delivered a new turbine to the mine."

Rockman typed a note on his phone. "I'll look into it in the morning. I can say that the diesel fuel deliveries don't indicate that there is a third generator."

Another dead end. "Without power, the CVD equipment can't be in Sunset Peak." I felt let down. His investigation intrigued me, but I'd never see the end of it. I hated that about my job. Once I recovered the stolen item, I was done.

Rockman shook his head. I studied the grease board again. Rico Lobo's name seemed to jump out at me, like it always did. "Was Lobo gluten-free during his rodeo clown days?" I asked. That crowd tended to be fast food junkies.

His grip tightened on the beer bottle. "No. He was one of the guys."

"What changed? He's high-strung now. An unusual combination for an analytical computer specialist."

"A good point. Do you always look at personality and behavior traits?" he asked.

I nodded. "People can pretend to be someone else for a short period, but, like leopards, they never change their spots."

"I didn't see a psychology degree in your long list of accomplishments."

His quiet compliment made my stomach twitter. "Observation. Undercover operators are another story."

"You mean, like me?"

I looked him straight in the eye. "Exactly like you. Who are you really, Rocky Rockman?" Tension sparked between us.

He raised his beer bottle in salute. "The man who will solve this case."

I had no doubt. "At what cost?" Listen to me, seeing a human price.

"Whatever it takes." He doubled down.

Admirable. Time to refocus. "How did Blackwood get involved with the cardroom?"

"I don't know exactly. Phoenix Security has used cardrooms before. Blackwood recruited Rico to help at the cardroom. He's a brilliant mathematician. The Indians call him 'Two Socks.'"

My jaw went slack. Could the answer be that obvious? "When was Rico born?"

"1994." The fact that he rattled off the date without checking his notes told me everything.

"*Dances with Wolves* won the Oscar in 1991."

His blank expression told me he wasn't following. "Two Socks was the wolf in the movie. Lobo means wolf in Spanish. Volkov means wolf in Russian."

Rockman knew. His slight nod confirmed it. "Rico Lobo is Nikolai Volkov's biological son."

Another piece of the puzzle clicked into place. Whether that was good or bad remained to be seen. The Peak Mine was clearly tied to the CVD diamond operation.

"This is too much of a coincidence," I said.

Rockman gave me the "duh" look. "Nikolai's son was seven when his father died. His mother married Ivan Medved shortly after her first husband's death in 2001. She ran away from him in 2006."

No need to elaborate further. We all knew the part my father had played in that event. I did the math in my head. "Rico was 12 when she escaped from Ivan."

"Yes. They both disappeared until two years ago when Rico showed up at the Ft. Worth rodeo."

"Where he was a rodeo clown?" My disbelief must've come through. Rockman agreed with me quickly.

"He never appeared in the ring. He handled social media and IT work for them."

That better fit the man I'd met. I had to ask. "Why were you there?"

No denial. Just the pat answer. "You know I can't tell you that."

My teeth clenched. I hated secrets. Not my own, of course. "And now he shows up here in Sunset Peak."

Rockman knew more. He couldn't or wouldn't share. I got it. He needed courtroom-quality evidence to make his case stick. My job was recovering the Peak Diamond by whatever methods worked. Our goals pulled us in opposite directions.

"How many languages do you speak?" Rockman asked suddenly.

That came out of nowhere. "Seven, including English."

"Wow! I can barely manage Spanish."

"You don't use it enough." Neither did I, but languages came naturally to me. Something I could thank my absentee father for.

Gram's dinner call saved me from having to elaborate further.

The meal proved both informative and comfortable. Glimmer worked the table with her usual grace, moving like a seasoned beggar, rotating between each of us with practiced charm until someone slipped her a bite, then she'd trot off to her next mark. At this rate, a diet loomed for the little sausage dog sooner rather than later. I dreaded that day.

Rockman left a little after eight. I sent a yawning Gram and my food-comatosed dog off to bed. I detoured to the bathroom for an Aleve to soften the reminder that my 30-something-unmentionable body didn't recover from falls off horses as well as I did in my 20s before heading back to the kitchen to tackle the dishes.

I shouldn't have been startled to find my father there, sliding the last plate into the dishwasher. He moved like a specter in his plain navy uniform with his silver hair tucked beneath a baseball cap pulled so low it cast his face in shadow. This was not the look of a man delivering good news.

Chapter Twenty-Eight

NEVER CHOOSE SIDES. UNTIL YOU MUST—
WISDOM FROM A JEWEL THIEF

TUESDAY, 8:30 P.M.

"What are you doing here?" I asked.

"You're impossible to catch alone. I told you—*le shérif Rockman est en difficulté.*"

Perfect. "You mean, Chief Rockman is trouble for you." I caught my lower lip between my teeth. I couldn't correct him. Rockman's secret wasn't mine to tell.

"Is he really who you think he is?" the illusionist extraordinaire had the nerve to ask. "I have learned, *ma chérie*, that when *trop beau pour être vrai ...*"

Maybe Rockman was too good to be true, but that didn't make him a liar. Although he'd never really confirmed that he was an FBI agent, I had guessed it. Thinking back, the information he'd shared included all the same stuff the bad guy would know. And the thing about the drone targeting me ... Pretty unreal after rational contemplation. A talk with Sophie would help. My normally detached brain needed a reset.

"What do you know about the ghost at the Amethyst Inn?" My subject change didn't fool him. Dad had made his point, and he knew it.

"The old miner is just a story."

"Funny thing about that story is that guests keep seeing him. You wouldn't happen to know anything about that, would you?"

"*Peut-être.*"

"I'll take that as a yes. What are you looking for?" It had to be something important for Dad to come out of hiding again.

"*Ma chérie*, you are just like your mother."

His practiced charm bounced off me this time. I folded my arms across my chest. Game time over. I needed real answers. "What are you looking for?"

He hesitated long enough to gauge my reaction. "A flash drive."

Of course, he was. Any wonder why I felt like the cast in a Hollywood spoof? "What's on it?"

He looked furtively around. No one in sight. What did he expect? I tapped my foot, waiting. "Blackwood kept a ledger of every diamond he replaced and sold to private collectors."

"How many other diamonds are missing?" My stomach dropped. This could be catastrophic for the diamond industry and collectors.

"I don't know the exact number. The CVD technology has been operational for over two years."

No need to say more. A whole lot of time to create copies.

"It is important to have the information. The police may have the drive in their evidence room without realizing what they have." His words sounded far too reasonable.

"Come on. Everyone knows what a flash drive looks like." Yet Rockman hadn't mentioned one.

"This is not a traditional flash drive. It is a small digital key hidden in his ..."

"... lighter." The man's cigar habit always left a lingering smell of hot cinnamon buns around him.

Dad's quick smile annoyed me. Yes, I was starting to finish his sentences, too. I shook off my annoyance. "Why do you want the information?" But I knew. He was a jewel thief.

His smile never touched his eyes. "I have no interest in stealing counterfeits. It would destroy my reputation."

A flip excuse, nothing more. There was definitely more he wasn't telling me. I pressed on. "Where was the drive last seen?"

"Blackwood had it with him the night he died."

Perfect. "And you know this how?"

His tell—the ever-so-slight twitch in the corner of his right eye. "You were there." My accusation escaped an octave higher than necessary.

He tipped his hat back, exposing his unaltered expression. Maybe the first time I'd seen him unmasked. "I did not kill Blackwood. He wanted me to steal the Phoenix Red."

"The largest pink diamond ever cut, lost ten years ago during the Argyle mine thefts?"

"It's in a private collection."

"Whose?" I asked.

"He hadn't told me yet."

"The perfect crime. The stone was illegally obtained. The collector can't report it as stolen."

"The collector will never know the stone is missing. The copy is flawless. I compared it against the GIA report."

Of course, he had. The man was a jewel thief. My greatest fear was playing out exactly as I'd imagined. Natural diamonds replaced by CVD fakes. I tried to process the information, but it didn't make sense unless ... "You said you came to Sunset Peak to protect Hope and me. That you were targeted ..." Had it all been a lie?

"I was targeted for a job to pay my debt."

"I see." Hope's husband had said the same thing. Was this the first bit of truth my father had told me? Why did I feel so used?

"No, you don't. I refused. I'd rather be hunted than be party to this ..."

He raised his hands in anger. "Diamonds are ..."

My glib father at a loss for words?

A long minute later, his voice softened, a reverence creeping in that I'd never heard before. "... life. Their fire and beauty speak to something deeper, something that transcends mere wealth." His eyes grew distant, almost wistful. "Each stone holds light captured from the beginning of time, *ma chérie*. To touch one is to touch eternity itself."

In that second, I got why my mother had given up everything for him. He wasn't a poet or even a romantic soul, but he did strike a chord. I savored the feeling for a hot moment before reality knocked.

Best I get this back on track and find out what he needed me to do. "Why is all this important?"

"If the police don't have the flash drive, then whoever took the Peak Diamond has both the drive and the Phoenix Red."

"Or Blackwood stashed it somewhere close by," I suggested. "Which explains why the mysterious ghostly figure is haunting the Amethyst Inn."

"*Oui.* There is a fifteen-minute gap from when I saw Blackwood to when my surveillance resumed. It was unfortunately the murder window."

"You've been watching him?" Like he'd been watching me? I needed to see his base of operation. The fifteen-minute time block gave me a location circumference ...

"*Mais, oui.* Before you ask, I didn't record my visit."

Hence the gap. Rockman's team may not have indoor footage, but I wondered if they had the surrounding area. This mess was his job. If he really was a good guy.

That fifteen minutes still mattered. "Did you smell anything unusual?"

"Not that I ..." His eyes shut, visualizing. "*Un momento.* I recall peppermint. As if Blackwood wanted to cover his noxious cigar smoke."

My pulse jumped. Dad saw it, too. "We are too much alike, *ma chérie*."

"We are not." I didn't lie for sympathy or hide the truth. Well, maybe I did a little, but all for a good reason.

"Believe what you will, there is another stone made and ready for replacement."

"Not my problem. I've been hired to find the Peak Diamond. My job ends there. I have no interest in the Phoenix Red." But I lied, and he knew it.

Dad stepped back. "You need answers just as much as I do."

I was an idiot for even entertaining this idea.

WEDNESDAY, 12:01 A.M.

Sophie agreed. Tired as I was, of course, I couldn't sleep. While Glimmer snored like a Marine, I tossed and turned, rehashing every event and clue. Midnight Arizona time, I gave up. I dressed in jeans and my lucky, blue-striped Oxford and carried the crime board into the kitchen. I dialed Sophie as my tea water boiled. American coffee just wouldn't do.

"Top of the morning to you." Hesitation touched Sophie's greeting. "Do tell me you have a spot of tea in front of you."

"Seeping." Before she could launch into proper tea etiquette, I turned on the video feed.

"Oh, dear. Perhaps a trip to the spa is in order."

Perfect. I looked as bad as I felt. "I hope that's a suggestion based on information versus aesthetics." I poured the hot liquid from the glass teapot into the horse head shaped mug. "Tell me you have something on Rockman." More than anything, I needed to know if I could trust him.

"Well, you were correct, Chief Rockman shows up in all digital academy versions. Not in original print."

"A neat setup. FBI?" How could I tell her without actually doing so?

"Perhaps. No matches in my database searches. Do you have a limiting parameter?"

"Criminal Investigation Division."

Sophie whistled. "You're not asking for much."

"I know. It's the secretive division of deep cover ... You'll figure it out. You always do. That's what I love about you. He has a drone he calls a Camouflage Surveillance Device."

"That's old news."

Nice to know. "Can I have one?"

"When you learn to use a computer."

It felt like a reprimand. "A computer? Can't you control the drone for me?" I took her silence as a yes. "I'd like a hummingbird. It fits my need for speed." That bird flew twice as fast as other birds. I'd love to follow Rockman and my father. "How about two bird drones?"

"You need to deal with your daddy issues."

I cussed. That's exactly what it was. Me not trusting men. I changed the subject. "Did you get a look at the shipping manifests for the mine?"

"By no means complete, but there is a water turbine I find interesting."

"The Peak Mine did flood—way back when. Maybe it's just a safety thing," I suggested.

"Perhaps. I will continue the hunt. No chatter pertaining to the Peak Diamond."

"It's like whoever has it plans to keep it." Bad news for me and the insurance company. "Does Sterling & Sons insure the Phoenix Red?"

"That stone has been missing for years."

"Maybe the better question is: did Sterling pay a claim on it?"

Sophie's typing filled the silence. "Indeed, we did."

"It appears it will be the next theft. The stone counterfeiters also have the necessary GIA reports to create two additional Jazz-era diamond pieces insured by Sterling & Sons." I didn't have to report Hope's involvement. "I'd say we're being targeted."

"It would seem we have an informant in our ranks." The steel in her tone conveyed so much more than anger—Sophie didn't abide betrayal. She'd find him at all costs.

Chapter Twenty-Nine

KNOW THE END GAME—WISDOM FROM A JEWEL THIEF

WEDNESDAY, 9:30 A.M.

I parked in my garage behind Starlight Estate Jewelers and walked diagonally across Canary Trail toward the bright yellow awning-trimmed restaurant. The tuxedo cat greeted me with its usual grin as I entered the Canary Café. The breakfast rush had slowed, so finding Goldine Block, the *Peak Examiner*'s tenacious reporter, proved to be easy. She sat in a back booth tucked beneath another iconic Tweety and Sylvester movie poster, engrossed in a suspiciously familiar stack of paperwork. Not exactly besties, she'd texted me requesting that I join her here, which intrigued—as well as concerned—me.

I crossed the yellow-and-black checkered floor to the bird-themed booth. Overhead, a toy cat dangled from the ceiling on fishing line, "pouncing" toward a ceramic canary perched on the light fixture. The sight never ceased to force my smile.

I placed my Starlight Estate shop's coffee mug on the tabletop with a "Morning" to Goldine and slipped into the unoccupied bench seat across from her. Glimmer leaped up beside me and curled up for a nap.

Goldine's head snapped up. She hastily concealed whatever documents she'd been examining.

"Word is you're tracking down the Lost Miner." I kept my comment deliberately vague. No point giving her an easy out.

Instead of denial, Goldine swept her cascade of rich honey-blonde hair into a claw clip and settled back against the cushions. Her tall, elegant frame moved with a graceful confidence that made her seem better suited for a television anchor position than chasing down gritty investigative leads. "Something's happened to Sunset Peak's water supply."

I appreciated the woman's directness. "Why do you think so?" I expected to hear about the famous Old Miner's ghost.

"The Amethyst Inn cancelled my hot springs appointment on Monday."

That explained why she'd been hanging around Blackwood's murder site. She'd been at the scene of the crime, so to speak. "They cancelled half of their appointments," I said.

"Do you know how long those appointments take to schedule nowadays?" Goldine exhaled in a huff. She didn't wait for my response before she added, "Six months. It's crazy. Now they are taking half of the appointments they used to."

I shrugged. "Opal, the front desk receptionist, said it was due to the drought."

"Opal is covering up what's going on." There was the burning accusation.

"A conspiracy theory?" Opal deliberately lie? She didn't have it in her.

"Rainwater doesn't affect geothermal springs whose source is groundwater heated by the Earth's mantle." Goldine removed the documents she'd hidden in her lap. "This may indicate the water table is falling."

I glanced at the data. "Possibly." Although part of my under-grad curriculum included water supply, I'd hardly call myself an expert. "Many things could cause the phenomenon."

Goldine slid a pristine white business card across the polished wood surface. The embossed lettering read: *Vortex Engineering. Doctor Iam Fantastic.*

My laughter escaped as a snort. "Seriously? Iam Fantastic? That's got to be the worst alias I've ever seen."

"It might actually be a typo. His real name is Ian." Goldine's mouth still twitched with amusement. "But that's beside the point. These cards were scattered all over Whiskey Row."

I gestured for her to continue.

"I tracked him down yesterday. Turns out he is a doctor. His PhD is in hydroelectric energy."

My gut twinged. "What does he look like?"

"Average height, maybe five-nine or five-ten. Silver hair swept back like he stepped out of a cologne ad. Pale gray eyes that probably charm the ladies." She paused, studying my expression. "Sound familiar?"

My stomach clenched. Could it be my father? He was a jewel thief, not an engineer. Besides, the man's continued longevity required that he blend in. I kept my voice steady. "Did this guy mention why he was in Sunset Peak?"

"Not directly. But here's where it gets interesting." Goldine pulled out her phone and showed me a grainy ring photo of a shadowed figure entering a van.

My concern remained steady. I couldn't tell if I knew the man or not.

"One of the Peak Mine's security vehicles picked him up from Whiskey Jack's last night."

"I didn't know the mine's security team ever left the compound."

"They don't. According to the night clerk at the Amethyst Inn, this Ian—or Iam—character showed up a day ahead of schedule and played tourist around town. The bartender at Whiskey Jack's thought I might want to know about our mysterious visitor."

Her source network impressed me. "Where's this leading, Goldine?"

Instead of answering, she spread several black-and-white photographs across the table. I recognized the circular stone structure immediately—the old wishing well located in the Amethyst Inn's courtyard—the same one I'd tossed countless pennies into as a kid, making wishes that sometimes actually came true.

She laid another yellow map on the table. "This is the 1920s mining camp." She tapped the center photo. "That well goes down a hundred feet to reach the water table."

I studied the images, trying to piece together her logic. "The underground water system is well known. The mining disaster of '36 occurred because excess rain caused flash flooding."

"I know. Where is the water now?"

The question hung in the air like a cloud of smoke. "Natural depletion, maybe. Underground aquifers don't last forever," I replied.

Goldine braced her elbows on the tabletop, her amber gaze drawing mine into the haunting, crystalline depths, and making the café's chatter fade into the background noise. "Or maybe someone's redirecting it." Goldine unfolded yet another yellowed survey map, this paper crackling with age. Her French-manicured nails drew my attention to the double lines drawn between the hills. "This shows the original underground river."

My pulse quickened as the implications hit me. A hydroelectric expert. Disappearing water. A mining company with military-grade security. "I need to get inside that compound and see what they're really doing up there."

"I figured you'd say that." Goldine's high cheekbones seemed to catch the light as she smiled.

"We're not getting in the front door," I said.

"True, but I think there might be a way in from the back side, near the inn." Goldine pointed to the original maps. "The old water tunnel system connects to the mine shafts here. Assuming the underground river has dropped, I suspect that it'll be navigable."

Trudging through standing water? I shivered. I hated dealing with the many deadly desert critters in the water. "We need to determine the entry point." Rockman and I had failed yesterday. What were the chances that today would be more successful?

Goldine removed a flimsy piece of vellum tracing paper from the information pile. "The librarian indicated that the old miner was dyslexic. If she was right ..." Goldine flipped the vellum tracing paper and laid it over the 1920s area map. The hills aligned perfectly. An X marked a rock outcropping at the base of the hills.

My enthusiasm bubbled over, and the familiar thrill of a case breaking open engulfed me. All thanks to Goldine's dogged research skills. "Why do you need me?" I asked. "You can run with this information on your own."

The blonde inspected her perfectly manicured nails. "My calculations put the entry point on the Amethyst Inn's property."

Realization struck. "You need me to talk to Ruby." As co-owner with her husband, Ruby's permission met all the legalities.

She nodded. "The GM told me to go away. Not politely either, I might add."

"You can be a bit of a sensationalist," I pointed out.

Goldine exhaled. "I get enthusiastic. I'm working on that. You're Sunset Peak's savior. The mayor can't afford to refuse your request."

My respect for Goldine's political savvy increased. "You're a good reporter with a lot of passion, Goldine. I don't care what anyone says."

"Thanks, I think. This isn't about the scoop, you know."

I believed her. "I get it. This one's personal." Just like it was for me. I dialed Ruby's number.

She answered on the second ring, her anxiousness apparent in every word. "Any progress locating the Peak Diamond?"

"Getting closer," I said, choosing to spare her the full truth.

While I'd collected pieces of information, the complete picture remained frustratingly elusive.

"When will you find it?" Ruby pressed.

"Soon."

"At least you're making headway. The chief seems less hopeful." Another telephone rang in the background. "This whole situation has our residents on edge."

"Give it time," I said.

"Something I have precious little of."

I cut off her complaints. "I need your assistance with a lead I'm following."

"Get in line. The chief already requested access to the Inn's property. I told him to use whatever means necessary."

Was Rockman one step ahead of me again? "I need the same access."

"For what purpose?" Ruby asked.

"I need to expand my search area to where Edward Blackwood may have visited before his death."

A flimsy justification under intense cross-examination. Fortunately, Ruby's preoccupation worked to my advantage. "If Blackwood hid the diamond somewhere nearby, Glimmer will locate it," I assured her.

Not only did Glimmer's ears perk up, but she barked her agreement. The mayor chuckled. "You'll find it, won't you, darling? I have complete faith in you."

Perfect. Like my dachshund wasn't already insufferable. I changed the subject. "I heard the Amethyst Inn recently purchased some additional property."

"That's correct," Ruby answered cautiously. "My husband has been trying to buy two lots adjacent to the inn for quite some time. The property was stuck in probate proceedings. We managed to finalize the purchase late last month."

"Planning to expand the inn?" I asked.

"Originally, yes. However, the ongoing water shortage may force us to reconsider our plans." The phone rang in the background again. "My husband will know all the details," Ruby said. "I have to go." She disconnected the call.

I turned to Goldine. "We are cleared to explore." I picked up the map. "Meet me in thirty minutes here." I pointed to the open area behind the spa.

We were getting closer. I felt it.

Chapter Thirty

THERE IS ALWAYS A WAY IN—WISDOM FROM A JEWEL THIEF

WEDNESDAY, 11:00 A.M.

I pulled into the Amethyst Inn's parking lot a few minutes early, finding a spot beneath a blooming palo verde tree. The profound silence struck me immediately—this spa was too quiet. Glimmer felt it, too. She lifted her snout toward the sky, nostrils flaring as she caught some scent I couldn't begin to figure out.

At the truck's tailgate, I began suiting up my companion. First came her custom blue mining helmet, then the waterproof boots that would shield her paws from jagged stones and whatever creatures lurked in the unexplored caverns ahead. The neon safety vest would make her a beacon in the darkness when my flashlight found her. While most dogs might cower at such an elaborate outfit, Glimmer owned it. She sat at attention beside me, her paw tapping the ground in eagerness.

I slipped into my own equipment—a sturdy denim jumpsuit, reinforced boots, and a matching blue helmet equipped with a high-powered headlamp. Just as I secured my utility belt and hoisted Glimmer's pack onto my shoulder, Goldine's vehicle appeared in the parking lot.

"Well, don't you two look ready for action," Goldine called out as she approached.

I studied her designer jeans and standard hiking boots with concern. "We'll be dealing with water down there," I said.

"I'm prepared." She patted her bulging backpack. "Brought waterproof boots, plus a flashlight and emergency glow sticks."

Maybe I should've qualified her experience first. "Abandoned mine shafts are home to coyotes, rattlesnakes, mountain lions, and critters you've only seen in horror movies."

"I'll be fine," she said, but the shiver that ran through her told me everything I needed to know. I hoped that what Goldine lacked in experience, she'd make up for in grit. She'd need it.

"You have the map. Lead on." I gestured toward the mesquite-clumped hillside.

Compass in hand, Goldine set a steady pace across the dusty terrain. I shaded my eyes against the glare, watching a turkey vulture circle overhead. Drone or the real thing? Hard to tell. Maybe a good thing Rockman knew where I was.

We walked in comfortable silence, our boots crunching softly on the gravel as we climbed the rocky hillside. The hot wind whispered through the towering saguaros, and I remembered exactly why I hated hiking. The twelve-pound Glimmer pack strapped to my shoulders wasn't helping my mood either.

Sweat trickled down my spine, making me question this whole endeavor, especially when Goldine stopped abruptly at what looked like a random pile of weathered rocks.

"We're here," she announced.

I stared at the nondescript stone heap, which showed no hint of a mine shaft or cave entrance. Goldine didn't seem to notice the lack of promising features. With her attention focused on the map, she nearly walked straight into a barrel cactus. Only dumb luck saved her from a face full of spines.

My confidence wavered. Was this just another wild goose chase?

Glimmer had other ideas. The small dog poked her nose

against my neck from inside the backpack, panting in the heat. She had to be miserable in that thick fur coat. I unclipped the pack and set her on the ground, where she immediately began sniffing—first right, then left, moving with such determination that she nearly tripped Goldine in her haste. Fortunately, I managed to clip her retractable leash to her vest before she took off after whatever had caught her attention.

Goldine stumbled, finally becoming aware of her surroundings. "What's Glimmer doing?"

"She's getting her bearings." Goldine's frown made me qualify my statement. "Glimmer's a scent hound—like a bloodhound."

Goldine's expression was priceless. "But she's so ..."

"Low to the ground?" I suggested. "She was bred to hunt badgers in tight spaces. This dog's sense of smell is ten thousand times better than most dogs."

"10,000? You mean, she can smell a cave?"

"In theory, yes. The dog knows a cave is nearby. She also knows a rattlesnake lives there, a squadron of javelina walked by, and a mountain lion napped under the tree."

"Are you saying she doesn't know what we want her to find?" Goldine asked.

I nodded. Fail to understand a dachshund at your own peril. I'd learned that the hard way.

"But Glimmer has been in mines before," Goldine said.

"Diamond mines. The association is different."

Glimmer's head suddenly snapped up. She barked once and jerked hard on the leash, dragging me toward another rock outcropping about a hundred yards further up the hillside. The Amethyst Inn's land or the mine's? Hard to tell in the open desert.

Goldine and I followed with renewed energy as the dog disappeared under a gnarled mesquite tree. I let out all twenty feet of lead before Glimmer's head popped out on the other side, her snout decorated with wispy cobwebs. She circled back to my feet, barked twice, and sat with the satisfied air of a job well done.

"She's found something." I pulled out my shears and began cutting back the ancient, twisted branches. Sure enough, a rotted wooden beam spanned what looked like a narrow opening in the rock.

"A coyote den?" Goldine asked.

"Possibly. Though I'd put money on a scorpion nest." The break in the granite appeared natural enough, but Glimmer's excited barking suggested otherwise. She punctuated her disagreement with sharp yips as I hacked away more debris, sending lizards scattering and startling what looked like a pack rat into a blur of motion. At least it wasn't a coiled rattler. I really hated them.

What had started as a single mound of boulders, entwined with thick mesquite roots, began to take on a different character as I cleared away years of accumulated plant matter. My pulse quickened as the rocks revealed themselves to be arranged in a decidedly human pattern.

Goldine joined in the excavation, and gradually our "rabbit hole" took on a more defined shape. Had we actually found the mine's escape route, or was this something else entirely?

I switched on my high-voltage headlamp and peered inside. The opening was barely larger than a ship's porthole, divided almost equally by thick, gnarled roots that had grown across the gap over the decades. Inside, the narrow entry appeared to open into a larger chamber beyond. Unfortunately, neither Goldine nor I would fit through that tight space.

Glimmer, however, was a different story. She waited patiently until I leaned against a nearby boulder to catch my breath, then made her move. Before I could react, she tore the leash from my hands and darted into the hole, her lead bouncing against the gravel as she disappeared into the darkness.

I stood frozen for a long moment, too stunned at the dog's outrageous behavior to move. Finally, reality kicked in, and I lunged forward, shouting, "Get the chief. Tell him Glimmer found something. He'll know what to do."

Not that Rockman would offer much help. The man wouldn't get his linebacker shoulders in that entry hole without heavy equipment. But knowing he was out there might. Goldine didn't argue. Her phone in hand, she turned tail and sprinted toward cell service.

I cleared the mesquite root with a mini hatchet, opening the cave's entry enough to squeeze my hips through. At least I thought I had until my utility belt caught, putting my nightly calorie-packed cocktail in jeopardy. I ultimately made it through after stripping to my bikini underwear. If that overhead vulture was a camera, I'd have given someone a show.

Inside, I redressed and savored the momentary shade after hours under the relentless Arizona sun, my sweat-soaked shirt suddenly clammy against my skin.

Blinking in the dimness, I caught the pungent smell of bat guano mixed with mineral scents and the freshness of moving water. I switched on my hard hat beam. The tunnel stretched ahead into blackness, far bigger than I'd expected, its walls painted in streaks of white, orange, and deep red by centuries of rising and ebbing water.

Today, only a small stream chattered along the back wall of the cavern. I waded through ankle-deep water, surprisingly cold through my waterproof boots, while shafts of light pierced fissure-openings above, creating cathedral-like beams in the dusty air. More of a brook than a steady stream, I could see the lined water marks on the walls—reminders that this peaceful trickle had recently been much higher. If this was the Amethyst Inn's groundwater supply, they were in big trouble.

The real question was Glimmer's interest. Why would a trained diamond dog disappear into an underground waterway adjacent to a silver mine?

I called the dachshund's name softly. The sound ricocheted through the stone passages, but silence answered back—no familiar bark, not even a whimper. Something was wrong. I could feel it. I had to find her.

I pressed forward where the passage narrowed. My headlamp swept across the rough walls, and suddenly the darkness erupted. Bats poured from their roosts in a frenzied cloud, their wings beating frantically as they spiraled around me in the confined space. I killed the light immediately, plunging us all into absolute darkness. Their distress calls echoed and faded as they settled back into the shadows.

My shivers abated. Bats brushing against my arms gave me the creeps.

Relaxed, I heard a distinct whirring and whooshing sound unlike anything I'd heard inside a mine before. I flicked the light back on, keeping the beam aimed at the ground, and picked my way along the rocky path toward the source. Eighty paces brought me closer to the vibrating hum.

Around the next bend, the mystery revealed itself. Massive gates channeled rushing water through industrial turbines, the entire system carved into the heart of the mountain. The Peak Mine ran its own hydroelectric operation, completely independent of any power grid. No wonder Rockman's searches for unusual electrical consumption had turned up nothing.

I took three photos before two figures dressed in mine security jumpsuits materialized beside a control panel, carrying tablets glowing in their hands. Their hats hid any hope of recognition. Had Dad penetrated the fold? I couldn't be sure.

I melted back into the tunnel shadows. Getting spotted here would end whatever slim advantage I still possessed. Besides, I had a strong suspicion about where my diamond dog had vanished to.

I backtracked to my entry point. Logic dictated calling for backup, but Glimmer's disappearance changed the rules. Partners don't get left behind.

I swept the headlamp across the ground, searching until I spotted one of Glimmer's distinctive boot prints pressed into loose sand. The trail wound deeper into the labyrinth of passages, each step taking me further from any hope of retreat. Then an electronic beep pierced the silence ahead.

My hand moved toward the Glock, but it was too late. A red dot appeared on my chest, steady and bright in the blackness.

"Don't make me shoot you, Miss Hunter."

I went completely still. That good-old country boy voice—I'd heard it yesterday at the mine entrance. The pieces fell into place with sickening clarity. I hadn't just stumbled into this operation by accident. They'd been waiting for me.

Chapter Thirty-One

HONE YOUR WITS. THEY KEEP YOU ALIVE— WISDOM FROM A JEWEL THIEF

WEDNESDAY, 1:00 P.M.

Captured and disarmed a hundred feet underground with only a twelve-pound dachshund as backup? My situation had moved well beyond bleak and into the realm of impossible.

Stay alive. That was rule number one. I'd been here before, and I'd survived. Hostage training had drilled the basics into me: keep calm, follow orders, don't give them a reason to pull the trigger, plan your escape. I had that part covered. Although I couldn't see much in the inky darkness, I'd mentally mapped my way back to the point I'd entered.

My next step was to establish a human connection with my captor. Unfortunately, when I tried a few conversation starters, the Alabama accent that drifted from behind me chuckled softly and said, "Nice try, Miss Hunter. We've had the same training."

Of course, I'd be dealing with a professional who knew exactly what I was trying to do and found it amusing.

I contemplated a different approach until I heard a familiar mechanical whirring followed by a subtle rattling that made everything click into place. Glimmer had been right all along.

Another guard opened a metal door set deep in the rock, and fluorescent lights changed the semi-darkness to high noon. I blinked, allowing my eyes time to adjust. We'd entered what could well be any dust-free, high-tech laboratory in the U.S. White walls and tiled floors hid any sign of the rugged mountain location. Numerous CVD machines lined the walls, their industrial hums confirming their activity. Lab-coated technicians moved between complex control panels, fine-tuning gas mixtures while others examined rough stones that looked convincingly natural on long, stainless-steel tables. I noted the location of two exits, the door we'd entered through, and an elevator, each with an armed sentry. Three emergency escape routes were discreetly hidden in the room.

"Impressive setup you've got here." There was no point playing ignorant—we all knew what this was.

"High praise from a De Beers auditor," came a voice from the shadows. My blood went cold as Rico, the nervous computer guy, emerged, cradling Glimmer against his chest. Someone had fashioned a crude muzzle from a leather strap, keeping her from barking, but my dog's eyes burned with retaliatory indignation as he scratched behind her ears. "Smart little thing. Found our operation right away."

Of course, she did. Glimmer had even tried to tell me. "She's trained to do that," I said, watching the weiner dog struggle against the restraint.

Rico had shed his awkward IT persona completely, replacing it with someone comfortable running a multimillion-dollar deception. Was he the head guy or was Washburn?

"So, I see you've 'discovered' the Peak Mine's long-lost alluvial diamond deposits," I said, keeping my voice steady. No way I'd get a photo. I'd need a sample of the uncut CVD rough. I needed to keep them talking and distracted. "Clever setup passing off manmade stones as natural finds. You'll make a killing."

Rico's smile held depths I hadn't seen before. There were layers to this situation that I was still missing.

"I don't get why you had to replace the Peak Diamond, though. You could have made millions selling small commodity stones that no one bothers to create diamond plots for, with no risk."

Something shifted in his expression—a flash of raw fury that made me instinctively step back. His pale eyes went cold, and, in that moment, I understood what my father had been trying to tell me. This wasn't about the money—it had never been about the money. For Rico, this was personal.

"I'd like an answer to that question myself." Washburn emerged from the shadows behind me, his coveralls identical to those of his security team. He moved with the fluid grace of someone accustomed to staying invisible.

Rico neatly changed the subject. "I retrieved the dog."

Glimmer's low growl rumbled through the cavern, drawing every eye. I covered my grin with a cough. My little dachshund had perfect timing. She gave me a minute to observe the dynamic between Rico and Washburn. Rico might think he was the boss, but Washburn ran the show.

"You don't have the real Peak Diamond." I kept my voice level. "You're counting on Glimmer to track it down." I didn't specify the conditions the dog would need to succeed. Glimmer might be the only card I had left to play.

"Then I suggest you convince us she's capable of finding it, Hunter." Washburn's smile was razor thin. "Otherwise, you become a liability we can't afford."

I straightened my shoulders, my gaze locking with Rico's. "There's another reason to keep me breathing."

"Your sister will serve the same purpose." Washburn's tone never wavered, but I caught Rico's subtle flinch. I played with fire, but I needed to stall until someone arrived—assuming anyone was coming at all.

"You're making a mistake if you think my father will risk his neck to save me. I haven't seen him since ..."

"Moscow," Rico picked up right off where I'd left off. Sweat glistened on his forehead despite the cool temperature.

"I don't remember you there." Not surprising since I'd tried to forget most of the experience. I'd survived. That was the important part.

"I wasn't there," Rico replied.

Washburn hadn't been either, but understanding gleamed in his dark eyes. Why was I still in the dark?

"You mean this whole mess is about my father?" I shook my head. "I can tell you he isn't worth the trouble."

Washburn's hum agreed. Glimmer whimpered. Rico's intense hold crushed her small body.

Washburn frowned. "Give me the dog. It's an asset, not some bloody teddy bear." He placed Glimmer on the stainless-steel table beside the uncut diamond rocks.

Rico didn't argue. Bad move. He lost the power struggle to Washburn in that minute.

"Did you put this whole bloody operation at risk to flush out *Le Renard Argente*?" Washburn asked.

Rico popped a peppermint candy into his mouth. I'd have a panic attack, too, the way Washburn leveled his weapon. No guard moved in his defense. They waited for the outcome. Rico didn't flinch this time.

Time to de-escalate, lest Glimmer and I end up dead-center in a shootout. "What did my dear old dad do this time?"

"He killed my mother," Rico insisted.

"Your mother was killed in a suspicious hit-and-run accident. I'd be asking your gangster stepfather. That practically screams with his involvement," I suggested.

Wrong thing to say. Instant anger turned Rico's pale complex ruddy. "I don't believe you. He protected us."

There was only one way Rico knew that. "Is that what he told you?" The crap adults told children ... At that moment, I swore to be honest with my own. If I ever had any. "Your mother died the minute you gave Ivan your father's notes for this." I motioned around me.

"No!" Rico's lips pressed into a tight line.

Washburn reholstered his weapon. Something in his manner signaled agreement, or at least the possibility that I'd been right. He turned to me. "Your father killed Blackwood."

I shook my head. "He did not. Even you know that it's not his style." At least Dad had said he hadn't killed Blackwood. I'd believed him—hopefully, not to my detriment. I waited for Washburn's nod before facing a seething Rico.

In that second, I saw the hatred in the younger man's eyes, and catching my father was only the tip of the proverbial iceberg.

In his usual bull-in-a-china-shop manner, Washburn missed the entire exchange. He nodded to one of his men. "Take her to the cave."

"The cave?" The guard repeated, instilling terror.

Of course, they had a subterranean torture chamber. I pushed away images of medieval dungeons crawling with bats. I closed my eyes and prayed—something I hadn't done in a long time. Hope appeared in my mind, followed by my two nieces and Rockman's rugged face. Strange how clarity came at moments like this. I felt no regret about the path that led me here. My life had come full circle: fleeing Sunset Peak in search of purpose, only to have my history corner me mere miles from where it all began.

The guard's palm found my shoulder blade, steering me toward the elevator. One last chance to get a sample of the diamonds. I stumbled as we passed the sample table. Glimmer's rumbling growl provided just enough distraction and gave me time to palm a stone.

I was in big trouble now, I realized as the elevator door started to close. This mess required nothing less than a miracle, which arrived a heartbeat later.

An explosion hit like a thunderclap, shaking the ground to its foundations, followed by a groan so deep it seemed to rise from the earth's core.

Glimmer launched herself from the counter, her sleek body slipping through the closing elevator doors just as the floor fell out beneath me. I lunged for her, but my fingers found only air as we plummeted together. The guard's scream bounced off the shaft walls, and I knew it was over. I sent my forever love to my sister as only a twin can, as the crushing impact swallowed all sound.

Chapter Thirty-Two

HIDE IN PLAIN SIGHT—WISDOM FROM A JEWEL THIEF

WEDNESDAY, 5:00 P.M.

Moisture on my cheek and the sound of rushing water dragged me from the blackness. I couldn't be dead. I was freezing cold, soaking wet, and every inch of me hurt.

Disorientation lasted only a heartbeat longer before my vision sharpened in the emergency lighting. Glimmer lay on my chest, using me as an island while water cascaded through every crack and seam of the mangled elevator's cage. The explosion must have caused the dam to fail. Another of Dad's timely interferences? I prayed this one hadn't gone too far. Had he made it out?

Nothing I could do about it now. My survival instinct kicked in. I was going to drown if I didn't get out of here. I moved a drenched Glimmer to my shoulder and crawled to the guard's lifeless form, confirming what I already knew. I holstered his weapon in my own, took possession of his flashlight, key fob, and phone, then stood. A sledgehammer pounded against the inside of my skull, threatening to take me right back to my knees.

My surroundings spun a full revolution before I slipped the weiner dog under my shirt. Man, her wet body was cold, but necessary. I needed both hands to force open the trap door and climb onto the top of the crumpled metal cage. Crimson emergency strobes revealed the nightmare: torrents of water hammering down from two directions, creating a whirlpool that would drag me under before I could reach the escape ladder bolted to the shaft wall at least fifteen feet away. Not a chance I'd leap that distance.

I glanced at the severed elevator cable swaying above my head. I could swing on it, but was the cable secured, or would my weight pull it from its anchoring? No way to tell. The water covering my feet and lapping at my ankles decided for me. Staying here was not an option.

No time for second thoughts. I ripped off my sleeve, wound the fabric around the cable, and locked both hands around it, launching myself and Glimmer with a stunt-worthy force toward the emergency ladder.

Fortune smiled upon us. My shoulder slammed into the wall, killing my swing momentum just as my free hand clamped onto a metal rung. Every muscle screamed as I held on with all my strength while my feet frantically searched for a foothold. I found it just in time, and I hung there long enough to catch my breath.

We'd made it. Glimmer knew it, too. Her wet nose peeked from beneath my shirt and she licked my cheek. Not a time to celebrate, I glanced upward. Bad idea. The red security lights lead into blackness. Renewed panic kicked in. How far underground was I?

My practical mind crushed my fear. I had no choice. With the sound of rushing water and Glimmer's heart beating against mine, I put one hand over the other and climbed.

My hands burned from cuts, and my arms felt like spaghetti when daylight suddenly flooded the shaft, blinding me. I heard the fire chief, Chili's, voice a moment before I recognized his red head. "Taylor. You're alive."

Relief blew the tension right out of me. We'd made it. Chili took the dachshund from my grasp.

Before I climbed the last step out, Rockman's concerned face blocked the light. He hauled me up the last few feet, his muscles straining. "Don't ever do that to me again."

His gruff words, thick with emotion, sent my pulse pounding in triple time. I collapsed against his solid chest, feeling safe for the first time in a long time. I clung to him, refusing to let go until my scolding sister pushed him aside.

"I-I thought you were dead." Tears streaked Hope's cheeks as she crushed me against her.

"I'm okay," I choked, hardly able to get a breath. "Is Goldine okay?"

"Yeah. She's at the Amythest Inn." Hope's grip remained unchanged. "What were you doing in the mine? You could've been killed in the flood."

"A flood? There was an explosion." I'd heard it—I was certain. I managed to step back. We stood at the edge of the parking area, ground zero for the rescue operation. Both checkpoint gates hung wide open, while emergency vehicles surrounded the mining trucks parked in front of the office building. The sheer number of personnel darting about churned up clouds of dust that made me cough.

"What explosion? The water alarms suddenly went off like Fourth of July fireworks." Hope shuddered in horror. "Chili thinks it's even worse than '36."

No denying that. "Who made it out?"

"A couple of miners who'd been working on the upper level. You're the first from the lower levels," she explained.

"Mines have flood safety procedures. There are other exits." I'd seen them.

"How did you ..." her voice broke.

"I was lucky. I was in the elevator when the explosion hit." No need to traumatize her further by telling her why. I squeezed my twin's hand. "I think Dad was down there, too. He posed as Iam Fantastic and ..." My voice broke. "He saved me, Hope. He sabotaged the dam."

"A dam? How hard did you hit your head?"

"Washburn was running an extensive CVD diamond operation on the mine's lower level. Powered by a hydroelectric dam."

"Built underground and in complete secrecy?"

My sister's gape told me how farfetched and crazy I sounded. "I've got photos." I patted my soaked-through jeans. "Oh no! I need rice. Quickly." I waved my phone.

A fireman handed me a plastic bag half-filled with white powder. "Desiccant. It'll work in a day or so." I dropped my lifeline inside and sealed the bag. My photos likely hadn't uploaded to the cloud from underground either. This was my only hope. Otherwise, it was my word against the miners.

"Washburn is MIA," Hope added.

"He was in the CVD room below. So was the IT guy and about five members of the mine's security team. There were also three lab technicians." I cut off Hope's objection. "I don't think the lab guys will show on the mine entry logs."

Hope peered into my eyes, clearly trying to decide the extent of my injuries. "I-I'd better get you to the hospital." Louder, she said, "You've had a concussion."

I likely had, but ... "I'm not delusional. I know what I saw." Even if I did look like roadkill, I didn't care. Glimmer and I survived.

She wanted to believe me, but her skepticism looked comical. "Did you find the Peak Diamond?"

I shook my head. My single mission had been to locate the Peak, and it remained frustratingly out of reach. "I failed to achieve my primary objective."

A sudden burst of activity on the west side of the office building drew emergency workers in force. Glimmer pressed her front paws against my calf, then padded toward the commotion, and Hope and I trailed behind her across the gravel yard. We kept to the shadows. After everything we'd endured, neither of us had the energy for another struggle. Good thing I'd remained unseen as two paramedics emerged, supporting Washburn's slumped form between them as they guided him to the ambulance. His blood-stained trousers and the harsh rattle of his cough painted a grim picture of his ordeal.

I felt no sympathy. The man had ordered my imprisonment. Two security guards limped out next, followed by a lab technician stripped of his protective gear. All suffered facial lacerations and bruises, and walked with unsteady gaits, but they'd survived thanks to the emergency protocols implemented after the previous catastrophe.

Minutes passed before Glimmer's low growl announced Rico's emergence into the afternoon sunlight. His hiking clothes hung in shreds, and two paramedics flanked him as they led him toward a waiting stretcher.

The dog's nose twitched, sampling the air from every direction. Hope remained silent beside me until Rico popped a peppermint into his mouth.

My sister's sharp gasp made me turn. Her accusation cut through the afternoon air, drawing every eye to her and me. "It was you. You killed Blackwood."

Chapter Thirty-Three

KNOW WHEN TO WALK AWAY—WISDOM FROM A JEWEL THIEF

WEDNESDAY, 4:00 P.M.

Rockman materialized at Hope's side, slightly winded. "Who?"

I answered for her. "My sister thinks she's solved ..."

"... Blackwood's murder," Hope huffed out.

"You did?" Rockman directed his brow arch my way. Like I could control Hope on a roll.

"Yes. The IT guy ..." Hope's voice trailed off.

I gave her time to organize her thoughts and answered for her. "... has stomach issues. He chews activated charcoal tablets and peppermints." I paused for a hot moment, then nudged her. "Rico was in Blackwood's room right before his murder, wasn't he?"

Hope nodded. "I remember the distinctive sharp peppermint smell."

She was right. Altoids didn't clear your nasal passages as well as Rico's candy choice did.

"The smell came from the bathroom in Blackwood's suite. He must've been hiding there when I arrived. I didn't connect it until now." Hope's relief freed her until Rockman cleared his throat.

Ooops! That tic throbbing above his eye meant trouble. He'd caught us both concealing critical investigation information. I expected his anger. Not calm acceptance. "I take it you intend to amend your crime scene statement, Mrs. Allegro."

Hope swallowed noisily. "Y-yes, of course, sir."

I had to be too tired not to have seen that misstep coming. Hope had just identified a credible suspect.

I touched Rockman's arm, delaying him from questioning Rico. "I found the CVD machinery fueled by a hydroelectric dam in the mine. Rico, Washburn, and the security team were in on it."

Rockman's jaw muscle pulsed. "The flood?"

"Was no accident. I heard an explosion. I think the dam gave way." I didn't dare say anything about Dad. "I have photos. Well, kind of. My phone got wet ..." I handed him the desiccant-filled plastic bag containing my phone.

Rockman's smile warmed me. "We can fix that."

I figured as much. His lack of concern worked for me. I believed him.

"The photos are of the dam. I didn't get the lab and the machinery, but I have this." I showed him the CVD piece of rough I'd taken from the mine. "I'll certify that CVD signature matches the fake Peak Diamond. You'll need to send down divers, but this and my photos should get you a warrant."

No thanks needed. He was already on his phone, calling in backup like a fed—exactly who he claimed to be.

It must've been my relief that made me light-headed. Hope steadied me. "So, you got a sample CVD diamond. I should've known."

Of course, she'd eavesdropped on my conversation with Rockman. I shook off lingering thoughts of the man.

"I can't figure out why Rico would kill Blackwood? The two men were partners," Hope said.

My sister made a valid point. Rico may have been the technical brains of the group, but Blackwood had been the sales leg in the CVD operation, finding the marks and fencing the stolen merchandise. His contribution was as important as Washburn's, who handled the mine security and cover operation. They had the perfect setup. All they needed was a logistics expert to deliver the merchandise and ...

"Sh ... oot!" My cuss slipped out so loudly it drew everyone's attention.

Hope punched my already-aching shoulder. "Do I need to wash your mouth out with soap?"

"Ouch. I said shoot."

Her hands on her hips, she scolded, "Everyone knows what you meant."

"Come on. I'm not shocking anyone. Everyone's heard it before." I rubbed the abused muscle.

"No excuse for a poor vocabulary."

I couldn't win this one. "I need to talk to Dad."

Hope's annoyance turned to frustration. "And how do you propose to do that?"

A good question. "I don't know exactly. But standing around here isn't helping." To prove my point, a pair of black SUVs sped into the rescue area.

"Let's go. I need a shower." I tapped my leg. The doxie fell in beside me as I followed Hope to her SUV.

She climbed in behind the wheel. "Where are we going?"

"To the shop." I placed Glimmer on the center console and slid into the passenger seat.

"It's four o'clock. Hardly private," Hope pointed out.

"Lock up for the day and send Sunny home early. That should send Dad the right message."

Hope reversed out of the parking spot. "What makes you think he's still alive? Never mind watching the place?"

"Dad's a survivor. He'll find a way to contact us when he's ready."

"A drop point would be easier," Hope muttered.

And so spy craft. "Not our dad's style. He'll want answers, too," I said with a confidence I didn't feel. "Rico jeopardized everything when he copied the Peak Diamond. Claims he did it to settle the score for what happened to his mother."

"So, Dad lied?" Her tone held no surprise.

The truth felt murkier than that. "I think he's holding back information. Plus, Rico bragged to Washburn about getting his hands on the dog." I ran my fingers through Glimmer's soot-tangled fur. Both of us desperately needed to clean up. "Washburn tried to purchase a diamond dog during my visit with Rockman, too."

"Why? CVD and natural diamonds have identical carbon molecular structures. Any diamond detection device should find it." Hope chewed her thumbnail. "Can Glimmer differentiate between lab-grown and natural stones?"

"I've never tested him with it. If the CVD manufacturing gases leave trace scents not found in natural diamonds ..."

Hope's spine straightened. She loved possibilities. "We will need another CVD diamond to test Glimmer's nose." She extended her hand. "I'll hide the rough piece you have in the shop while you two bathe."

I placed the knobby, grayish-brown stone in her hand. We had a plan.

As Hope approached the town square, she took the left onto Canary Trail and pulled into the alley behind Starlight Estate Jewelers. She parked in her assigned space. Her hand touched my arm before I could open the door. "Want company going upstairs?"

Even after today's chaos, my sister worried about shielding me from my own phobia. "I can handle it. This fear of returning to my ransacked apartment is ridiculous anyway. Time I dealt with it." Brave words, but heartfelt. "I'm willing to bet Washburn sent someone to my place to get Glimmer."

Hope scratched the dog's head. "It's a good thing you

brought her hiking to find me. You know, you don't always have to be the strong one. We're sisters. I've got your back, just like you've mine. It's okay to lean on me."

Glimmer added her own supportive bark. Their combined affection wrapped around me like a security blanket. I blinked back a tear. "I'll manage." And I knew I would, as Glimmer and I climbed the rear staircase to my apartment.

My fingers barely trembled as I turned the key and peered inside. No panic seized me, irrational or otherwise. No scattered clothes littered the floor. Nothing personal marked the space as mine. Even the practical IKEA furniture made it feel like a budget hotel room. Was this really what my life had become? I had to do better.

Our shower routine reminded me exactly why I'd sworn off sharing bathing time with a dachshund. Glimmer commandeered the entire rain shower, refusing to share. She planted herself directly under the spray and refused to budge, no matter how much I demanded personal space. Only when I finally turned off the water did she consent to move. The doxie's shake sent droplets flying across the shower walls in violent arcs. My attempts to tame her fur with the blow dryer met with such fierce resistance that I eventually surrendered, leaving her with a wild, Einsteinish look.

Taking cues from her no-fuss approach, I slipped into worn jeans and a cotton shirt, allowing my wet hair to dry naturally into untamed waves that brushed my shoulders. I retrieved my backup Glock from its hiding place. Not because I felt unsafe, but rather because, without my weapon, I felt naked.

Twenty minutes later, we found Hope hunched over the high-powered microscope in our shared office, studying the CVD specimen. She straightened as we entered, dislodging Dee, who'd been on her lap.

"What's the decoy doing here?" I asked.

"I wasn't sure what kind of trouble you were in and what I'd need to do after I found you. So, I dropped her off here," Hope replied.

So much for stealth. Hope's defensiveness struck a chord. "You like having the dog around, don't you?"

"Yeah." Hope lifted the weiner dog, balancing its chest in her palm, and snuggled her close. My sister's silly smile told me everything. "She's really sweet."

I grinned at my mirror image. "And opinionated and bossy and ..." I scooped Glimmer into my arms. "... a great companion for life."

"Our friends are going to kill us. They'll never be able to tell us apart now," Hope said.

"Put a pink collar on Dee," I suggested.

Dee barked. Not sure if it was agreement or an objection. Glimmer, with her usual perception, understood the decoy's new role. My dog graciously allowed Dee to sniff her. When the dogs settled, I pointed to the microscope. "What did you find?"

"This rough is flawless," she announced. "No visible CVD markers whatsoever."

The implications hit me like a cold wave. "Every cutting house will process and laser-ID these as natural diamonds."

Hope's identical blue gaze held mine. "The flood may have destroyed the machinery, but the technology still exists." She lifted the one-inch stone, rotating it between her fingers so it caught the light. "This single piece could trigger a global financial collapse."

A bit of an exaggeration, but the price of diamonds did affect wealth management. Was that the point? No diamonds needed to be manufactured either. The threat alone could bring down governments in producing countries. Had someone orchestrated this from the beginning? I watched Glimmer methodically cleaning her paw, wondering if my lowrider partner held the key to preventing disaster. Time to find out.

"Did you locate the copy of the Peak Diamond in the safe?" I asked.

Hope nodded. "It's hidden in the store."

I called Glimmer over and slipped her Hunter Investigations vest over her low-to-the-ground frame. She immediately transformed—ears perked, body rigid with attention, ready for work. Taking the CVD rough from Hope, I held it beneath my dog's sensitive nose.

Glimmer sniffed the diamond, then cocked her head in obvious confusion. My heart sank. Not exactly the confident start I'd hoped for.

I lifted the stone again. "Glimmer, hunt."

Her tail began its rhythmic wag. She tested the air, nose working left and right, then bolted from the office. Adrenaline surged through me as I hurried after her through our elegant office and into the main showroom, where late afternoon sunlight streamed through the picture window, transforming the display cases into sprays of sparkling diamonds.

The dachshund had somehow wedged herself behind the largest glass case. She reared up on her hind legs, front paws clawing at a wall vent, and barking intently.

Hope's sharp intake of breath told me she found the copy diamond. My dog might be the only thing that could stop an economic catastrophe.

Chapter Thirty-Four

THE SIMPLEST ANSWER IS OFTENTIMES THE BEST—WISDOM FROM A JEWEL THIEF

WEDNESDAY, 7:30 P.M.

Despite my burning desire to contact Rockman, I couldn't risk it. My invitation to Dad complicated everything. Bringing those two men together would not end well.

An hour crawled by as Hope and I prowled the showroom like caged animals, our footsteps echoing against the polished floors. The unspoken questions hung between us like a desert sandstorm: Was Dad even alive? Had he been hurt in the flood? Now that his work here was done, did he have any interest in seeing his daughters again?

At least, that's what was eating at Hope. The deep creases etched in her forehead betrayed her anguish. Our father's decision to meet with me alone had left her hurt and questioning everything. I wished I had answers for her—I wished I had answers for myself.

"I'm heading to the Canary Café to pick up takeout," Hope declared with forced determination.

My stomach growled its response. "Nothing like stress eating to solve all our problems."

"We've already rearranged the sales case twice and obsessively triple-checked Sunny's orders." Hope's tone suggested our store manager's meticulous organization was somehow a personal affront to her current mood. "I can't just hang out here. I need to do something."

"You're right. Sophie will be back at her computer in a couple of hours anyway. Maybe we'll have real answers then."

Hope wrinkled her nose in mock deliberation. "So, what's it gonna be? Chili cheese fries or loaded nachos? Because if we're going to feed our frustration, we might as well do it right."

And give indigestion its proper due. "Nachos. But pile on the extra jalapeños."

"On the side," Hope finished automatically, not bothering to write anything down. The Canary Café would probably have our order ready before she even made it across the street. We really were creatures of habit—predictable to a fault.

Glimmer chose that moment to add her own emphatic bark to the conversation. Dee just sat there taking it all in. She'd get into the swing soon enough.

"I've got you covered, girls. Sirloin patties, medium rare, with a side of fresh blueberries." Hope slung her oversized mom tote bag over her shoulder and headed for the front door, Dee following in her wake.

I glanced at Glimmer, sitting by my feet. "You know Dad's going to show up the second Hope leaves, don't you?"

Two and a half minutes later, I heard Glimmer's low, rumbling growl a split second before the alley door entry alarm chirped its warning. I moved toward the backroom doorway, my right hand instinctively hovering over my backup Glock. "I'm not explaining to Hope why you refused to meet her."

"*Au contraire, ma chérie.* I wish to meet her very much." His voice carried that familiar inflection, but when he limped into the dimly lit showroom, everything else had changed. Each step sent a visible wince across his face, and he cradled his right arm against his chest like a broken wing.

"You need to see a doctor." The debonair European charmer I'd expected had been replaced by a back-alley brawler who looked like he'd lost his last fight.

"I am relieved you escaped, too, *ma chérie*."

I gestured to a chair. "Vodka?" I turned toward the bar, watching him gingerly settle into the leather seat through the mirrored wall. He was in worse shape than he'd let on. Glimmer sensed it. She leaped into the chair beside him, lying across the armrest instead of landing on his lap. The dog tended to be an excellent judge of character, so her acceptance meant a great deal to me. Despite Hope's concerns, I couldn't be all wrong about him.

I offered him the vodka shot. "I'm glad you're okay. Relatively speaking. What went wrong?"

"Nothing. Your arrival forced me to move up the timetable."

He had saved me again. I suppose I should be grateful. "My arrival! How was I supposed to know ..." But I had known, deep down. "Iam Fantastic? That's the name you used to alert me. Seriously?"

"What would you have preferred? Yuri Fat Her?"

I cracked a smile. The man's sense of the absurd matched mine. "How about a phone call or a text? You have a burner phone, I assume."

He held up his shot glass. I poured him another generous portion. "How did you get out alive?"

"I took the geyser through the hot spring. I suspect stories will circulate about Jules Verne's lava monster, Hortense, making an appearance at the Amethyst Inn."

His dead seriousness promised a memorable tale. "You're not a hydro engineer. How'd you do it?"

"Simple, really. I dropped a wrench in the turbine."

My turn to be impressed. "That's it?" Why hadn't I thought of that?

"The simplest answer is oftentimes the best."

"Wisdom from a jewel thief?" Hope's question replaced our easy camaraderie with a decided iciness.

I downed my vodka shot. Oh boy, Hope in a huff promised fireworks. I took a step back. Glimmer followed my cue and scooted to my side.

"*Ma espoir. Tu es le portrait de ta mère.*"

"Don't call me your hope. I am not your hope, nor the image of my mother. I look exactly like my sister." She'd placed our dinner bag on the coffee table and crossed her arms, taking school-marm disapproval to a new level.

"*Mais non,* you have a light all your own, *ma espoir*. Those who do not see it are blind and foolish."

"And what is it you see?" she asked unimpressed, not giving an inch.

I wanted to shake her—to tell her that Dad had saved my life more than once, but my protection wouldn't help him if he wanted a relationship with her. He needed to win her over on his own.

"A woman whose love holds together her family," he replied without hesitation.

Emotion curled in my stomach. Dear old dad could turn a phrase. Did Hope believe him? Was I a fool to?

"Why? Why have you stayed away for so long?" Betrayal came out in her every word.

"I have made some bad choices, and, for that, I pay the price of a man with no home." His pointed look focused on me.

I straightened. This wasn't about me—or was it? Is that why he'd shown himself? To stop me from repeating his mistakes? We worked on different sides of the law, but the basics remained the same. Rockman pulling me out of the elevator shaft came to mind. Did we have a chance?

"You haven't answered why." Hope regrounded the discussion.

Dad took a deep breath. "I have dangerous enemies who will use you and your family to get to me. My absence is what protects you all." He let his words sink in before adding, "If I could do it again, I would be the father *mes petites filles* needed and the husband your mother made me want to be."

That was the point—the desire to be your best self with someone else.

"I understand if you never want to see me again. Know, *ma espoir*, I will love you to the moon as I do your mother."

Even my naturally suspicious mind couldn't find fault with his answers. Hope remained undecided. I sent her my twin warning through our unique mental link: *Accept him as he is. You can't change him. No one can.*

I wasn't expecting a response, but Dad's voice echoed in my mind: *Merci, ma chérie. I am humbled that you understand.*

I did understand. But two voices in my head? I swallowed the curse that threatened to escape, knowing Hope, especially in her current mood, would make good on her threat that I eat soap.

"Enough," I said aloud, cutting through the mental chatter. "You two can work out your issues later. Right now, we have a killer to catch, and I need answers."

Both of them turned their attention to me, the weight of their combined focus almost tangible.

"Dad, I need to know more about Rico's mother. Who was she? And why did you save her from Ivan Medved?" I asked.

He masked whatever he was thinking with a wistful smile, then seemed to sink even deeper into his chair. He tapped his empty glass against the armrest. I poured him another vodka and fixed one for Hope, too, sensing she'd need the liquid courage before the evening ended.

Dad cleared his throat like a storyteller from centuries past, ready to weave his tale. "This is about opposites," he began. "Twins, just like you two."

I pressed closer, afraid to miss even a syllable.

"Angelina was golden-haired and stunning—the kind of woman who could make any man forget to breathe. Katarina had raven-black hair and a razor-sharp mind. Different, yes, but they shared one thing." He paused, studying our faces. "Eyes the color of sapphires, as brilliant blue as the Hope Diamond itself."

And the twin bond. I understood it, and, from the way Hope shifted beside me, so did she.

Dad took a slow sip, his eyes moving between us as he waited for understanding to dawn. It did.

"The story begins with Nikolai and Ivan—university friends in Moscow who collaborated on CVD diamond technology research."

My stomach clenched as the fragments began forming a picture.

"After graduation, Nikolai joined Almaz."

"Russia's largest CVD diamond manufacturer," I explained for Hope's benefit. "Did Nikolai keep developing his diamond project there?"

Dad nodded. Glimmer had found her way onto his lap, practically purring as he stroked her head. "In Siberia, Nikolai met Angelina. They married within months. What matters is that Ivan stood as Nikolai's best man at the wedding."

"And Katarina, her maid of honor," Hope added.

"Ten years later, Nikolai died in what authorities called a tragic accident. Angelina's house was ransacked, and Rico barely escaped a kidnapping attempt."

Hope's gasp hung over us. "Did the police capture ..."

"Justice in Russia is easily bought." Dad's voice carried bitter experience. "Angelina needed to protect her son. She was sure someone from Almaz was after her husband's research. She turned to the one person who could keep the boy safe."

"Ivan," Hope said.

"*Oui.* They married quickly, and he legally adopted the boy."

"Ivan now had his hands on all of Nikolai's CVD research," I said, the pattern crystallizing.

Dad's nod sent a spark of satisfaction through me. Clarity felt within grasp. I knew where this was going.

"In theory, yes. But Nikolai had written everything in a personal code."

"And Rico broke it?" Hope's skepticism cut. "A kid decoded his dead father's scientific notes? That's impossible."

"He didn't crack it." Dad paused, savoring the moment. "Angelina did."

"And handed a global crime syndicate the breakthrough technology of the century," I said.

The full scope hit me while Hope's mind focused on the human cost. "The beauty queen? No wonder Angelina reached out to her twin sister. She must've felt trapped and used."

"*Exactement.*"

"But how did you get pulled into this mess?" Hope pressed.

"I occasionally handle recovery work for a, uh, Russian ... insurance firm."

"Ivan's rivals." The statement hung between us—no question needed. I grasped the reality of his world. All too clearly.

"You work for the Russian mob!" Hope burst out.

"*Ma espoir,* I was hired to retrieve a certain young woman's necklace from Ivan's collection." His stare challenged us both to dig deeper into the details.

I didn't want to know. My sister couldn't let it go. "So, you stole a stolen necklace from a thief? This is insane."

Of course, the necklace had been the cover. Dad's real mission had been to extract Angelina. Oddly, that he was far more than some common jewel thief didn't surprise me. But this wasn't the time to go down that road.

"Who was your client?" I asked, but I knew. I'd have done the same thing at any price.

"Katarina," Hope said simply. No judgment in her voice. She finally understood. "You brought Rico, too?"

"Yes. At first the boy wouldn't come. Nearly got us all killed refusing to leave." Dad's jaw tightened with old anger. "Ivan had already decided Angelina knew too much."

"She left the visual identification signature in the process," Hope said, understanding flooding her voice.

"No. Her twin sister did that." The final piece clicked into place for me.

Dad's grin spread wide, revealing decades of admiration and something deeper than mere pride. "Together, those two women sabotaged Ivan Medved's empire."

Talk about an enlightening moment that Hope ruined by saying, "Yet here we all are. So, who actually has the real Peak Diamond?"

Dad shook his head, frustration creeping into his expression. "I don't know. I damaged the stone moments after it arrived at the museum."

How he'd orchestrated that was a story for another time. My thoughts raced through the timeline. "Which means the switch happened sometime between your grading thirty days ago and the diamond's arrival at the museum."

"Only four people touched it during transport from the vault to the museum," Hope said, her insider knowledge from the planning committee providing valuable intel. "The bank president, the mayor, Chief Rockman, and Officer Pepper. They stayed together the entire time, giving nobody a chance to make the switch."

"Unless they were all in on it," Dad suggested.

"Impossible," Hope shot back. I nodded my agreement.

"Or someone accessed the vault directly," Dad offered.

"The security system is impenetrable. Nobody gets in without leaving a digital footprint." Hope's voice carried absolute certainty.

Dad's wry smile told a different story—one born from years of experience. "Someone can," I said, the truth crystallizing. "Two people, to be exact."

"And who is that?"

The familiar voice at the exact moment Glimmer growled made my blood run cold. Even Hope would forgive me for cursing now.

Chapter Thirty-Five

THE GRANDER THE FINALE, THE BETTER—
WISDOM FROM A JEWEL THIEF

WEDNESDAY, 7:30 P.M.

I reached for my Glock too late. Washburn's weapon was already pointed at my father.

"I wouldn't, hey." Washburn's distinctive accent coursed through my veins.

I might have tested my fast draw skills, except for the red target shining on Hope's chest. Someone had my sister in their sights. Dad saw it, too, and he responded like a seasoned pro. Or a man with a death wish. I'm not sure. He didn't flinch. His tell didn't even activate. He sat in the chair like he'd been sipping tea at a high society garden party.

"It is a pleasure to finally meet you face to face, Washburn. We have been like two ships passing in the night for too many years."

Had Washburn been the one hunting Dad? Or Rico?

Washburn's sardonic smile scared me. For someone who'd been fighting for his life just hours earlier, his recovery bordered on miraculous. Apart from the white bandage stark against his forehead, his dark clothing transformed him into something almost inhuman. He was an adversary to respect.

"Weapon down," Washburn ordered.

I obeyed, showing my open hands as I slowly laid my weapon on the coffee table. At the same time, I surveyed my options and gave Glimmer the hand signal to stay in the chair beside me. She'd create the distraction when I needed her.

"I'd wondered if you were some kind of spook, hey. You're a bloody difficult bloke to pin down, *Le Renard Argente*. Imagine my surprise when the intel came through that you were holed up at your daughters' jewelry shop, right under my bloody nose. Quite fitting, that."

"Indeed. Do give Ivan my regards." Dad's smart-aleck reply drew another evil smile.

"You'll get the chance to share your feelings in person, hey," Washburn replied.

That his orders included taking Dad alive helped. I needed to get Hope to safety first. We were cornered, and we knew it. Washburn blocked the back exit, and the sniper, likely one of the man's special forces security folks, the front.

Ma chérie, save yourself.

I ignored his request. There had to be a way out.

"And you've got the dog, hey." His gaze fixed on Dee, sitting pretty in Dad's lap. "Must be my lucky day."

Thank goodness for the decoy dog. Hope's phone rang. She glanced at her iWatch. "It's Gram," she squeaked.

"We're late getting home. Our grandmother wants to know when to put the shrimp tacos on the grill," I said quickly. "They'll get too well done if it's too soon."

"Don't try anything," Washburn ordered. The target remained fixed on Hope's chest, a sobering reminder.

Tell her we're tied up at the shop.

I prayed Hope got my message.

She answered the call with a pause. "Hi, Gram. Sorry. We're tied up at the shop. Put the shrimp tacos on the grill right away. We'll hurry." She disconnected before Gram could respond.

I breathed easier. If Gram got the message, help would be on the way.

Be ready to hit the ground.

The slight jerk of Hope's head indicated she understood.

I needed to buy time. Narcissistic Washburn would talk about himself. "Why did you kill the dentist?"

Washburn shook his head. "That's on you, hey." He pointed to Dad. "Using the same gas we used to lure the gamblers made the dentist look guilty."

"I see you continue to practice shoot first and ask questions later," Dad said. "Exactly like when you broke into Taylor's apartment."

"My sources put the dog here," he replied, clearly annoyed.

"Why do you need her?" Hope asked.

"To find the Peak Diamond," I suggested.

"How do you expect the dog to do that?" Hope asked. "You need to give her some place to start."

"Listen here, lady, you better hope that dog can find the real Peak Diamond or I don't need any of you." His escalating anger didn't bode well.

I changed the subject, lest Hope's honesty get us in deeper trouble. "So, let's figure this out. When did Blackwood orchestrate the diamond's switch?"

All eyes focused on Dad. His chuckle broke the tension. "I'm not your thief, Washburn. The stone had already been switched when I damaged it."

"You! You started this whole bloody mess. Should've known, hey." The brief crack in Washburn's composure gave me hope. "How'd you know it wasn't real?"

I waited for Dad's answer. He'd brushed off my questions, and I'd let him.

"The weakness in your system is in adding the blemishes. Your CVD specimens will break on those imperfections," Dad replied.

My heart skipped a beat. There was only one way he would've known that. He'd been working with Angelina and Katarina.

And now you know the truth, ma chérie. This was never about the Russians. It is two sisters' justice.

I got it all too well. The photo started this journey. "The photo the chief showed you of you, Blackwood, Rockman's Uncle, and Nikolai—who took it?"

For a split second, Washburn looked like a hunted animal, and I knew. "It was Ivan," I said. "The five of you cooked up a scheme to replace the most sought-after stones in the world, but Nikolai couldn't do it. He wanted out, and Ivan killed him for his research. Except he couldn't interpret it. Ivan had to fake Rico's kidnapping, causing Katarina to run to him for protection. Now Ivan has acquired the technical know-how through Nikolai's son."

Glimmer's rumbling growl warned me.

Dad heard it, too. Help was coming. Surprise would buy us seconds. "First, your logistics expert. Next Blackwood. You are dying one by one," he added.

Washburn flinched. Exactly what I'd been waiting for. "Glimmer, hunt!"

Hope dove for the ground. The little dachshund shot like a cannon out of the chair, biting Washburn's calf. I hit him in the chest at the same time, sending him flaying backward. The distraction worked. His shot hit the ceiling.

All too late. I heard the impact as the sniper's shot hit its mark. My heart about stopped.

Two swift return shots got the shooter, but my sister lay on the wood floor in a puddle of blood, unable to move, our father weighing her down, shielding her, shot in the back.

Chapter Thirty-Six

LEAVE BEHIND NOTHING BUT A MEMORY— WISDOM FROM A JEWEL THIEF

ONE MONTH LATER, 9:00 A.M.

Dad will always be an enigma. He'd blown into my life when I needed him most and disappeared, without a trace. I suppose I respected that. He'd taken a bullet for my sister, saving her life. For that, I will always be in his debt.

I don't know exactly what happened to him—if he even survived that night. My gut says he's okay, that he walks with a dignified gait now, and that he'll show up again the next time I need him. I pray he found peace in the life he chose. I do sometimes wonder if he was real at all or simply an angel sent to protect us.

I'll never forget the last time I saw him. The paramedics had loaded him into the medivac helicopter. Hope held his right hand, and I his left.

Mes filles, je vous aime.

Hope and I drove frantically to the hospital, following the helicopter until we lost it in the clouds. Forever. The chopper never arrived in Phoenix or at any other area hospital. In fact, the FAA had no record of any helicopter, medivac or private, anywhere near Sunset Peak that evening. Even Rockman's FBI contacts came up with no answers.

How he pulled that disappearing act told me everything I needed to know about his backroom contacts.

If that wasn't odd enough, Rockman and I went to the Sunset Peak Bank the following morning to examine the vault access records. No need for a warrant, the access information was neatly printed and sitting on Dale's desk beneath his assistant's resignation letter and a box with my name on it. The woman had disappeared into the night like another ghost, leaving the real Peak Diamond and a single note. The bold letters read Спасибо. Thank you in Russian and the initial K.

I assumed the K stood for Katarina—it seemed the most logical choice—but Karo had also vanished. The FBI tracked him to a private airfield outside of London, but then lost his trail completely.

Blackwood's lighter, which allegedly contained the complete list of replaced diamonds, remained unaccounted for. Not my job to recover, as Sophie had reminded me.

As I put the finishing touches on my bill for the Peak Diamond's recovery, Sophie called me. No greeting. Her explosive news spilled out in a rush. "Ivan Medved was gunned down in Sochi this morning. Shot with a 9mm pistol. A CVD diamond was found in his mouth. Ballistics matched the weapon to the one that killed Blackwood."

Angelina's vengeance was now complete. I wondered if rock, paper, scissors decided who pulled the trigger on Medved. That had to be the problem with accumulating enemies. Both my father and Rico had cause, too.

All those involved in her sister's death had now been punished. Rockman's uncle would be the first released from prison with good behavior in twenty years. Washburn would serve life for killing the dentist and whoever else Rockman uncovered.

"Have you located Blackwood's lighter?" I asked.

"No. Its existence remains rather a mystery, I'm afraid."

Or a secret no one wants released. "Any word on *Le Renard Argente*?"

"No. How's your sister coping with it all?" Sophie asked.

"She's decided that 'shoot' is no longer a curse punishable with a lye soap mouthwash. She says it so often that the twins have quit saying it at all. Something about it being uncool now."

"Reverse psychology?"

"A reprieve until they discover something else to torture her with."

Sophie chuckled. "Twins."

"Yeah. Gram's laughing her head off and keeps telling Hope to just wait."

"For what?"

"The twins' next big plan, I imagine. It's a good thing Rockman forced my sister to go to therapy."

"And you?"

"My shrink suggested I take up meditation."

"Blast ..." Sophie spluttered tea all over her keyboard. I was certain of it. I would have done the same. Me, meditating? I couldn't quite wrap my head around it either.

"How's it going then?" Sophie finally asked.

"I'm a work in progress." I meant it. "Can you fast-track my payment? I'm breaking ground on my new home next week."

"Ten acres adjacent to your family's spread, I heard. And Rockman? He's a proper gentleman."

I hoped not. I had much more interesting plans for that sexy bod. The important thing was that I wanted to believe he was a good guy. "He's based in DC. Long-distance relationships rarely work out."

"I hear there's a post in Los Angeles ..."

A tingle worked its way to my toes. An intriguing thought.

"I have a job for you," Sophie said.

I sat up taller. Glimmer did, too. "My bags are packed and I'm ready to go." An escape to Monte Carlo or Tokyo sounded exactly like what I needed.

"Scottsdale, Arizona. Phoenix PD jurisdiction. I understand if you'd rather give it a miss. Your ex-husband's the lead investigator."

Buck shot! This one ought to be a pain in my ankle.

The End.

* * *

Be sure to follow pupfluencer Glimmer the Diamond Dog on her quest to keep her human safe. You can find her on Facebook and Instagram.

* * *

Join Hunter and Glimmer in their next adventure...

The Water Diamond

A stolen bracelet. A missing heiress. A secret worth killing for.

When a priceless Art Deco bracelet vanishes during an exhibition at Phoenix's historic Wrigley Mansion, diamond detective **Taylor Hunter** and her extraordinary dachshund, **Glimmer**, are called to investigate. But what begins as a glittering whodunit quickly spirals into a dangerous chase stretching from the scorching Arizona desert to the fog-draped cliffs of Catalina Island.

To solve today's murder, Taylor must first unravel the disappearance of a young heiress in 1929—a century-old mystery entwined with two matching bracelets. Together, they hold the

key to a legendary treasure. But someone else is hunting, too...
and they're willing to kill to keep the secret buried.

In **The Water Diamond**, past and present collide in a cozy
adventure brimming with intrigue, charm, and danger. Because
every diamond tells a story—and some stories refuse to stay
hidden.

Acknowledgments

The Gem Hunters has lived in my imagination for years, born from a lifelong fascination with all things that glitter. Hunter is the woman I've always dreamed I could be—fierce-hearted and street-smart, worldly yet grounded in family. She has the courage of a lioness and the wisdom to know that sometimes our greatest treasures are found not in distant places, but in coming home.

My journey into the world of gems began a decade ago at the Gemological Institute of America in Carlsbad, where fascination deepened into true appreciation. Through this series, I'm excited to share some of the remarkable discoveries I've made along the way, hoping readers will find the same wonder in these precious stones that captivated me.

And yes, diamond dogs are real! These incredible animals can detect diamonds buried up to 50 feet underground. While no dachshund has been officially trained for diamond detection, I chose this breed because they're natural scent hounds, originally bred to hunt badgers in underground burrows. If any dog could sniff out buried treasure, it would certainly be a determined dachshund.

Heartfelt thanks to my "sisters" Pam, Becky, Dee, and Ann—you sustain me when words fail. To Lori Roberts Herbst, your guidance has truly made me a better writer. This book wouldn't exist without all of you. Special recognition goes to Sharon Jacobson and Mia, the sweet inspiration for Glimmer.

I'm deeply grateful to Sergeant Jeff Daukus of the Glendale, Arizona, Police Department for his expertise on police procedures. You're a true hero and friend—any remaining errors are mine alone.

Melissa Martin, thank you. You keep me sane.

Finally, to my husband Rocky whose unwavering patience and support make everything possible.

Telling Hunter's story has been pure joy.

Award-winning author C.B. Wilson's writing journey began with a childhood rebellion—after reading a Nancy Drew mystery, she decided she could write a better ending.

A passionate animal advocate, C.B. created the beloved Barkview Mysteries series, which combines her love of puzzles and pups. This popular ten-book series follows Cat Wright, a feline-loving former investigative reporter on a mission to find her perfect canine companion. Each mystery showcases a different dog breed while exploring the question: is there really an ideal dog for every person? C.B.'s commitment to finding every animal a forever home drives this heartwarming series—and you'll likely discover adoptable dogs at her book events. Take a stroll through Barkview and help Cat decide if there's truly a perfect match waiting for this dedicated cat person.

Her new series, Gem Hunters, sparkles with adventure. Drawing on her Gemology degree from the prestigious Gemological Institute of America and her fascination with all things that glitter, this series features Taylor Hunter and her extraordinary Diamond Dog—a sassy Dachshund named Glitter who can detect diamonds buried fifty feet underground. (Yes, this is a real profession!) Join Hunter as she recovers stolen gems across exotic international destinations, where glittering treasures hide deadly secrets.

C.B.'s most ingenious plot twists strike while she's horseback riding through the Arizona desert. When not crafting mysteries, she's an avid pickleball player and self-proclaimed chocoholic who believes the best stories—like the best chocolate—should be savored slowly.

To connect with C.B. Wilson:
www.cbwilsonauthor.com

facebook.com/cbwilsonauthor

instagram.com/cbwilsonauthor

tiktok.com/@author.cb.wilson

bookbub.com/profile/c-b-wilson